PRAISE FOR AMULYA MALLADI

"Malladi examines India's surrogacy industry with honesty and grace. This slice of life will touch all women who have struggled with conception and/or poverty. [A] thought-provoking novel [that] will be a sure hit with book groups."

—*Booklist* (Starred Review) on *A House for Happy Mothers*

"Malladi writes a poignant novel from two difficult perspectives that spans several complex and often controversial topics. This title would make a great book club selection."

—*Library Journal* on *A House for Happy Mothers*

"The story provides an intriguing glimpse into the surrogate industry and casts light on the emotional toil those involved face."

—The *Associated Press* on *A House for Happy Mothers*

"A feel-good story that warms the heart."

—*Redbook* on *A House for Happy Mothers*

"Amulya Malladi brings Denmark's capitol into brilliant color in this intriguing novel about a marriage on the brink, a wife's precarious emotional stability, and the international business deal that could either save or ruin everything. *The Copenhagen Affair* reminds us that we must each decide what we are willing to risk to build our fortunes and find our true happiness."

—Julie Lawson Timmer, author of *Five Days Left, Untethered,* and
Mrs. Saint and the Defectives on *The Copenhagen Affair*

"Amulya Malladi's *The Copenhagen Affair* is an entertaining romp of a read! As we travel with Sanya on her search for happiness, love, balance, and the meaning of life, we end up, as she does, completely captivated by a swirl of infidelity, corporate intrigue, and the very particular habits of Copenhagen's café class. Along with surprises, twists, and humor, Malladi gives us an intimate look at a city she clearly loves and knows well. I was captivated to the end."

—Nancy Star, bestselling author of *Sisters One, Two, Three* on
The Copenhagen Affair

"Compulsively readable, *The Copenhagen Affair* had me turning pages well into the wee hours. The story of Sanya's unraveling is familiar to anyone who has ever felt the overbearing weight of depression, but how she heals from her downward spiral is anything but ordinary. From gossipy coffee shops to gritty blues clubs to the dining rooms of the Danish elite, Sanya's impulsive, exciting, [and] often humorous journey through the colorful streets of Copenhagen is full of surprises. I could not put the book down!"

—Loretta Nyhan, author of *All the Good Parts* on
The Copenhagen Affair

THE COPENHAGEN AFFAIR

ALSO BY AMULYA MALLADI

A House for Happy Mothers
The Sound of Language
Song of the Cuckoo Bird
Serving Crazy with Curry
The Mango Season
A Breath of Fresh Air

THE COPENHAGEN AFFAIR

AMULYA MALLADI

LAKE UNION
PUBLISHING

Text copyright © 2017 by Amulya Malladi
All rights reserved.

Published by Lake Union Publishing, Seattle
www.apub.com

Amazon, the Amazon logo, and Lake Union Publishing are trademarks of Amazon.com, Inc., or its affiliates.

ISBN-13: 9781503940314
ISBN-10: 1503940314

Cover design by David Drummond

Printed in the United States of America

For Copenhagen, jeg savner dig

Chapter 1
The Implosion

It's a common mistake to assume that emotional baggage will disappear if one changes geographies. There are many who think that a change in weather is all that is needed to set everything that is wrong with a person right.

Harry, Sanya's husband of two decades, was under the very same misconception. He came upon the idea after a joint therapy session with Sanya's shrink, whom she started to see after her dramatic nervous breakdown three months earlier.

"Copenhagen," Harry announced with aplomb like it was a panacea. "We'll move to Copenhagen for a year. It'll be an adventure."

"I know nothing about Copenhagen," Sanya said.

"And therein lies the adventure," Harry said.

Harry explained that his company, ComIT, a Silicon Valley IT consultancy where he was a partner, was going to buy a company in Copenhagen, IT Foundry, also an IT consultancy, to get a foot in the European door.

ComIT had already done a fair amount of due diligence, and now Harry had offered to go and finish the acquisition and run the company as interim CEO. Once he established the business and found his successor, which he believed would take a year, he and Sanya would come back home to California. This was a win-win, according to Harry. He would solidify his standing as partner with this project, and it would improve his wife's health.

"Look, I *have to go*. It's the opportunity of a lifetime. Not everyone gets a chance to expand a business into new markets like this. And I'm not leaving you alone here. Can you please not be selfish about this and see the bigger picture?" Harry said.

Sanya was baffled. *Oh, Harry, really,* she thought. *You've been leaving me alone through sickness and in health for years, and* now *you can't leave me alone? And I am the selfish one?*

If Sanya cared enough, she would've said something in protest, but she didn't care enough, not since the *incident,* so she further sank into the couch, wanting nothing more than to go back to bed.

"It's the happiest place on earth," said Sanya's eighteen-year-old daughter, Sara, who had driven up for that weekend from UCLA, where she was a political science major.

What Sanya found out later was that Denmark was also the country with the highest consumption of happy pills; after all, they invented the antidepressant. They had the highest rate of female suicide and the second-highest consumption of beer per capita in the world. They used to be the top beer-drinking country but lost that status when Czechoslovakia split and the title went to Slovakia.

To move or not to move was a question that Sanya's addled brain couldn't compute, and she, as she had always done, let someone else make another decision to impact her life without her interference.

Sanya's life was, and probably would forever be, fragmented between Old Sanya and New Sanya, pre- and post-nervous breakdown. Old Sanya was happy, positive, a director of strategy at a financial consultancy, and a veritable pushover with a *please everyone all the time* disease who lived in a three-thousand-square-foot house in the prestigious Montclair neighborhood of Los Gatos in Northern California. New

Sanya was depressed, unemployed, unresponsive, and intractable, and lived under her duvet cover regardless of geography.

So what happened to positive, cheerful, life-loving Sanya? It was physics. The second law of thermodynamics states that entropy is the quantitative measure of disorder in a system. In any closed system, the entropy of the system will either remain constant or increase. If marriage is considered a closed system, then the physics of it starts to make sense. Entropy or disorder increases in a marriage—day after week after month after year.

And what happens when disorder completely takes over the system?

It implodes. Boom it goes, and a new system comes into existence—not a better one, just a different one—like the one under the duvet cover where the colors were muted, the sound hollowed, the world small, keeping pace, one breath after the other, where creation exists in only that one moment of inhale and exhale, nothing before it and nothing after.

Since it was Sanya's first nervous breakdown, she didn't quite know what to expect. One minute she was a whole person and the next she was a broken, scattered caricature of herself. Of course, it didn't happen from one moment to another; it took years of buildup for that last straw to fall on her back before she broke.

The nervous breakdown was theatrical in its execution. Hysterical, movie-style.

It happened the morning the partners of her consultancy invited her for a meeting. They were all there, all ten of them. People she had worked with for nearly a decade and a half. She had started as a junior consultant and worked her way up to director of strategy, but the elusive partnership had never been offered to her. Brian, who was hired three years after her, was one of the ten partners. He was a star. He was fast-tracked. His type usually was.

Sanya worked for a financial consultancy in San Francisco's posh Embarcadero Center—they did financial process optimization. Sanya was a finance expert. She looked at the books. The money legalese. She fixed accounting procedures for many, many companies around the United States and even some in Europe.

She was considered to be hardworking, pleasant, someone who didn't challenge authority, went with the flow, and never negotiated a raise or a bonus. She was a workhorse. She was good at what she did. Clients specifically asked for her to be on their projects. She was considered to be a good middle manager, a good leader. People wondered why she was still *just* a director and not a partner. She never wondered. She knew why. Every day Sanya went to work she waited to be *found out*. Every day she thought, *Today will be the day when they will know that I'm not as good as they think I am.* When one lives with that kind of low self-esteem, they expect the worst, and when it is handed to them, they feel relieved not to wait for it anymore.

So after being passed over, ignored, and generally underappreciated, when Sanya was offered partnership for being a financial consultant who had been bringing in a lot of business to the company based on her reputation and skill, instead of saying "Thank you, this is great," she burst into tears and didn't stop crying until they knocked her out with a benzodiazepine in the emergency room. There had been plenty of drama in the meeting room that morning. One partner asked to call security, no one knew why. One called 911. Another asked Sanya to get a grip. Through it all Sanya just sat there and cried hysterically like a Victorian ingenue from a period film, wiping snot off her face with the sleeve of her charcoal-gray Hugo Boss suit.

Once she stopped crying, she also stopped speaking. It went on for nearly a week. When she finally was able to talk, slow and stilted and with effort, a psychiatrist wanted to know if she was suicidal. Ten days after the incident in the meeting room, once the mental ward people were sure Sanya was not a danger to herself or the people around her, they released her into the general public—and that's when she took residence under the covers, alone, cocooned and insulated inside her new closed system.

❖   ❖   ❖

Sanya learned about entropy and closed systems from her best friend, Alec, who was a physicist at Stanford.

"Think of your closet," he said. "You spend a whole weekend cleaning it up, and it's neat and nice and looks like the inside of a Benetton store. The first week, you try to keep order. You put clothes where they belong and it works. But the folded T-shirts are getting a bit unruly, and you start mixing your pants with your skirts, and soon your blouses are everywhere, and you throw in that sweater that was lying on the bed before you went to sleep. A couple of months pass, and your closet is disorderly again. A closet is an isolated system. It's not going to get any cleaner than it was when you started; it can only get messier."

Sanya felt that Alec was talking about her life, her marriage, which was a closed system where the entropy had increased exponentially with every passing day.

"You're right," she told him, "my pants are mixed in with my skirts and my blouses with my jackets."

Among all of Sanya's friends, Alec was the only one who didn't like Harry. The others thought he was amazing. This good-looking man (*How on earth did you land him, Sanya?*), this successful man, this charming and stylish man was just what every woman Sanya knew thought she wanted. Harry believed that Alec was jealous of him. Alec was single, balding, not particularly good-looking, geeky, and ideal as a friend for a man's wife, as Harry put it, because he was no threat at all.

Alec, on the other hand, felt Harry didn't consider Sanya an equal. "Of course he does," Sanya would protest, and then Alec would remind her of the many instances where Harry treated her like his at-home secretary.

"Can you make sure those suits are dry-cleaned? And I think I need a new suit bag. Can you pick one up for me? I need it before next Monday; I have meetings in New York," Harry would ask on his way out the door, the same door Sanya would be out of a few minutes later to go to work, just like he did.

Of course she would take care of the suits and the luggage. Because that's what she did. She took care of Harry and Sara. Sanya didn't particularly like to hear what Alec said because it made her sound like one of those pathetic wives on *Oprah* who wanted to find the wind beneath their wings and become her own person. The fact that she had become a doormat to her successful husband made her cringe. She wasn't even sure when it happened.

Alec came to see Sanya when she was catatonic in the hospital and then after, when she took up residence in her bed. He had sat stroking her hair, saying nothing. No judgment. Sanya felt that he blamed himself a little because he hadn't seen this coming; he had thought she was tougher.

❖   ❖   ❖

Sanya's parents, both of them successful doctors who had emigrated from India in the seventies, were disappointed in her as well because they also assumed that she was stronger. Earlier they used to be disappointed that she was not a doctor and that she was also not getting anywhere in her career. Her lack of ambition was just not what they expected of a Bhargav, and now they felt the size of their disappointment had increased several hundredfold.

Sanya's mother, Naina Bhargav, an obstetrician and gynecologist, and her father, Raghuram Bhargav, an anesthesiologist, lived and worked in Boston and understood the chemistry of what had happened to Sanya's brain, but they were horrified that their daughter was now popping antidepressants and seeing a therapist. Also, they were appalled that their *happy* and *positive* daughter was now a hostile nutcase who seemed to not care about her job, her life, her family, or her home and spent an inordinate amount of time under a duvet.

Her younger sister, the wonderful Mira, who was married to the impeccable Vinay, was gleefully upset—a part of Mira was probably relieved that the competition was over. She had won. She was a successful pediatrician with her own practice in Boston. She had two beautiful boys. She had the handsome *Indian* neurosurgeon husband (Sanya was married to a corporate white man). She had full control of her mental faculties. But Mira loved her sister, so she worried and called Sanya to make her feel better in her own style—which lacked compassion, to say the least.

Sanya had her sister on speakerphone outside the duvet while she lay inside, and when Mira started to talk about how she always knew Sanya was the *flaky* sort and had predicted that something like this would happen, Harry, who had been listening to their conversation, if you could call it that with Mira doing all the talking, picked up the phone and told her to not call again for a long while.

He did that, he told Sanya, because he felt Mira was being condescending, and that she was not saying what his wife needed to hear during her *difficult* time. Which was nuts! Mira had always been like this—how did he miss that for two decades? Every time they had a family get-together, size-zero Mira, who still fit into her before-kids jeans, would tell Sanya just as she loaded her plate with food about a new diet she knew her sister needed to try. You know, to get rid of all that *belly fat*. Just two months of programmed starving and Sanya would look great in the dress she was currently wearing (which was very nice but didn't *quite flatter the middle area*).

Sanya's mother would agree with Mira. Harry would ignore Mira and Sanya because he would be busy playing *whose dick is bigger* with Vinay, as they both ran marathons and liked to discuss their stats. Sanya's father, who liked to stay away from any controversial female conversations about body image (or anything else, for that matter), would not defend potbellied Sanya.

Instead of asking Mira to go fuck off, Sanya would look at her potbelly and feel a rush of shame and ask for the details of the diet. Instead of asking Harry to defend her—say something, anything—she would remain silent.

It wasn't like she was obese or unhealthy. She was a size eight. She jiggled a little bit here and there, but she was like any other woman in the world with some body parts that excelled and some that did not. But Sanya would not challenge her family and never told them that they made her feel small and irrelevant, even though they believed they were being helpful by *pushing Sanya to be a better person*. She never fought back, and in fact she never acknowledged, even within the confines of her consciousness, that she was playing dead and submerging every negative feeling she had about the people around her and herself.

❖ ❖ ❖

The biggest fraud she committed upon herself and the people around her was to hide the real Sanya, who was not happy or positive but afraid and unsure, and had used the technique of lying down and letting her life and the people in it run all over her so as to not deal with herself or her inadequacies.

Living such an inauthentic life meant that there was a pressure valve that would eventually have to give out to release the steam of Sanya's personal mendacity. So when the pressure became unbearable, boom she went, and imploded with a bang.

Chapter 2

Exiled

They moved to Copenhagen in early May, nearly four months after Sanya's mental collapse. The weather matched her mood, and she watched the gray skies and the pitter-patter of unrelenting pins-and-needles rain from the window of their bedroom as she peeked from under the fluffy Georg Jensen white down comforter. Even though it was May, Harry informed Sanya that people had told him the weather might stay fall-like, windy, rainy, and gray until nearly June and maybe beyond if they were unlucky.

Despite the uncooperative weather, so drastically different from sunny, blue-sky California, Harry was pleased with his decision to move. Because now Sanya sometimes ventured out of the bedroom and sat down to watch television, which is what she was doing when Lucky, Harry's best friend and right hand at work, came to discuss matters of great corporate importance with Harry, in this case, a dinner party.

"Can you please keep your voice down? I don't want anything, and I mean anything, to screw with her recovery," Harry whispered to Lucky.

Sanya could hear them. Of course she could. She had imploded; she hadn't gone deaf.

Their new apartment in Copenhagen had two living rooms connected by glass doors that could not be closed due to some hiccup with the hinge that the landlord still needed to fix. The men sat in the small living room that had been converted into an office while Sanya sat in the large living room watching television. Since everything in Denmark was subtitled, she didn't have to get used to watching *Friends* in Danish. *Friends* in German, she had discovered on a rare business trip to Frankfurt, was just not the same.

"Then don't take her with you for this dinner," Lucky whispered back. "These are important people."

"I can hear you," Sanya called out.

Amply medicated, she was amused that their five-room apartment had a layout called "pork chop." Lucky, with the help of real estate agent Lilly Nielsen, had found the place in the unpronounceable Østerbro area, one of the ten districts of Copenhagen, just north of the city center, where the buildings were over a hundred years old. The double living rooms were in the front with a narrow hallway ensconced by a small bathroom, bedroom, and at the very end of the "chop," a kitchen and a maid's quarters, which now was a spare bedroom.

The furnished apartment had been seriously renovated and modernized. The living room couch—Sanya's domain—came from some big-time Danish designer, and Harry favored a red chair shaped like an egg from the same designer. The coffee table was glass and metal, all clean lines and minimalistic. Lilly Nielsen had even gone on about the faucets in the apartment.

"It's all Arne Jacobsen," she told them. Like that meant something to Sanya. She didn't know Arne Jacobsen from her ass.

"And the china is Royal Copenhagen, the silverware Georg Jensen. The furnishings are from Illum Bolighus," she said to them with a sparkle in her eyes. "This is as upmarket as it gets."

Harry had enthusiastically shown his appreciation for the coolness of the apartment, as well as the location. He loved it all, he told her. It was just the way he had imagined a European capital would be. Old dwellings divided by narrow streets. Green copper turrets with specks of gold. Red rooftops. Clothing stores with unfamiliar names displaying dark and beige-colored clothes on mannequins. Cheerful wine bars advertising their selections of Italian, French, and Spanish wines. Outdoor cafés outfitted chairs with blankets and had gas and infrared lamps in case it got cool in the summer evenings (spoiler alert: it did). Bicycle lanes on all the main roads and more bicyclists than one could count crowding the streets during rush hour. Small cars that expert parallel parkers squeezed into smaller spaces. Unlike Paris, Lilly told them, here people did not dent the cars when they parallel parked, so Harry's new Audi A5 would not be damaged on the street, because obviously when one lived in a city that was nearly a thousand years old, there was a scarcity of parking.

"I'm sorry," Lucky said to Sanya, including her in their conversation.

Lucky, too, was being careful with Sanya, as Harry was. Lucky had *always* been there, since business school. Lucky was Harry's fixer, his whip. Attached to Harry's hip. And it was inevitable that Sanya and Lucky had also developed a relationship, an odd one where they knew each other well but only through Harry.

Harry and Lucky were alike in many ways. Like Harry, Lucky was also fit. Unlike Harry, who ran every morning come hail or rain and did at least one marathon a year, Lucky was into CrossFit. He had a penchant for slim-cut gray suits. Never blue or black. He wore crisp white dress shirts with cufflinks. His ties were gray with black stripes, gray with white stripes, gray with polka dots. He slicked his black and plentiful hair back with enough hair gel to give Danny Zuko a run for his money.

"Lucky, I'm not going to flip out over dinner. And it's been forever since I had a nervous breakdown, so stop stressing about it," Sanya said flippantly. "Where is this dinner?"

Harry smiled his Colgate smile. No cosmetic help. Never a cavity.

"At the American ambassador's residence," Harry said. "This guy whose company we're buying, IT Foundry, he'll be there with his wife."

Sanya nodded. "What time?"

"If you're ready by seven, that'll be great," Lucky said carefully. "And you'll meet Mister Ambassador, of course, and his wife Cindy, Cynthia Wells. Anders Ravn, the owner of IT Foundry, as Harry said, and his wife, Mandy. Also invited . . ."

There were going to be how many people at this dinner? Sanya felt anxiety spread its tiny fingers around her windpipe and slowly choke her. In defense, she raised her hand as she walked toward them. "You're killing the suspense, Lucky. Let me get there and find out. If I know everything now, that'll just ruin the fun."

As she left the room Sanya heard Lucky say, to her satisfaction, "She's not going to take that attitude to dinner, is she?"

You bet she is, Sanya thought gleefully.

Chapter 3

Sanya and Harry, a Happy Couple?

Harry met Sanya at UC Berkeley. He had just broken up with a girlfriend—like fifteen minutes before he came to the Starbucks on Oxford.

A woman was standing in line in front of him. She wore pearl earrings, the kind that dangle. He could only see her dark hair and her earrings as he stood behind her. But once they were at the counter, she turned around, a dazzling smile on her face, and he fell hard. He followed her when she left with her latte, abandoning his coffee that the barista was making for him.

"Hey," Harry said when he caught up with her outside the coffee shop.

The woman looked around her, as if he were talking to someone past her. "Me?" she asked.

"Yes," he said. "Have I seen you before?"

"How would I know if you did?"

"You're right," Harry said. "Can I buy you a cup of coffee?"

She held up the Starbucks cup and smiled. "I already have coffee."

That was when Harry felt foolish. He stuffed his hands in his pockets and nodded. He turned around and was walking away when she called out, "But you can buy me a glass of wine tonight."

He had gotten her name, number, and address, and that evening he took her out to Blake's, one of the student hangouts in Berkeley. They had beer instead of wine.

He had been fascinated with her. She had gotten into Tufts, she told him, but had decided to come to Berkeley to get away from Boston. Harry had gotten into UC Berkeley with sheer hard work, which had earned him a scholarship that alleviated most of the tuition burden; for the rest he had taken a loan, and he was working as a waiter on weekends to pay for living expenses. Sanya didn't have a job to pay for living expenses. She didn't have to take out a loan to pay for school. Her father was a surgeon.

That evening as they sat in the Rathskeller, Blake's subterranean beer hall, with a jazz band, which made it difficult for them to have a conversation, he found that he couldn't look away from her. No other woman had had this effect on him. There was something about Sanya, something about them together that had created, no, demanded instant intimacy. She was vivacious, a happy person who exuded contagious, positive energy. She made him happy by just being there.

Harry's parents had divorced when he was eight. His brother had been fifteen. Too old for Harry to have a relationship with. Harry had been shuttled between his parents, but after a while his father moved and Harry stayed with his mother and her new family: her new husband and his two college-aged daughters. He thought of them as *her* family because he didn't feel included. It wasn't like he had a horrible childhood. He wasn't exactly neglected. No one beat him. He was always well fed. He had the freedom to do what he wanted. There were no hysterical scenes or fighting when he was a teenager. When he left for college, his mother moved with her husband to the East Coast—they all just drifted apart physically as they had emotionally.

He had been an independent child, and he had grown to be a self-confident and independent man. But he had been alone all his life. He'd had relationships, but none of them had made him feel like he belonged. That changed when he met Sanya. She was warm and loving and embraced him. Sanya became his family. She was there for him. She was on his team. Those early days he hungered for the intimacy they had and made love to her whenever he could. It wasn't just that the sex was good; it was the closeness. He loved feeling close to her. She was *his*. And his alone.

In the beginning, it hadn't been love. It had been security for Harry, and he knew it had been his physical appeal for Sanya. He had found that out when they were on their way to Boston, where he was going to meet her parents for the first time.

"I know it's shallow, and you're so much more than that, but god, Harry, you look like you walked out of a fashion magazine," Sanya had told him.

Harry hadn't been surprised. He knew how he looked. He had eyes. And he had ears, so he had heard it before. A blond Paul Newman, one girlfriend's mother had said of him.

"It's not shallow," Harry had said, and flicked her pearl earrings. "You look like an Indian princess. *My* Indian princess."

She was his Indian princess, and he was her cross between Prince Charming and Barbie's Ken.

"My parents always assumed that I'd marry an Indian," Sanya had told him. "You're going to be a rude shock." And that's how he found out that she was *dropping* him into a sea of Indians, without warning her family about his *whiteness* or their closeness, at her parents' annual Diwali party where all their friends would be.

Harry should've been terrified, but he had felt immensely proud of Sanya. He had noticed how she always deferred to her parents over the phone, seemed to be in some ways living like she was still their child and not a grown woman. Many sentences started with "My mother will just lose it if she finds out . . ." No, this Sanya who was taking him to meet the entire Walpole Indian community during the festival of lights, she was rebelling against her family *for him*.

And when he heard Mira's whispered, "God, he's *very* handsome. What does he see in you?" he had understood Sanya's need to show him off.

Beneath surface attractions, Harry and Sanya found common ground. Plenty of it. Good food. Good wine. Workaholism. Business acumen.

For Harry, Sanya was the perfect wife. She never turned him down for sex, even after they were married, even after they had Sara, and even . . . she just never did. She didn't nag about his travel when he started working all hours of the day. She didn't complain when he started an executive MBA at Haas—commonly called a divorce education because it was like having a second and a third job atop the first job he already had.

His career had thrived, thanks to the fact that Sanya was completely undemanding and wholly responsible for running the *home* and *family* parts of their lives. It didn't go unnoticed by Harry that Sanya's career, which had started out with a lot of promise, stopped flourishing around the same time Sara was born. But that was what happened to women, he had rationalized. And he made more money than Sanya, so he had to keep pushing. He had also noticed, and then ignored, the fact that Sanya had fallen back into the old routine of being the pleaser; her one act of rebellion, which was marrying Harry, had faded, but that was part of growing up, wasn't it?

His passion for Sanya had been that mad-for-you, can't-live-with-out-you kind. The type that people look back upon years later and wonder, *Where did it go?* Because now, twenty years later, the passion was tenuous. Love had become comfort, had become commonplace, and had shrunk to nothingness. They had been moving apart for so long that there was a giant abyss between them.

Harry didn't even acknowledge it existed until Sanya's mental collapse. After some joint therapy sessions he started to see her life, torn at the seams as it was, and because he didn't know how to deal with it or even where to start to fix any of it, he did nothing when she hid under the covers in her bed.

It had taken a while for Harry to become serious about Sanya's condition, even after the nervous breakdown. Part of it was that he wanted to be in denial. A month after the *incident at the office*, one morning he had kissed her cheek as he always did, and she had opened her eyes to look into his. She was lying on her stomach, not an elegant pinup sexy position, but a bedraggled I-own-this-whole-bed position.

"Hey," he said. "You're awake."

This was the first time in a month Sanya was awake in the morning, and it made everything inside him squeeze. *Yes,* he thought, *she's going to jump out of bed and say, "Of course I'm awake, and I'm going to go ahead and have a great day."*

But that was Old Sanya. The one who wanted to make everyone around her happy—and he worried that she'd done such a good job of it that all the happiness had drained away from her, and she was left with nothing. And it was his fault because he had stopped paying attention to her, to them.

"No," Sanya whispered, "I'm still sleeping."

She looked so helpless that he had looked at her with disgust; he hadn't been able to stop himself. And that was when tears started to stream down her face. Harry had stood up in shock at his own insensitivity, but unable to say anything to fix the situation, he had said a hasty good-bye before leaving. He hadn't been able to stay, hadn't been able to face Sanya's tears, and she hadn't been able to stop crying. He did what he always did when things didn't work his way: he pretended everything was normal because he didn't know how to handle the abnormal situation they were in.

The next day he went away on a business trip and was gone for a full three days.

He didn't call her. He never called when he was on business trips, so why should he now? Nothing was different. He didn't want to accept that there was a new Sanya in his life, a woman he didn't understand very well. And then there was the fear that he had *never* understood his wife, not because she had hidden something from him, but because he was lacking in intellect to know her inner workings.

Naina, Sanya's mother, called him on day three.

"I called and she mumbled something, and now she won't pick up the phone. It goes straight to voice mail," she told him. "Do something."

"I'm in Houston. What do you want me to do?" Harry had snapped.

"Get her help," Naina had yelled at him. "She's your wife. So pull up your pants and be a man."

Harry got four calls—one from Sanya's mother, one from her father, one from Mira, and one from Vinay. Everyone was worried.

Harry hadn't known what to do and called Alec. He never liked Alec—mostly because he knew Alec didn't like him. He looked down upon Harry. Alec was the intellectual, and Harry was the corporate whore.

Alec went to see Sanya after his call with Harry and told him later that he had had to ring the doorbell for a good fifteen minutes before she opened and that he had been close to calling 911, worried that she'd hit her head or worse.

"How the fuck do you leave your wife when she's just had a nervous breakdown?" Alec had demanded when Harry had called him to check on Sanya. "She could hurt herself."

Harry had panicked then and called his assistant to change his flight. He had to get home ASAP.

He got a text message from Alec as he made his way to the airport.

She's unwashed, starved, and sick. Looks like shit. Managed to get her into the shower. Get your ass back home. Taking her to therapist.

It gnawed on Harry that it was Alec who took her for an emergency appointment with her therapist. It was Alec who fed her. Of course he did, because Harry had run away, scared, a coward.

When Harry came home, he found Sanya sobbing softly on a couch and Alec sitting next to her, reading a book, her hand in his.

"You need to go for a joint therapy session with her," Alec said as he disengaged from Sanya and stood up. "And you need to stay at home and not wander off on business trips."

"I have a job," Harry said defensively.

"Yeah, you do, as her husband; so get to work, buddy, and don't screw this up any more than you already have. She didn't get here all by herself. You pushed enough," Alec said.

Sanya didn't even look up while they argued. Her eyes were swollen shut because of the nonstop crying. *Had she been crying for three straight days?*

"Don't blame me for this," Harry said to Alec, but his voice was shaky.

He was afraid to be with his wife because he didn't know who she was, because this woman lying there with swollen eyes was not the happy woman he had married.

"Get your shit together," Alec said, "and *be* with her for the first time in your marriage. She needs someone to be with her. And if you won't be with her, have the balls to say so, because then I can take care of her. She needs help."

"This is not my fault," Harry said. A part of him was bewildered that this was happening to him, that his life had become this unbearable trial.

"She's sick, and just like you wouldn't leave your wife if she had the flu, you can't leave her now," Alec said, then sighed. "Well, you would leave her if she had the flu, so maybe you're doing what you've always done. But right now, you can't run away from this."

Harry straightened. "Thanks for helping out, Alec. I'll take it from here."

"Yeah, you do that," Alec said, and then gave Sanya's unpliable body a hug and left.

It was a wake-up call for Harry.

Sanya wasn't just having a bad day or a bad week or a bad month—Sanya had flown over the cuckoo's nest, and she needed saving from herself.

Harry pulled Sanya into his arms then and promised her, "I'll take care of you."

Chapter 4

The Emmerys on Strandvejen

The morning after Sanya brazenly decided that she would be going to the dinner party to spite him, Harry appeared to be more hopeful than ever that his wife was coming out of it and would be her old self again very quickly thanks to the magic of changing geographies.

"It's nice out today. I had a really good run. Looks like summer is making an entry in Copenhagen," Harry remarked as he put on his tie in front of the mirror that hung on the bedroom door.

Sanya, who was still in bed, didn't respond. She'd stopped responding to idle chitchat. She was done with that nonsense.

"If the weather holds, maybe you'll come running with me tomorrow morning?" he asked.

What?

Harry went for a run every morning at six, no matter what and no matter where. He would run for thirty-five minutes; then he'd come back, make himself fresh orange juice, drink two glasses of it (he didn't drink coffee early in the morning; coffee was for people who woke up at seven, still groggy, trying to get to work on time), and eat a bowl of muesli, the organic kind they sold at Whole Foods, with organic plain nonfat yogurt. Then he'd take a shower, after which he'd put on a Brioni suit with an Hermès tie. He used to wear Hugo Boss, but that changed when he became a partner. His ties, however, were always Hermès, block colors, the monotony broken recently with patterns like tiny seahorses and dolphins. Hermès did really cute animal prints.

Sanya, on the other hand—by the time she'd drag herself out of bed, her hair looking like it belonged on a worn-out broom until it was tamed—would look at *perfect* Harry in abject despair. She couldn't compete with him. She couldn't live up to him. And because she couldn't, she would try to please him so he wouldn't realize that she was a complete failure, just like her mother and sister unfailingly reminded her, and leave her.

Sanya found that the advantage of having an implosion was that she no longer looked at Harry like he was a god offering her the miracle of life. Her brain functionality did not extend to matters such as these because it was in survival mode.

"Do you have any plans for today?" he asked, trying to make conversation.

"What do you think?" Sanya asked, looking at him pointedly.

Harry almost met Sanya's eyes, she knew, because he wanted to take her up on her challenge, but then at the last minute he looked away.

"It's a beautiful day outside; I hope you'll go out and explore," Harry said. "It's a really lovely city. You'll like it."

"Have a nice day, Harry," Sanya said, and she might as well have been saying *fuck off*.

Harry grinned like he had an ace up his sleeve. "Well, I'll be home around six. We have that dinner at seven. The one you told Lucky you *really* wanted to go to. So be ready."

She heard him whistle as he walked through the narrow corridor into the living room. *Son of a bitch,* Sanya thought, and then she sighed and said, "I don't have anything to wear."

To rectify her lack of an outfit for the dinner at the American ambassador's residence, Sanya called Lilly Nielsen, the real estate agent who had helped them find their new home. At the apartment showings, she had looked smart in a Chanel suit.

"I'll pick you up at one," Lilly said.

"I don't want to go to a department store," Sanya warned her.

"Of course not," Lilly said. "I'm going to take you to the street where all the rich people shop."

With the word *rich* hanging around her, Sanya opened her wallet to find she had a Wells Fargo bank card, an American Express card, and a Visa bank card called a Dankort. Lucky had given her the Dankort the other day and advised her to use the Danish bank card to avoid foreign currency charges. He had also given her a PIN for the card, which Sanya had typed onto the notepad in her iPhone. For someone who used to play with numbers in long Excel sheets and could remember revenue figures and calculate percentages inside her head with ease, she was certainly struggling with four measly ones to unlock the bounty in their Danish bank account. But how much bounty was there, and what did a dress cost in Copenhagen?

Unsure of her financial prowess anymore, Sanya called Harry. He picked up on the first ring, a new habit forced by her condition, because the last time he'd missed a call from her it had been when she was alone in her office meeting room, wailing her guts out and waiting for the paramedics and/or Harry to show up.

"Are we rich?" Sanya asked him.

Harry paused for a moment. "You can buy a new dress for tonight, but if you're planning on picking up a car, I'd very much like Lucky to check it out first. They charge a two hundred fifty percent tax on cars in Denmark."

"I hardly leave the house; why on earth would I want to buy a car?" she asked.

"I'm fine with it if you want to buy a car," he said.

"I don't want a car. Lilly wants to take me to the street where all the rich people shop," she said. "She thinks I'm rich."

"We're okay," Harry said.

"Am *I* okay?"

"As long as *I'm* okay, *you're* okay," Harry said.

"I guess since I am living off you now," Sanya said. Despite the fact that she currently couldn't hold down a job, a part of Sanya, the one that used to be financially independent, felt caged.

"Oh, for god's sake," Harry snapped. "Look, we've been together for way too long, long before prenuptials were fashionable, to be having this conversation. Not that either of us had any money when we met anyway."

"Do you want one now? I'm sure your whippersnapper lawyer . . . what's her name? Tara Hansen? Maybe she can put one together, a postnuptial agreement," Sanya suggested.

"You're being silly. I'm glad you're going shopping," he said, changing to a safe subject.

"I'll be glad if I make it downstairs when Lilly comes to get me," Sanya said seriously.

Anxiety is depression's good friend, and sometimes they party together.

❖　❖　❖

"You look good," Lilly said in her accented English when Sanya sat down on the plush leather seat of her BMW 645.

"Thank you," she responded automatically, and then added, "you look good as well."

A tall, slim blonde, she really did look good, and, though roughly Sanya's age, she seemed much more sophisticated than Sanya had ever been.

"Strandvejen is the most exclusive street in all of Denmark. *Strand* means 'beach' and *vejen* means 'road,' so it's 'beach road,'" Lilly said as she expertly navigated traffic on Østerbrogade, the main street in Østerbro that turned into Strandvejen, after the large and famous Tuborg beer sculpture.

Lilly, who was a good saleswoman and therefore an excellent conversationalist, probably realized that Sanya wasn't much of a talker and spent the entire time they drove showing off Strandvejen to her.

Lilly pointed to various shops and cafés as they drove down the beach road.

"You'll love Birgitte Green. Everyone shops there," she said, and by *everyone*, Sanya knew what she meant. "Birgitte Green's store has all the right brands, and she takes care of her customers. I also shop at Trois Pommes, you know, for everyday stuff. You should check it out. And if you like to read, there's a lovely English bookstore across from the Bang & Olufsen shop, Books & Company. The owner, Isabel, is a good friend of mine. And Øresund is just down the street, so the views are just spectacular from some of these places. I've sold many apartments in the area. This is the *it* street."

"I'm not a high-end-clothing kind of person," Sanya said, gesturing to the jeans and sweater she had chosen for the shopping trip—though "chosen" was a euphemism in this case. Sanya had spent an inordinate amount of time worrying about what to wear so she wouldn't be cold or uncomfortable.

"What kind of clothes do you like to wear?" Lilly asked.

"Just . . . regular stuff," Sanya said, and didn't elaborate. When she used to work (just a few months ago), she tended to wear suits or work dresses. She favored Hugo Boss at bonus time; otherwise, Ann Taylor, J.Crew, midrange brands.

"I wear Chanel when I work because I do real estate at the high end of the market," Lilly said. "The rest of the time I like a pair of jeans. But dinner at the ambassador's residence warrants something special."

Sanya realized she should never have said yes to this dinner. It was hard enough to leave the house, remember to lock the door, remember to take house keys, remember . . . oh, so many things. She had just wanted to piss Lucky off in the moment, so she had acted impulsively, and now the joke was on her.

"I have a showing at three," Lilly said, as she parallel parked on the busy street, Strandvejen. "So . . . I may have to leave . . ."

"I'm not picky," Sanya quickly said. "It shouldn't take that long."

❖   ❖   ❖

If Sanya had imagined an expensive European boutique, Birgitte Green is what she would've imagined it would look like. When they came in, Birgitte asked if they'd like a glass of champagne. They turned her down, but it was *that* kind of store, ornate and classy, an exclusive little space with no mannequins but stylish and expensive clothes displayed on hangers with coordinating shoes underneath them; jewelry on large, dark stones; and a green-and-white floral upholstered antique couch artfully positioned in front of the dressing rooms.

Birgitte immediately sized Sanya up with her eyes and pulled together a couple of dinner-party-worthy dresses and hung them in a dressing room with a speed that Sanya found admirable. She and Lilly spoke to each other in Danish, leaving Sanya completely out of the conversation. Sanya would find out later that Danes did that kind of thing all the time and didn't consider it rude. Sanya didn't, either, considering her eagerness to avoid being asked questions or participate in small talk.

The first dress Sanya tried was in her comfort zone. A little black dress. It draped without clinging, and she felt luxurious in the obviously expensive fabric. It was simple. A small bow in the back was the only embellishment. It had a V-neck in the front and a lower one in the back. It came right above her knees. It was demure and classy. It hid all the dodgy areas (the belly fat) and accentuated the tits and ass, which had not gone south yet, well, not Deep South, anyway. The price tag was gigantic even though the dress was seventy percent off.

"I don't think this is the dress," Birgitte Green announced after a long moment during which Sanya waited for a pronouncement.

Birgitte stood with her arms crossed, eyeing Sanya up and down speculatively, while Lilly sat looking through her phone, completely disinterested in the Prada, Gucci, and Célines around her. Sanya felt a pang of guilt for wasting her time.

"Try the LWD," Birgitte suggested, pointing to the white dress she had chosen and hung on Sanya's dressing room door.

"And what's that?"

"The little white dress," Birgitte said. She was another Lilly. Tall, blond, and gorgeous. The national look of Denmark. "With your dark complexion, you'll glow in white. Trust me."

Sanya looked at her watch when she saw Lilly look at hers.

"Lilly, you don't have to wait for me," she told her, even though her heart was in her throat and a panicked voice inside said, *How will I get home?*

"You can take a taxi home," Birgitte suggested.

Take a what? Sanya couldn't even remember her address. This woman obviously knew nothing about anxiety.

Sanya licked her dry lips and tried to stay calm. "I'll go to the café you showed me on the way here. The one you said *everyone* goes to? Harry can pick me up from there. What was it called?"

"Emmerys," Lilly said. She gave Sanya a hug and wished her luck and left ten minutes before the clock struck three.

Sanya tried on the white dress. It was one of those lace numbers that came right below her knee. Sanya felt uncomfortable in it, even if it was a Miu Miu.

As she watched Sanya in the dress in a mirror outside the dressing room, Birgitte made small talk and wanted to know if Sanya had bought a house from Lilly.

"We're renting."

Birgitte nodded. "I think this is a good dress but . . . let's try something else."

She went to a rack and got Sanya a yellow dress with big red flowers. There was no way, Sanya thought, that she was wearing a yellow dress. It was too fucking happy. But she didn't want to be rude—Old Sanya was still there lurking in the corners—so she went into the dressing room again and put on the happy dress. It was a dress with a tight bodice and a full tulle skirt. Sanya felt she looked like a cross between a ballet dancer and a tequila sunrise.

"Oh, it's lovely," Birgitte said. "Your skin color just works with everything."

"Actually, I prefer the black dress," Sanya said. "I'm more of an LBD kind of girl."

Birgitte smiled at her. "Are you sure? This is really . . . you know? *Va va voom.*"

Sanya nodded and then shook her head but didn't say anything. She went into the dressing room and changed out of the happy outfit back into her jeans and sweater.

"Are you an Indian expat?" Birgitte asked Sanya as she changed.

"I'm American," Sanya said.

She *was* American, but when she said so, some people, particularly Europeans, who didn't always understand the intricacies of being ethnic-looking and still being American, raised their eyebrows and she'd have to explain. "I'm ethnically Indian. My parents immigrated to the United States in the seventies. I was born and raised in the United States."

"And your husband is . . . American?" Birgitte asked curiously when Sanya came out of the dressing room, holding the black dress on its hanger.

Sanya knew Birgitte was eager to learn Harry's ethnicity, but she wasn't about to satisfy her by blurting, *He's blond and white, just like all of you.* So Sanya nodded vaguely and looked at the clothes she had just tried on and felt claustrophobic. She had hit her wall.

Ultimately, Sanya bought the little black dress. Birgitte seemed dissatisfied with her choice. Partly, Sanya thought, because the LBD was seventy percent off and maybe partly because she really felt that Sanya glowed in the LWD or the tequila sunrise dress. She showed her disappointment amply as she packed up the dress.

Join the disappointed-with-Sanya club, lady, Sanya thought. *Maybe there's room in the back.*

❖   ❖   ❖

Thank goodness Emmerys was just a couple of hundred steps away from Birgitte Green, because Sanya was having heart palpitations that she would get lost.

People were sitting outside in the spring sun against a backdrop of the window display of homemade jams and jellies and *bio vin,* which Sanya guessed meant organic wine. Chilled from the short walk, she joined the line inside with her dress in a cloth bag hanging on her arm. Birgitte had shown her how to hold it upright on its hanger so it wouldn't get creased, but her words were lost in Sanya's fog of fatigue.

She should have been tempted by the pastries and countless types of bread, some so warm she could smell them, but after the shopping ordeal, all she could stomach was coffee.

The place *was* popular, because Sanya had to stand in line for ten minutes before she could order.

"You take cards?" Sanya asked, because she had no cash.

"Yes, Dankort," the woman behind the counter said.

Sanya nodded and stayed calm. She had just gone through the drill with Birgitte. And once again she checked her iPhone for the PIN. *How muddled is my mind,* she thought, *that I can't remember four little digits?*

As soon as she took her latte to a table and settled the bag with the dress on the chair next to her, a woman approached Sanya. "Hi," she said in a strong American accent. She carried a paper bag with a baguette sticking out of it.

"Hi," Sanya replied.

"You must be Sanya," the woman said. "I'm sorry for being so forward, but I saw your name on your Dankort."

Sanya stared at her blankly.

"I'm Mandy," she said and held out her hand to shake, the one not holding the bread. Sanya shook it absently, still waiting for the strange woman to explain who she was.

"Mandy Ravn," she elaborated. "Anders Ravn's wife."

Her name meant nothing to Sanya.

"May I join you?" she asked. Sanya sure as hell wanted to say no, but before she had a chance, Mandy cheerfully sat down, and Sanya had no choice but to sit down as well.

Maybe Sanya still looked confused as to who Mandy was, because she continued, "My husband is the CEO of IT Foundry. Your husband, Harry Kessler, is here to acquire his company."

Did this woman really just have to name my own husband for me? Sanya nodded and smiled like a fool.

"You went shopping, I see," Mandy said brightly. "Birgitte has great clothes."

"Birgitte?"

"Yes, the woman who owns Birgitte Green," Mandy said and pointed to the logo on the cloth bag that held her dress.

"Right, of course," Sanya said.

"Is it for the dinner tonight?" Mandy asked.

Sanya nodded. Obviously Mandy would be at dinner, and that's when it struck Sanya there would be a person seated to her left and one to her right and one across from her . . . *Oh boy.*

"You'll love Cindy," Mandy said and smiled. "This is my life here in Copenhagen, you know. I keep losing my wonderful friends. I was so close to Amaya, the Spanish ambassador's wife, and then they were sent back home. This is how it works with expats."

"We're here for just one year," Sanya said in warning. *Don't make friends with me, and actually I'm not really here, I'm still under the covers in my bed at home in Los Gatos.*

"We'll make the best of that year," Mandy said, and then looked at her watch in a deliberate move. "Oh, I have to go. I have to pick up my daughter—I just rushed in to pick up some bread. It was nice meeting you, Sanya, and I look forward to tonight."

After Mandy left, Sanya drank her coffee quietly. Two men in suits came to sit at a table in the corner. It appeared like they were having a meeting. For Friday afternoon, the place was pretty packed. Maybe they left early from work on Fridays, Sanya thought. And as soon as she thought about work, she realized she hadn't texted Harry yet because Mandy had distracted her. She sent him her whereabouts and her need for transportation back to the apartment. He texted back saying he was in a meeting; could he pick her up at four thirty? Always scared now of Sanya *suddenly* losing her mind, he offered to come earlier if that's what was needed.

Do you know where Emmerys is? Sanya asked. He wrote back, Yes, the one on Strandvejen?

Of course there was more than one Emmerys. *Why does everything have to be so complicated?*

In desperation, Sanya turned to the man who had just arrived and was settling down at the table next to hers. "Excuse me, is this the Emmerys on . . . Strand . . . vejen?"

The man looked at Sanya for a moment, and she immediately noticed the scar on his right cheek. It was a deep, old gash, starting from the base of his ear and ending midcheek. "Yes," he said.

His skin wasn't as dark as Sanya's, but he was tan. His hair was jet black. He wore a suit. A dark suit with pinstripes. His tie was bright orange and so were his socks, which peeked out from between the hem of his pants and his black leather shoes. They would've seemed incongruous on anyone else, but they entirely suited the man with the scar.

"Thank you," Sanya said, a little dazed that she was intensely curious about this stranger.

"It's pronounced *Staandvahen*," he said as he got comfortable in his seat and picked up his cup of espresso. "We roll our *r*'s, and our *j*'s are *h*'s."

Sanya nodded. She sent Harry a text message to confirm her location, and when she looked up, the man was watching her keenly. He asked, "Are you okay?"

"Of course," Sanya replied immediately. It was her standard response because Harry asked it so often.

When Sanya had been in the psychiatric ward, unable to speak, Harry had told her that he blamed himself for neglecting her. *Not your fault*, Sanya had wanted to say. *It's physics.*

"I can't lose you," he had said. "I know who I am without you. I don't like the man I am without you."

Even though Sanya's senses were numbed, what he said had crept through her consciousness, and she had wondered what she was without him. After so many years of togetherness, she wasn't sure what was him and what was her and what was them. When she looked at their living room in Los Gatos, she wasn't sure whose taste it reflected. Their identities had intermingled even though they'd lived separate lives together for so many years.

Harry had promised, as he held her listless hand in the hospital, that he would be more careful with her. And that's why he asked so often if she was okay. Sanya wasn't sure if it was going to be enough to heal the wounds within, to survive the onslaught of an honest Sanya, a Sanya who was permitting herself to feel not just what was safe and allowed but . . . *everything.*

"You have this look on your face," the man explained.

"What look?" she asked. His scar was compelling, and Sanya felt an urgent need to connect with him.

She took a deep breath. Her therapist in California had said to take deep breaths when she felt the next moment was going to be a mountain. *I need to find a therapist in Copenhagen,* she thought, then, *I'm not ready to be without one.*

"I'm fine," she said, breathing evenly. "I imploded a while back, but I'm fine now."

The man smiled then. His teeth were crooked here and there. Normal. It made Sanya smile as well.

"That's good to hear."

"How did you get that scar on your cheek?" The question was out before Sanya could weigh it, measure it, check it. For the first time in what felt like a hundred years, Sanya was curious, and what a thing to be curious about.

"I was in an accident," the man said.

"A knife fight?" she asked with eyes wide. He looked like someone who could be a character out of *Carmen.* A Spanish soldier fighting for his lusty lover.

The man laughed. "Nothing that romantic," he said. "I fell into an open well when I was a child and got hurt."

"How old were you?" she asked.

"Ten," the man said.

"Were you scared?" Sanya could see this man as a ten-year-old in a well, alone, a big bloody gash on his cheek.

"Of course," he said. "But not for long. My parents heard me scream, and they came running to pull me out."

"How did they bring you out of the well?" she wanted to know. It was suddenly imperative that she construct this incident in her mind, as close to reality as possible.

"My father put down a ladder and then helped me up," the man said.

"Do you like your scar?" Sanya asked.

The man nodded without hesitation. "It's a good scar," he said.

"Yes, it is," Sanya agreed.

Another man in a suit walked in and waved at the man sitting next to Sanya. The man rose, folded the Danish newspaper he was reading and placed it on the table next to his empty cup of espresso. Sanya's latte had been served in a tall clear glass. His espresso was in a small white cup on a saucer. His biscotti and his sugar packet were untouched. It was as if these details were the first things Sanya had seen in many months in color, not in black and white.

He left with the man in the suit without saying anything to Sanya, but it wasn't rude. Her intimate conversation with a stranger had been . . . comfortable. *Yes, that was the word,* she thought as she watched him walk out through the doors of the café.

❖   ❖   ❖

Sanya had finished her latte and contemplated calling Harry to check where he was when he came into the café. Before Sanya could draw his attention, a woman screeched his name. A redhead with glossy, curly hair. She had a large Emmerys box atop her table. And instead of wondering how she knew Sanya's husband, or why she was so elated to see him, Sanya found herself wondering what was in the box. Cake? Pastries? One of those twisty cinnamon rolls with chocolate on top?

Before she knew it, Harry was introducing Sanya to the redhead, Penny. She had a Danish name, *Per-ni-la,* but everyone called her Penny, she told her, because the Danish name was too difficult to pronounce, especially for everyone in London. That's how she made sure Sanya knew that she had lived in London and her husband was British and couldn't pronounce her name properly, either.

"I look forward to seeing you at dinner tonight," Penny said.

Great, another person who was invited to that blasted dinner. But the panic Sanya had felt with Mandy was gone. Her mind was still on the man with the scar on his cheek.

"And we have to get to know one another," Penny continued. "You must come to our annual party at our summer house in Sweden. It's by a lake. We stay overnight and go skinny-dipping in the lake."

Penny looked at Harry when she said skinny-dipping. Women always showed interest in handsome Harry. Sanya had long ago learned not to pay attention, and that old habit came into gear.

"Got to get home. Pastries for the kids," Penny said, holding up the Emmerys box.

"What kind of pastries?" Sanya asked.

Penny looked confused. "Just something chocolate, you know." She left hurriedly, as if running away from Sanya.

"Do you mind if I have a cup of coffee before we leave?" Harry asked.

He got himself a black coffee and a second café latte for Sanya. Now that Penny had gone, they could talk about her.

"Penny is Anders Ravn's cousin," Harry explained. "Anders Ravn—"

"Is the CEO of IT Foundry, I know," Sanya said, and explained how she had met Mandy just a short while ago. "She sat exactly where you're sitting. This is a *very* happening café."

"Apparently, it's the most popular bakery on the street, for bread and business meetings," Harry said. "I met Penny last week at the IT Foundry office."

I didn't ask for an explanation, Sanya wanted to say.

Harry drank his coffee, eyeing his wife carefully. "Are you okay?"

"Of course," Sanya said with more verve than she had in a long time.

Harry went completely into defensive mode. He did that, Sanya thought, maybe because he was not sure what her new effervescence meant, and probably it meant nothing good considering how she had been for the past four months. "You don't have to come to dinner tonight, if you're not feeling up to it. Your eyes . . . they . . . you look tired."

Her eyes looked wild was what he wanted to say, but he was too polite to tell his crazy wife she looked crazy, Sanya thought, as she controlled a giggle that almost escaped her and would prove his point.

"I am tired," she agreed, even though she was exhilarated.

"I can make your excuses for tonight," he continued.

"I bought a little black dress," Sanya told him, and pulled out the dress from its bag to show to Harry. Cracked-up people didn't buy new dresses, right? "The saleswoman wanted me to buy a little white dress, but I got what I wanted."

Harry smiled. "The dress will look lovely on you."

"I didn't tell the saleswoman at the store, but the little white dress made me look like I was ready for the funny farm. This dress hides my belly . . . and . . . I think it also hides . . . you know . . . the rest, in my head," Sanya said.

"You have the sexiest belly in the world. I love your belly. You're a woman with a woman's body," Harry said. "And thank god for that."

Sanya's excitement turned into confusion, and she felt like Ingrid Bergman in George Cukor's version of the movie *Gaslight*.

Just a few years ago when they were at an office thing, one of the partner's wives, Elizabeth, had been wearing a skin-hugging dress.

"How is she my age and looks like that? I mean, she has no belly at all," Sanya had said.

"She works out. If you worked out, you'd have a flat belly as well," Harry said.

"Do you want me to have a flat belly?" Sanya asked as she sipped her champagne, watching Elizabeth as she mingled with guests in her nearly two-dimensional body. What she didn't say was, *Will that make you happier with me? Will that make you want me more?*

"Sure," Harry said and then shook his head. "Look, if you want a flat belly, go get one. I don't understand women sometimes; you look at other women with envy, but you don't want to do anything about your situation."

Sanya had been hurt, and instead of saying, *You're a piece of shit and the correct answer is: You're perfect as you are, Sanya,* she said, "You're right; maybe I should get a trainer."

Harry had smiled and patted her shoulder. "That's the spirit. Lose some weight, build some muscle, you'll feel better."

Sanya never got a personal trainer or the flat stomach; and she never discussed it with Harry again . . . until now. And now Harry was saying, sexy belly? Love it? Woman's body? He'd never said such words before. Who was this Harry? Was Harry changing, as she was? Or was he faking it for New Sanya's benefit?

Chapter 5

Dinner at the Ambassador's Residence

The American ambassador's residence was famous, they learned from the ambassador's wife, Cindy. It was called Rydhave, where *ryd* means "clear" and *have* means "garden." Perched on a hill along Strandvejen north of Copenhagen, it had a lovely view of Øresund, the strait that separates Denmark from Sweden, a view the guests enjoyed as they had their drinks in the patio upon arrival. The villa even had a bomb shelter, a leftover from when it was owned by a German foreign minister during World War II, when Denmark was occupied by the Nazis.

"We use the bomb shelter for storage. My skis are there," Cindy said as her guests nibbled on delicate blue crab beignets and drank Napa Valley Schramsberg Mirabelle Brut.

The guests also included the Ukrainian ambassador and his former trophy wife, Anya, who met all the stereotypes. She was a "former" trophy wife because when he'd married her he'd been forty-eight and she had been twenty-two, but now he was sixty-eight and she was no longer quite so shiny a prize.

Her blond hair was tied up in a loose knot, and soft, sexy curls surrounded her face. Anya had big breasts and the cutest Eastern European accent, mixed with a little French lilt, which she explained was a remnant of the French finishing school she had gone to. Her father was a Russian prince of some sort, wealthy in both currency and history. She had no children, though Mister Ambassador had three from his former marriage, and that was "more than enough" for her.

The dinner seating was typical Danish style—in Mandy's translation, "One boy, one girl."

Sanya sat across from Anya, who sat next to Harry. Penny flanked Harry's other side. Sanya was sitting in between an empty chair, which belonged to Anders Ravn, who was late, and the Ukrainian ambassador, whose name eluded her. But she figured she could just call him Mister Ambassador, and she could call the American ambassador Mister Ambassador, too. She was all set.

The dinner table was lavish with beautiful white calla lily decorations in Waterford vases, artfully arranged to not impede the line of vision between the guests and placed atop a thick Fadini Borghi patterned design white tablecloth. The white plates were decorated with big blue flowers that Sanya recognized as being the well-known Danish Royal Copenhagen plates; and next to the plates were oddly shaped Georg Jensen silverware that Sanya was familiar with because they had the same ones in the apartment.

The servers wore white gloves as they poured water from Erik Bagger (another famous Danish designer) carafes into crystal water glasses. Cindy informed them that the water and wine glasses were designed by Frederik Bagger, the son of Erik Bagger, who had recently started his own design company. They had chosen his glasses for the residence to support him, as they knew him very well.

"Frederik and his partner, who is also CEO of the company, Michael—they're both very good friends of our older daughter, Sharon," Cindy explained. "Such ambitious and hardworking boys; and the designs are actually very good, aren't they?"

Everyone around the table agreed that the designs were indeed very good.

The wines served were a 2008 Littorai Thieriot Vineyard Chardonnay from the Sonoma Coast, where Mister Ambassador was from, and a 2007 Domaine Armand Rousseau Père et Fils Chambertin Clos-de-Bèze Grand Cru, an expensive burgundy that Cindy *adored* and was serving even though it wasn't American. The white was matched to the first course and the red to the second.

Harry was successful in the Bay Area, but he was not the man who got invited to dinner at an ambassador's residence. The invitation probably came because of Anders and Mandy Ravn, who flew in these circles and wanted to take care of Harry, their new buyer. Here in Denmark, Harry was finally a big fish in a small pond, and Sanya knew that Harry wanted to be a big fish in any pond.

"Your husband is very handsome," Anya told Sanya as she openly flirted with Harry, who seemed comfortable basking in her attention.

Sanya was thankfully being left alone. The Ukrainian ambassador was speaking mostly to the American ambassador at the head of the table; and even as the first course, venison bouillon with delicate slivers of venison steak and chives, progressed there was no sign of Anders Ravn, Sanya's dinner companion.

It was becoming patently obvious that Sanya was not part of any of the discussions around the table.

"If I'd known he was going to get held up in a meeting, I wouldn't have seated you next to him," Cindy stage-whispered across the table.

"You know how Ravn is," Mandy said, obviously taking offense. "He always wants to be on time, but duty calls."

"Ravn is never on time," Mister Ambassador, the American one, said.

"I agree," Mister Ambassador, the Ukrainian one, concurred. "I waited for him for over half an hour at the golf course last weekend."

"Cindy, you have the most excellent chef," Mandy said, diverting attention from her errant husband. "When you leave I'm going to steal him."

"No, no, I have dibs," Penny said.

Sanya looked at Harry. These people could afford chefs. These people were not like them. They were out of Harry's league, but Sanya could see how much he wanted to fit in. *Poor Harry,* she thought. He must be scared shitless that she was going to fall apart right here at the dinner table and embarrass him.

"We're not leaving yet," Cindy said. "Another two years, and after that we'll see. Y'all better start being nice to me now if you want my Antoine. I did suggest to him that he could come back to Atlanta with us, but his children are here. Another love slave. Do you know what a love slave is, sugar?" she asked Sanya, who tried to avoid the *deer caught in headlights* expression because she was surprised to be addressed and just shook her head blandly.

Before Cindy could explain, another guest interjected.

"Man meets Danish hottie at some holiday on some beach and then follows her to Denmark. They marry or cohabit, whichever. They have children. They get divorced. They *always* get divorced. The father has to stay in this *dejlige lille land,* 'delightful little land,' for the children," Mark Barrett, a Brit and Penny's husband, said as he drank beer from a glass. Everyone else was drinking wine.

"And the reverse is true as well; a lot of women end up staying in Denmark with their Danish husbands," Penny said. "Mandy, what do you say, are you a love slave? Or maybe you'd like to be."

Mandy waved her hand at Penny as if she'd said something naughty.

"Oh, Mark, all y'all Brits are just too funny," Cindy said, and let out a laugh.

Christ, who were these people? The men had careers. The women dabbled in fashion and chefs. None of the women, including Sanya, worked. Except for Penny. She was apparently a designer and had her own clothing line that she'd started after she'd retired from modeling for the big fashion houses. She actually said that to Harry: "I walked for *all* the *big* houses."

And the former model was peddling her clothes actively.

"Mandy, you have to come to the store, because I have this one-of-a-kind turquoise-and-cream dress that will look divine on you."

"Cindy, you loved my leather jacket, the black one with the purple lining that I wore for the *Elle Denmark* gala? I have another one just like it but with a scarlet lining and it was made for you."

Harry liked women with careers, corporate ones, and Penny was an expert at the art of the pitch. No wonder Harry was all eyes and ears when he talked to her. Anya, the big-busted Ukrainian with the sex-kitten French accent, wasn't getting anywhere with Harry. Still, Sanya had noticed, and god knows who else had, that she rubbed her ample bosom against his sleeve each time she leaned over to tell him something.

During the break between the first and second courses, Mark claimed the empty chair next to Sanya, beer in hand.

"How are you doing?" he asked. "I introduced Lilly to Lucky, and I wanted to make sure everything went well on the housing front."

"Oh. How do you know Lilly?" Sanya asked.

"I'm a real estate investor," he said.

"It's a very nice apartment," Sanya said. She didn't tell him that she had just seen Lilly. She didn't want to prolong the conversation.

"And I hear that Lilly took you shopping today," he added.

Faster than jungle drums!

"She's very nice," Sanya replied.

Mark laughed. "She's a barracuda. Bloody good at what she does, and she knows her shopping. You look wonderful in that dress. But maybe next time you should go to Penny's boutique. It's in the center of the city."

Next time? Sanya turned away from Mark and looked blindly at the tablecloth.

"The man was caught with his pants at his ankles and the woman between his legs," Mister Ambassador from Ukraine was saying. "He paid through his nose for the divorce. I'm telling you, divorces have become so expensive it's better to put up with the wife than to get rid of her."

"Or have a tight prenuptial agreement," Penny added. "In our case it was just sensible, you know. I'm sure you have one, too, right, Harry? It's very popular in the United States, isn't it?"

Harry said something about how when they married there was no need for a pre-nup, a repeat of what he had just said to Sanya over the phone in the morning. Sanya felt a twinge of hysteria rise inside her.

"Oh, this is such a crass discussion," Mandy said. "So, Sanya, what did you do back in California?"

Everyone turned to look at Sanya.

Harry tensed. "Sanya was a consultant," he said.

Gallant Harry!

"A financial consultant," he added.

The women nodded politely. Sanya, who hated that Harry had to save her, spoke calmly, decelerating her heartbeat from galloping horses to strolling Victorian ladies. "I worked as a financial consultant, specializing in corporate financial procedures," she said, and saw the blank look on everyone's face. They were not expecting this from Sanya.

"How . . . nice," Mandy said.

"I went to companies and cleaned up their financial processes, you know, how they recorded revenue, gave out payroll and bonuses, how they spent money," she added.

Sanya decided that she sounded articulate and felt her spine straighten with a little pride.

"I can't wait for this acquisition to be done with," Mandy said. "I'm trying to convince my husband that we should buy an orange orchard in Spain and live there happily ever after. But he's not interested. He wants to start something new. Once a businessman, always a businessman."

"Orange orchards are business," someone said.

"But not that much money these days, which I'm sure Ravn knows," Mark said as he walked back to his chair.

"Again all this talk about money," Mandy said. "I miss the days when money was simply not discussed."

"We're not talking about money; we're talking about your husband's ambitions, luv," Mark said.

"I have only humble ambitions," a voice that didn't belong to anyone at the table said.

"Oh, Anders," Mandy cried, her voice dripping with affection.

Sanya looked up, curious to see this Anders Ravn. It was the man with the scar on his cheek. She was mesmerized. She watched him walk around the table, hugging and air-kissing and shaking hands. He came to her last as he took his place next to her.

"Anders Ravn," he said, and held out his hand. Sanya took it.

"It's a pleasure to meet you *again*," Ravn said.

The room fell silent at the word *again* and waited for Ravn to elaborate. He didn't. The tension built in the room, so vivid that Sanya had to once again control her breathing and let the weight inside her dissolve just as she had learned in therapy.

"I met Sanya earlier today as well," Mandy declared to thwart the unbearable silence. "At Emmerys."

"How funny. Me, too," Penny said.

All Ravn had to do was say him, too, but he didn't. So Sanya didn't, either. Harry looked at his wife quizzically just for a moment but then let it pass and wore the mask of insouciance.

"Cindy, I'm sorry for being late," Ravn said. "But the loss, I believe, is mine, because I missed the appetizer."

The conversation flowed again, and the man with the scar and Sanya sat in their assigned seats in resolute silence.

Finally, he whispered to her, "Was the appetizer any good?"

She shook her head. "Did you know who I was this afternoon?"

"Yes," he said.

She didn't ask how he knew.

"I used to have a mole," she told him. "Right here." She pointed to the right side of her neck. "It was small, but I kept obsessing about it."

"Why?" he asked, looking at her neck.

44

"It protruded like a witch's mole," she explained. "My parents are both doctors, and they said if it wasn't life threatening, then it didn't need to be removed."

"But you wanted it gone," Ravn said.

Could he be as interested in her mole as she was in his scar?

"Absolutely. I was horrified with it, and I was scared that any day a hair would emerge out of it and make me look like a witch. So one day I took a scalpel from my mother's medical kit, and I cut it off," Sanya told him.

"There is no visible scar," Ravn said. "You did a good job."

Sanya laughed, and almost immediately she felt the heat of Harry's glance. She ignored it.

"No, I botched it. There was a lot of blood. My white bathroom was red. My mother sewed it up. She's an OB-GYN. Lots of delicate C-sections, you know, so that mommies can still wear bikinis after they have babies."

"I have two children," Ravn said. "Twins. A girl and a boy. They're both nineteen."

"I have a daughter. She's eighteen, and I've never worn a bikini," Sanya said.

"Why?"

She ruminated on that for a moment. "I'm too Indian to wear a bikini. But maybe it's just an excuse, because I'm not Indian except for the ethnicity. I don't like to show my body with all its lumps and bumps."

"Bikini or not, clothing only covers, it doesn't change," Ravn said.

"But it hides."

"If you have courage, you don't have to hide."

"And what if you don't have courage?" Sanya wanted to know.

"Then you lie down."

Sanya shook her head. "No. No. Then you *find* the courage."

Ravn smiled and then turned to the server and asked for a glass of burgundy. He didn't like California Chardonnay, he told Sanya, though he was perfectly okay with other California wines, even their red blends.

❖   ❖   ❖

On their way home, Sanya decided to not be perverse and told Harry how she met Ravn at Emmerys that afternoon, but she hadn't known *he* was Ravn. She caught his sigh of relief behind his practiced nonchalance.

Harry was the competitive type, and he'd clearly taken note of Ravn's power and his fortune (Anya had let it slip at dinner that money had been in his family for generations). And then there was the scar.

Did Harry know her well enough, Sanya wondered, to know that the imperfection of the scar was attractive to her? Did he also realize that Harry's straight and neat lines, the ones that used to give her pleasure, had somewhere over the years become less attractive, less interesting? It wasn't Harry's fault, of course, it was just that Sanya had changed—she had started to crave jagged lines and disorder. She wanted edges rather than curves. She wanted to say the unsaid things. She wanted to feel everything at a time when she felt nothing.

Did he suspect that she not only didn't mind disorder, she wanted it, because she liked it? And did that scare him shitless like it did her?

He didn't say it out loud, but, watching him drive home in silence, Sanya could almost hear him think and wish, *Can't Old Sanya, the happy one, the organized one, the normal one, please come the hell back?*

The truth was that put-together Sanya might be gone forever. And though that should have scared her, this not knowing who she was anymore, this lostness, amazingly, it did not. This was the new normal—though normal was probably the wrong word under the circumstances.

Sanya smiled at the thought, tracing her finger along her face, over where Ravn's scar would be. Harry interrupted her not-so-private fantasy with a sideways glance, and she pulled her hand away.

Chapter 6

A Few Good Days in May

The day after the ambassador's dinner, Harry came back home early, and he was about to go up the stairs to the apartment when he wondered what was the point. She would be in bed or sitting on the couch watching television and ignoring him. The irony was not lost upon him. He had spent a large part of their marriage ignoring her, and now it was her turn. It didn't make it any easier to swallow.

Marriage, he had always envisioned it as a convenience. Sanya called it a pooling of resources, emotional and financial; it was the bulwark of her life, she used to say. She didn't say it now. She didn't say much to him now.

Instead of going up to the apartment, Harry decided to get a drink in the restaurant on the ground floor, the famous Le Saint Jacques. A small French brasserie that was an Østerbro staple, it was famously decorated like a cathedral, with genuine Russian icons and altar candles. Named after Saint James of Compostela, the restaurant was known for its coquilles Saint-Jacques, Saint James's scallops.

It was the end of May, and the official start of summer was looming large. The days had already started to stretch, with the sun rising at five in the morning and setting at nine at night. By the end of June, the sun would rise at three in the morning and set at midnight. It wasn't quite the midnight sun of the Arctic Circle, but it was close.

This is as different as it gets from life in Los Gatos, Harry thought. There, he never came home at four in the afternoon, but in Copenhagen, it appeared, when the weather was good, people left the office early. They called it work-life balance. And what the heck was that?

In the four weeks since they had moved to Denmark, this was the first day that showed promise of warmth; there was a smell of heat in the air, and Harry was reminded of California, of sitting on their patio with laptops, working. On weekends—there was no such thing as vacation—Harry would open a bottle of rosé, and they would drink barely a glass between conference calls, emails, and work.

But on this day, Harry sat outside Le Saint Jacques under one of the large green umbrellas, no laptop in hand. His phone was tucked in the inside pocket of his suit, and he had no desire to look at it.

Harry was not feeling at the top of the world.

There were several aspects of his life that were contributing to his melancholy.

The first was obviously his wife. She had gone from being able, capable, positive, and happy to this . . . what was this? Who was this?

The second was IT Foundry. Harry wasn't certain, but he was starting to wonder as they perused the books of the company whether maybe it was not such a good buy as they had thought. He had moved countries to bring his wife better health and himself better wealth, and it looked like none of it was going to pan out.

However, last night his wife certainly had been in a good mood, and not because of him, but because of that odious man, Anders Ravn, who was everything Harry wanted to be. Ravn had grown up wealthy; he had that polish of easy and old money. The very thing that Harry had had to cultivate, Ravn had had from birth. *Fucking silver spoon.*

When the waiter approached him, Harry ordered a glass of 2014 Clos Labade, one of the rosés served at Le Saint Jacques. And when the server prodded if he'd like something to eat, Harry glanced up at their apartment and then agreed that yes, as the server suggested, the dry-cured Provençal olives would go very nicely with the rosé.

Harry had never lived in a big city. He had visited on business nearly all the big ones, New York, Tokyo, New Delhi, Brussels, Sydney, London, Paris—you name it. But he had never lived in a capital city. And in Copenhagen the city was right at your doorstep. The sounds of traffic, the lights, the people. Not many sirens here, though, unlike the other big cities he had experienced.

He sipped his wine and watched the efficient citizens of Copenhagen. Some were on bicycles. Others walked past him, purposefully carrying shopping bags, speaking animatedly on their phones. There were mothers with prams. The sun was shining and the sky was blue, and it was as if the city had come alive and its denizens were stepping out of hibernation to wander out and smell the sunlit air.

One of them was a tall man with a military-style haircut. He pushed a stroller toward the outdoor seating area of the restaurant where Harry was sitting as he continued to talk on his cell phone.

"Who the F cares, Elsa? I don't," he said in English.

American, Harry thought.

"William will go to the *vuggestue* next month, and that's that," he continued.

He delivered some banal pleasantries in an angry voice, ended the call, and took a seat. The man ordered from the waiter in Danish.

He then peeked into the stroller, and, convinced the child was asleep, addressed Harry.

"*Dejlig sommer dag,*" he said in Danish.

"Excuse me?" Harry asked in English.

The man smiled as if he had found one of his tribe. "You're American."

"Yes," Harry said and drank a long sip of his wine.

"I'm Brady, from Fort Myers, Florida," the man said as he leaned, extending his hand. Harry shook it.

"Harry, from Los Gatos, California," he said.

The server came by again and Brady ordered a Kronenbourg, a French beer.

"I've been here ten years. How about you?"

"A few weeks," Harry said.

"My wife's Danish. We just had him," he said, and looked at the stroller. "William. He's eight months old. I'm on paternity leave, taking care of him. Elsa, my wife, she works at Widex, the hearing aid company, and she went back to work after eight of her twelve months of maternity leave."

Paternity leave? Maybe Bernie Sanders was right, this place was utopia. America didn't even have maternity leave, only a gratuitous twelve unpaid weeks offered by the largest companies. Even Marissa Mayer, CEO of Yahoo, took just a month or so off after she gave birth. Harry wouldn't dream of taking paternity leave—it would be the death of his career.

"Do you like being on paternity leave?" Harry asked.

Brady shrugged and then nodded. "I get to spend time with William, you know, but I want to cut my leave short by four weeks. The Danes are all family, family, but William has a spot in daycare, and I need to have a life, too."

His candor disarmed Harry, and when Brady moved from his own table to Harry's, Harry didn't mind; instead Harry pushed the olives between them as an invitation.

"It's a good life in Denmark for families," Brady said. "Daycare is subsidized, really cheap. We get days off for being sick and days off when our kid is sick. I just feel the longer I stay away from my work— I'm a marketing manager at a medical device company—the greater the risk they forget me. My wife thinks that's an American way of looking at things."

Harry remembered that Sanya had only twelve weeks of unpaid maternity leave after Sara was born. He had suggested that she become a stay-at-home mom, and he had expected her to accept the offer, but Sanya had rejected the idea outright. He had assumed that maternity leave was easy, even though Sanya behaved like it was a whole lot of work. It was just sitting around doing nothing. Little babies are not demanding; they just need to be fed and cleaned, not that he would know, because he'd never taken care of Sara when she was a baby or . . . actually ever on his own. Sanya was the one who'd driven Sara to soccer practice and AP classes and whatever it was Sara did. Wow, Harry thought, he had been a first-class asshole.

How come he hadn't seen this before? Maybe it was the Danish lifestyle, he thought, this time away from work, this time away from the hustle and bustle, this quiet time that allowed him to ruminate, to ponder and see himself more clearly. It was as if once they moved to Copenhagen, time had slowed down; the twenty-four hours in a day seemed longer and more stretched out.

"It's the weather here that gets to me," Brady said as he finished his beer. "Some years we go from the endless gray winter to fall, missing spring and summer entirely. It's not the cold; it's the wind that bothers me. And the lack of sunshine. Do you know how much sunshine we had this January? Just seventeen hours."

"Nice to know what to expect in a few months," Harry said.

Brady laughed. "Do you know what Danes say when the weather sucks in the summer? They say, *But we had a few good days in May.* This is one of those days."

Harry told Brady what he was doing in Copenhagen, and Brady said he had read about the impending sale of IT Foundry. He seemed impressed to be meeting with the acquirer of one of the famous and successful IT consultancy companies in Denmark.

"Do you miss America?" Harry asked.

"I do. But I was also burnt out. I was in the military. I worked for the CIA . . . I was into social media and big data long before it became mainstream, but I never listened to your phone calls or read your email," he joked.

"Do you miss the excitement of working for the CIA?" Harry asked, fascinated because everyone wanted to be a spy, didn't they? Did anyone think James Bond had a shitty job?

"Every day," he said. "I was the SCUD expert tracking warheads in North Korea, which was code for doing absolutely nothing. But then came the Gulf War, and guess what Saddam was launching? Yeah. So here I was nineteen years old and being called into the Pentagon."

The waiter came by, and they asked for refills. Harry didn't check his phone and instead decided to enjoy this conversation with a fellow American. What else was there to do than go upstairs, work, and be ignored?

"At the Pentagon, we would look at satellite images and track missile launchers. Once there was a picture of a highway, and we could just see the nose of the launcher—next day there was a crater there because we blew it up. And then there would be an air raid in Baghdad, which would be reported in the news," he said. "The press room was above us, and I walked by Wolf Blitzer all the time. It was . . . strange . . . it was exhilarating."

Harry asked why he left if it was so great.

"Even now when I look at photos of our newest conflicts, I feel like I'm in the middle of it again. I had nightmares for months about air raids and about the mistakes we made. That I'd by mistake marked a school to be leveled instead of a missile launcher. So I left. I was just twenty-one. For six months my parents took care of me, and then I went to Russia to learn Russian so I could continue to work for the government. Maybe I should've gone to the Middle East instead and learned Arabic, would've come in handy. But . . . you know, I was depressed. Clinically. It took a long while and sometimes I still . . . you know . . . feel the slide."

Fascinated because of Sanya, Harry asked, "How long ago was this?"

"Fifteen years ago," Brady said, and when he looked at Harry's shocked face, "Depression is tough. And it's like being an alcoholic. You always have it there, waiting for you to slide. Some days are good and some are not. I just need to stay away from trigger points like . . . all the fucking news these days."

"That must be tough," Harry said. "Thanks, man, for your service. I hope you feel better."

Harry wondered what Sanya's trigger points were.

"I am better. The thing is that we all heal and we all get better. The hard part is that you are different after you get better, and the people around you, and you yourself, struggle to accept those changes," Brady said. "But once you do, it works itself out. I have a baby, man, and a lovely wife. I've got six weeks of vacation. I see my friends in the United States, and they're working all the time. *I have a life.* It's great. And that helps keep the monsters at bay."

They inevitably moved from depression to basketball and then to football, and Brady told Harry which bars showed the games.

The baby started to wake up then. Brady stood and left cash on the table. "You stay cool, Harry," he said. "And welcome to Denmark."

Once Brady left, Harry paid for the wine with his Dankort in a card reader the waiter brought out to him. A couple had just arrived and he heard the woman say in English to the man, "You know, we have some great days in May, and this is one of them, so we must take advantage of it."

Chapter 7

They Leave Their Babies Outside

On the first day of June, the official start of summer, Sanya decided to leave the apartment on her own. The impetus to leave the apartment had been twofold. Her mother and sister had called together to discuss summer vacation plans in Provence but had segued into her mental health—which had not improved said health—and because, since she had met Anders Ravn a week ago, Sanya's bed had lost some of its appeal.

She went to the Café Bopa just down the street. She took with her for company *The Golden Notebook*, a gift Sara had picked up at Shakespeare and Company in Paris the summer before, when she had gone on a European holiday before starting college.

Was it coming to Europe that had brought on her first crush? Sanya wondered. Had her implosion opened her mind? Or was it simpler than that—did she know that Harry would forgive this emotional indiscretion because she wasn't emotionally stable and couldn't be expected to behave sensibly in her condition?

Café Bopa was named after the Borgerlige Partisaner, referring to a group of resistance fighters who conspired against the Nazis during the Second World War. The treelined Bopa Square was also home to

Café Pixie. The area in front of Café Bopa beyond the patio, where cozy tables covered in red-and-white-checkered tablecloths were surrounded by metal chairs, some rickety and some steady, was a pétanque court and a playground.

Sanya had just started to read Doris Lessing's epic novel about women and independence while she waited for a server to find her when the cry of a baby drew her attention.

The server came to her and then cheerfully asked if she was ready to order.

"There's a baby crying," Sanya said.

The server turned his head to the entrance of the café, and that was when Sanya noticed the six prams, one of which was shaking.

"There's a wailing baby inside that?" Sanya asked flabbergasted. "Where's the mother?"

The server shrugged. "In the café, probably. What can I get you?"

"The mother is inside?" Sanya asked, and then absently added, "I'll have a café latte."

"Sure," the waiter said. "Your latte will be thirty-five kroner. You can pay now, and I can get it for you."

Her eyes trained on the pram, she paid in cash this time because Harry had left several colorful Danish kroner at home.

Five minutes later, a woman came out to collect the red-faced baby.

"They leave their babies outside," a woman with short blond hair said with a British accent. "That's how they do it here." She looked up from her laptop, next to which was a copy of Somerset Maugham's *Of Human Bondage*, and smiled at Sanya.

"They just leave them outside?" she asked. "And nothing happens?"

"You mean no one takes the baby?" the woman asked and, when Sanya nodded, continued, "Denmark is very safe. Though one time in Østerbro, in the townhouse area near Svanemøllen, a rat got into a baby's pram and bit the baby's pinkie toe off."

Sanya was horrified.

"True story," the woman said. "I'm Chloe."

Sanya introduced herself, and they exchanged how long they'd been in Denmark.

Chloe was married to a shipping executive at Mærsk Group and stayed home with her one-year-old daughter and was working on her first novel.

Madeline, Chloe's friend who was an English literature professor at the University of Copenhagen, and who joined them shortly, was in her sixties and had purple hair. She was more hippie than university professor and spoke with authority about almost everything.

"We're in a writers' group," Chloe told her. "Do you write?"

Sanya shook her head. *Not really,* she thought, *not unless you counted reports and white papers on financial process optimization.*

Madeline seemed to be a genuinely happy person with passions that ran deep. "Life is meant to be lived," she said emphatically as she drank a glass of the house white wine. "My thirties were complete crap. Busy with my children and husband and all of that. Forties were better, but I still had to deal with that shit teenage phase with the girl, though the boy was easy. My fifties were delightful. I had many lovers."

"Lovers?" Sanya asked. "Are you still married?"

"Of course," she said. "I met my husband when I was twenty-one. Been married since then."

"Does he know about your lovers?" Sanya asked, and when she nodded nonchalantly, Sanya asked, "What did he say?"

"'Whatever makes you happy, my dear,'" Madeline said, and laughed. "He's a darling. But in my sixties, sex is just not happening. And how about you, Chloe? You and Johan doing better in the sack?"

Chloe snorted at Madeline's question. "Sex was never the problem for us except during that time after the baby," she said smugly, and then snarled, "it's this goddamn country that's the problem."

Ah sex, Sanya thought. How long had it been? Even before the breakdown it had become a once in a while thing after wine when they both felt that it had been too long and something needed to be done about it. After all, in a marriage if you were not having sex, it said something about the marriage, and it didn't say anything good.

"Everyone needs to have good sex these days," Alec said, when Sanya once asked him what he thought about a sexless marriage. "We brought sex out into the open, and the pressure to have it and for it to be fabulous is killing us. You watch television, and everyone is always having good sex. People rarely have bad sex on television."

Alec also suggested that the point was not if Sanya wanted to still have sex; it was if she still wanted to have sex with Harry. Those two things could be mutually exclusive.

Sanya used to love sex.

When Harry and she met, she was obsessed with sex. She wanted it all the time. She never, of course, let Harry know that she wanted it all the time; she waited for him to make the suggestion and leaped at the chance. She never initiated sex in those early days. She waited and she never turned him down.

Then she had a baby, and the sex was still okay. Not as great as it used to be, but okay. Harry stopped initiating sex. She started to initiate sex. She was apprehensive about it because he didn't always comply, and she wasn't so sure about her body post-baby. There were times when he said he had an early morning or he was too tired. So she initiated less and less; and she started to become less and less interested in sex with Harry.

They moved from one excuse to another until they didn't have to make excuses anymore because life got in the way and sex became a thing they did because they had to, not because they wanted to, not because it was an unquenchable desire that they needed to throw an orgasm onto.

They weren't tearing each other's clothes off and . . . it was the marriage cliché. They got married and they stopped having sex. They had children and they stopped having sex.

Sanya sighed. This marriage had many problems.

"You complain too much," Madeline said to Chloe. "Denmark on the whole has issues, granted. Look at how they vote for Dansk Folkeparti. It's a racist right-wing party, like your Tea Party," she explained to Sanya. "But Copenhagen is wonderful. It's full of diversity. Look at us, three women from three different age groups and places in life, and we meet here."

Chloe wasn't having any of it. "And none of us is Danish. How many Danish friends do you have?"

Madeline nodded in agreement. "Danes are not particularly friendly, I'll give you that," she said to Sanya. "They're hard to get to know. It's not just the language—it's how they don't seem to let people in. But I have now lived here for nearly three decades, and I have many Danish friends. I do. Have you met any Danes, Sanya?"

Sanya told them about Penny and Lilly. She didn't tell them about Ravn.

"The Hellerup crowd," Chloe said, shaking her head. "They are a different breed."

Madeline laughed then. "And you should know. Chloe, you live in Charlottenlund. So don't pretend that you're not one of them."

"I don't shop at Netto in a fur coat," Chloe protested. "In any case, Johan wanted to live there, not me. He's the one who's stuck on living in the right zip code so he can tell his colleagues about his villa. Like I care."

In California, strangers did sometimes talk to you when you met them, but here it seemed commonplace for people to just stir up conversation. It was the expats, Madeline explained to her, because they were the open ones who invited people to their homes and easily made friends, because they had to, because they didn't have old kindergarten or high school or handball team friends here.

"When we first moved to Copenhagen, I used to keep inviting Danes home, and they never invited us back. I thought they didn't like us," Chloe said. "But they kept coming over. I finally had to stop feeding people who never reciprocated. Now all our friends are like us, half Danish and half something else."

"Don't listen to her," Madeline said. "You'll find that Copenhagen has many delights. Denmark is an egalitarian society. Look at our government. We've actually had a female prime minister, and nearly half the parliament is women. The men are quite malleable here, and there is gender equality for the most part. Though in corporate Denmark, I'm told by friends, it's not the case. But men will cook and clean and take care of their offspring. Until I met my husband, I didn't know that men knew which side of the vacuum cleaner was up."

"Johan is wonderful," Chloe acknowledged. "I don't know about the other men."

Sanya felt so energized after meeting the women that in the evening when Harry came home, she suggested that they go out for dinner to Café Bopa. He was surprised at the invitation but nevertheless delighted that Sanya wanted to leave the house.

Sanya ordered a burger with all the works, even guacamole, and Harry did the same.

"The Danes leave their babies outside in prams," she said, pointing to one of the two prams outside Café Pixie, which was next to Café Bopa.

"Are you sure there's a live baby in there?" Harry asked.

"Yes," Sanya said, feeling like an expert on Danish society. "Danes probably grow up to be more independent than American children because they're not coddled. They learn to fend for themselves." Madeline had told her that.

"It's good to see you like this," Harry said.

"Like what?" she asked, more sharply than she intended.

She was being difficult. She knew what he meant. There was a perverse pleasure in seeing him in agony because of her.

Oh, Sanya.

Is this what marriage had become? She wanted—no, needed her spouse to be in the same shit hole she was in? Terrifying how the mind worked.

She felt a frisson of panic slide up her spine as she wondered if she hated Harry. She controlled the waves of anxiety and panic brought along with it because she needed to think, so as to not give in to the chaos in her mind.

Of course she loved Harry. Didn't she?

If one looked at marriage statistically, with number of years on the x-axis and affection on the y-axis, everyone started high, and then the curve went down and down and down as the years passed. Was there any other way for this graph to turn out? Who came up with the bright idea that once two people got to know each other really well, they'd love each other more?

The more you knew someone, the more you dug into their dirt, the more you saw and the less you loved. It was the mystery, wasn't it, that we were fascinated with? Like a scar on someone's cheek or a crack inside someone's mind.

"It's good to see you outside," Harry said calmly as the waiter arrived with their drinks. Harry was getting used to Sanya's shifting moods and was learning how to deal with them. A part of Sanya felt sympathy for Harry because she also had to learn to deal with her own shifting moods, from forcing herself to be happy consistently to not having any consistency at all. Sanya was drinking red wine, while Harry was drinking beer.

"Maybe we should have ordered champagne," Harry said, obviously feeling celebratory at their impromptu date night.

"I'm fine with the wine," Sanya said, not wanting Harry to celebrate quite yet.

They ate their burgers hungrily. Sanya realized she had not eaten all day except for the latte at Bopa in the afternoon. At this rate, maybe she would lose enough weight to attempt that bikini she and Ravn had discussed.

"I met two women today," she told him. "I even got their phone numbers. I think I made friends."

Harry nodded but didn't ask about the friends. He was being so pleasant that Sanya decided to throw him a bone. "How are things at work?" she asked.

If she had taken all her clothes off and said, "Take me, baby," he wouldn't have been more turned on than he was right now, Sanya knew. Talking business with her was better than sex for Harry. Though that didn't say much these days because it had been a while since they'd had sex.

"It seems to be taking forever for us to go through IT Foundry's books," Harry said.

"Why?"

Harry shrugged. "You can probably figure out the numbers better than I can, but our finance people just seem to have more and more questions."

Since Sanya had met Ravn, she had done research on IT Foundry and told Harry that everything she read said that the company was solid, reputable, and that Ravn was hailed as a top CEO for what he had achieved with it.

"Maybe you want to look at the numbers?" Harry suggested, and just as he did, Sanya shuttered down.

Back to work, are we, she thought, annoyed. But that wasn't what really irritated her. What bothered her was that Harry was tarnishing Ravn's reputation, and she wondered if he was doing it because he knew she was attracted to him.

Harry backtracked quickly. "But let's not worry about that now; I'm sure once the accountants look through the paperwork, they'll tell us what's up and what's down. Tell me about these women you met."

"Expats," Sanya said, even though she wanted to scream at Harry for making Ravn the villain in her story when she so badly wanted him to be the hero. "They're writers. I may see them again."

When they walked home, Harry put his arm around her, loosely, like he did this all the time. He was trying, she knew. Sanya wanted to applaud Harry for pulling his socks up and sticking to her, because a weaker man would've left her to stew in her own filth.

She smiled suddenly and leaned into Harry as they walked. She did love Harry. Especially *this* Harry.

Chapter 8

Penny and Mark Make the Papers

Mandy stifled a scream when she opened her morning newspaper. She immediately called Ravn at the office.

"Have you seen the headlines? Did you know about this?" she demanded.

"About what?" Ravn asked.

She told him. There was a long pause, and then Ravn said calmly, "Yes, I knew. I'm a little busy right now; can we talk over dinner?"

"But we're having Penny and Mark over, and those Americans," Mandy said.

"Then you can take Penny away to show her your bag or shoes or something and ask her everything you want to know," Ravn said, and then suddenly out of character, he burst out, "Those damn Americans are part of the fucking problem to start with."

"What? What did the Americans do? Are *we* in any trouble?" Mandy asked.

"No," Ravn said, calm again. "All companies get audited from time to time. Since Mark and Penny are co-owners of their individual companies, the media is having a field day. Can you please not be upset?"

"So this is not serious?" Mandy asked naïvely.

"Of course it's serious. But nothing is going to . . . *skat*, I'm busy," Ravn said.

He said he loved her and then hung up the phone before she could ask more questions. But he had for the first time in a long while called her *skat*, "darling" in Danish, so she believed him. Strange, wasn't it, that in Danish *skat* meant both "darling" and "taxes."

Mandy chewed on her lower lip as she read the article in Danish once again. Ravn joked that she didn't speak any Danish, and her oral Danish was only conversational, but she could read just fine, and she understood everyone very, very well. She chose not to speak the language, but it was a *choice*.

The headlines were simple:

Penny and Mark Barrett charged with tax fraud.

Penny Barrett, ex-supermodel and current designer and fashionista, and her husband, the real estate mogul Mark Barrett, might soon face prison time if the tax fraud charges against them are proven in court. Mark Barrett, who has sold some of the most expensive properties in all of Scandinavia, has some holes in his accounting, especially for some real estate deals in southern Sweden. The properties were leased out, and investigators are looking into whether Barrett did not pay taxes on the revenue.

The new government is poised to hit hard on the fashion-forward couple.

"No matter who you are, you have to pay your taxes in this country. We're not Greece," said Søren Pedersen, who, at twenty-six years of age,

is the youngest appointed tax minister in the history of Denmark. "I, of course, cannot speak about
this particular case, but we are looking into every
case thoroughly, and we will inform the media as it
becomes relevant."

The story went on to say that Penny was just as liable as Mark for
the tax fraud. Both of them could end up in prison for a good five years.

Oh god. This could happen. This could really happen.

She would have to take care of the children, Mandy told herself.
She didn't like Penny's children at all. Sophia and Annabelle, eleven and
eight respectively, were spoiled within an inch of their lives and were
miserable little divas—mini versions of Penny. If Penny and Mark went
to prison, at least there would be an opportunity to show these girls how
to behave properly. With Katrine and Jonas all grown up and disinterested in home (and their mother)—Jonas had even moved out and was
living with a friend in Frederiksberg when he wasn't traveling—Mandy
had all the time in the world to raise Penny's girls.

"Have you read this?" Mandy asked Katrine as she came into the
kitchen.

Katrine, still in the T-shirt and shorts she wore to sleep in the summer, scanned the newspaper article. "Are they going to jail, you think?"
she asked as she poured herself a cup of coffee.

"I don't know," Mandy said. "Would you like some breakfast?" She
looked at the kitchen clock. "Or maybe lunch."

"I'll just have a sandwich," Katrine said, and opened the fridge to
find some milk for her coffee.

"I don't see Kristian anymore," Mandy asked after Katrine's boyfriend.

"Kristian is backpacking in South America," Katrine said, and then
added calmly, as if she were unaffected, which she probably was, "with
someone else."

Her father's daughter, Mandy thought resentfully. *No emotions.*

Katrine was interning at Danske Bank for her skip year between high school and university. She was already signed up for college at Copenhagen Business School. Mandy wished Jonas had the same energy, but, like too many Hellerup boys, her son was unsure of his future. He was working at a pizzeria to pay his bills, well, part of his bills, as Mandy, without the knowledge of her husband, was paying her son's rent and his travel expenses when he took off with his friends for Nice or Ibiza or Thailand.

"Do you have a new boyfriend?" Mandy asked Katrine.

"No. Do I need one?" Katrine said, and put a wedge of a Serrano ham on a slice of dark rye bread. She made two open-faced sandwiches, one with ham and the other with a mild Danish cheese, and sat down at the kitchen counter next to her mother.

Katrine wasn't one to run away from a discussion, but she was also not one to reveal how she felt about anything. Both Jonas and Katrine had Scandinavian stoicism in their blood.

"Are you having a dinner party?" Katrine asked. "I saw salmon steaks in the fridge."

"Yes, Penny and Mark and some Americans who're here to buy Daddy's company are coming over," Mandy said. "Would you like to join us?"

Katrine shrugged. "Maybe. Shouldn't you be making something Danish for the Americans? You know, to introduce them to Danish cuisine."

Mandy cleared her throat. This is where she drew the line. "I want to keep it casual."

Katrine frowned. "Mom, Danish food is casual; you don't have to make a Noma-grade meal."

"We'll sit outside and Daddy will throw the fish on the grill," Mandy said. She hated Danish food. The pork, the grease, the brown sauce, oh, the horrible *brun* sauce and the potatoes—it was unimaginative and boring, and she wasn't going to serve that to her guests. If they wanted Danish food, she could recommend a few restaurants where they could get their fill of *bøf med løg*, beef patties with softened onions drenched in that detestable brown sauce.

When the kids were growing up, Mandy made it a point to serve them healthy and nutritious food. Not like the other Danish children, who grew up eating rye bread with crap on top—by crap, she meant the horrible *leverpostej*, a sort of liver pate that could be served warm with pickled cucumbers. The smell of that concoction made Mandy sick. But Danish kids were Danish kids, and no matter how much she had trained them, they had learned to eat rye bread with crap on top, as Katrine was for breakfast. For all their Noma, Geranium, and *best restaurant in the world* nonsense, Danes had no culinary culture and ate abysmal food bought at low-end supermarket chains such as Fakta, Netto, and the god-awful REMA 1000. Denmark was discount nation—and everyone wanted to buy the cheapest food they could get their hands on. Mandy shopped at Torvehallerne, the gourmet and expensive farmers market, when she had time, and when she didn't, she compromised with the high-end Meny supermarket in Rotunden at the Tuborg harbor.

Meat and fish were always bought at the butcher and the fishmonger. She had gone to Torvehallerne in the morning, early, to pick up the salmon steaks and lobster, because it offered the best of the best, and even if the price was steep, she could afford it.

Katrine laughed. "Your casual is *so not casual*. What's for the appetizer and dessert?"

"Lobster . . . also cooked on the grill," Mandy said. "I'll serve it with some nice garlic butter. We have poire belle Hélène with crème anglaise for dessert."

"You're such a great cook, Mom. I really appreciate all the effort you put into inviting people and throwing parties. My friends love coming here because they get good food to eat. And everyone is always welcome."

"Of course they are," Mandy said, sufficiently soothed.

"Don't worry about the paper, Mom," Katrine said, as she put her plate into the dishwasher. "Penny and Mark will be fine. Daddy will make sure." She gave her mother a rare hug in reassurance.

❖ ❖ ❖

For Mandy, home and family were her life. Her home was her business card. She had decorated it herself as part of her rehabilitation from middle-class girl from Oregon to pillar of high society in Denmark, and she liked to mention that as often as she could, not the transformation part but the fact that she herself had decorated her home, not some expensive, snooty interior designer. How many Hellerup wives could say that?

"Oh, that vase is beautiful," someone would compliment her, and Mandy would tell the story about how she picked it up in some small shop in Bali and how she had to haggle with the owner, a shrewd Balinese woman, to get it at a reasonable price. Everything in Mandy's house had a story around it.

The beautiful Navajo rug in the living room came from a trip to Sedona she and Ravn had taken before the kids were born, but that was where the twins were conceived. The painting of the woman with a basket of chilies was an R. C. Gorman original she had bought in DC at a gallery when they had gone as part of the Danish business delegation with Crown Prince Frederik and Crown Princess Mary.

The dining area had a Spanish air to it. The Miró was an original she'd picked up during a vacation in Bilbao. The Spanish ambassador to Denmark had taken them to a gallery where it was hidden among a whole lot of other paintings. The Merello was *not* her choice; it was Ravn's, she would say, and she wasn't sure where he got it. No story there.

The china and silverware were exclusively Danish because she had inherited some from Ravn's mother when she died, and you couldn't be part of the Ravn family and not acquire Danish designers. The furniture was mixed, some Piet Hein tables and lamps, some Arne Jacobsen, some old Finn Juhl, the father of the Danish design movement that Ravn liked (because his father had been a big fan).

Anyone who came to Mandy's house would eventually call her to help them decorate their house. It had happened many times. She had even led the team of designers Cindy had used to decorate the American ambassador's residence.

Mandy had also been on the board of ARoS, the beautiful museum in Aarhus. She was the sole socialite there among the many artists, gallery owners, critics, and curators. She had had to give it up when Jonas, four years ago, had that incident with almost getting kicked out of Ordrup Skole for selling laughing gas to friends at parties. Penny had been nonchalant and told her this is what kids did in Hellerup and Charlottenlund—it was almost a rite of passage—but Mandy had completely freaked out that Jonas was turning into a drug dealer and had for a year exclusively devoted herself to picking him up, dropping him off, feeding him, watching him, giving curfews, and even hiring a tutor to keep him on track. And she had succeeded. She would do what was needed to keep her family together and safe; and family included Penny.

❖   ❖   ❖

Penny was looking at sample designs for next year's spring collection when Mandy walked into her boutique.

"Are you okay? I saw the papers," Mandy said, rushing into Penny's office.

Penny hugged Mandy and kissed her on both cheeks. She closed the door so her staff wouldn't hear their conversation. They were already gossiping about the news.

"We haven't been charged," Penny said. "You know how the media is, always cooking up stuff. They're looking into Mark's company, but they're looking into everyone's company these days. The new government is just searching for scapegoats to show how their new tax laws are going to save Denmark from an economic crisis."

Mandy knew Penny, had known her for as long as she had known Ravn. Penny was scared; she could smell the fear. It was just too delicious not to feel thrilled about something bad happening to always-successful Penny. She used to be a supermodel, and then she had kids and kept her body without a tummy tuck or the torturous gym routine and running that Mandy had to do. And her husband was Mark Barrett, who used to be . . . beautiful and rich. He wasn't much of either anymore. Penny on the other hand had family money and what she earned herself as a model and businesswoman. Everything had just come too easy for Penny. There had to be balance in the universe, and apparently now there was.

"Have you talked to Ravn?" Penny asked, as her assistant came in and handed Mandy a cup of coffee before discreetly leaving the office.

Mandy sipped the coffee and shook her head. "I called him, but he said there was nothing to worry about."

"He said that?"

"And then when I said we were having the Americans—you know, Harry and that Indian wife of his—over for dinner, he said . . . I don't know if I should tell you," Mandy said. Between Penny and her husband, her loyalties were clear.

"We're family," Penny urged. "But if you're uncomfortable, don't; I'll just give Ravn a call."

Mandy smiled. "He said something strange, that the Americans were causing the problem. How can they cause a problem for Mark when they're looking into IT Foundry? How could they even be connected? It makes no sense. He really wants this sale to go through. He has so many plans for a new venture."

"What kind of plans?" Penny asked.

"I don't know . . . just plans," Mandy said. "You know how secretive he is."

Penny nodded. "He certainly is. So . . . do you want me to show you that turquoise and cream dress I have set aside for you?"

Chapter 9

Penny Hits on Harry

"Do you know where Café Victor is?" Harry asked Lucky, who was knee-deep in spreadsheets and looked more harangued than usual.

"What?"

"I just got a call from Penny Barrett, and she wants to see me for lunch at Café Victor," Harry told him. "What does she want, I wonder?"

"She wants to get into your pants," Lucky said acidly.

"I doubt it, and, in any case, I'm happy in my marriage."

"If you're as happy in your marriage as you say you are, why do you keep screwing around?" Lucky asked.

"I'll never leave Sanya," Harry said firmly.

"Maybe she'll leave you no choice," Lucky said.

"She makes me happy," Harry said. "Even like this, being with her is better than being without her."

They had always been a team. Harry was the idea man and Lucky was the enforcer. When Harry became a vice president, Lucky became a director. And now that Harry was a partner, Lucky was just a step away as associate partner.

"We have a meeting with Ravn at four," Lucky said. "So as long as you can be done with your pants-dropping by then, it'll be much appreciated."

Lucky liked to make it sound like Harry dropped his pants for just any woman who walked through the door. And even though it was true that Harry had not been faithful to Sanya, he'd only had *three* affairs, and that wasn't so bad in a two-decade marriage, was it?

"Today's newspaper broke the story of tax fraud charges against Mark Barrett. I had the IT Foundry secretary translate the article."

Denmark's equivalent to the *Wall Street Journal* was called *Børsen*, which meant "the stock exchange" in Danish.

"But why is Penny after you? Does she think there is a connection between Mark and IT Foundry?" Lucky wondered.

"That's what I hope to find out," Harry said. He leaned against Lucky's desk. "This is turning out to be rather interesting, isn't it?"

Lucky grimaced. "I don't know. It's a lot of time and money down the toilet if IT Foundry is not viable for purchase."

Harry shrugged. "Sanya and I needed this time. A little getaway from the California pressure cooker."

Lucky frowned.

Harry straightened his tie and said, "We save money if our due diligence shows that there was something rotten in the state of Denmark." He winked at Lucky and added, "I'll ask the secretary if she knows where Café Victor is."

"I'll tell you again: don't mix business with pleasure," Lucky said as Harry was leaving.

Harry patted Lucky on the shoulder. "I'm not doing that anymore. Also, I'm not interested in Penny. She's too *supermodel*. She's going to be dressed to the nines. Want to bet?"

Lucky leaned back on his chair. "Not that she'll be dressed, but that she wants to sleep with you. I don't think she's smart enough to figure out how her husband's crap is connected to Ravn's crap. I bet you fifty dollars."

Harry looked at his watch. "You're cheap. We meet at one. Why don't you join us at two, and you can see for yourself and pay for lunch."

Lucky shrugged. "If she sees me, she won't sleep with you."

"I don't want her," Harry said. "I'm trying . . . to be loyal to Sanya. I feel responsible. Maybe I triggered her . . . her . . . thing. Maybe it was my fault. So I'm planning not to cheat on her anymore. She's a beautiful, sexy, wonderful woman, and I'm lucky that she's my wife."

"Whatever lets you sleep at night, Harry," Lucky said.

❖　❖　❖

Penny arrived fifteen minutes late, as Harry expected. She didn't want to seem too eager.

It was another warm day in June, and there was talk in the IT Foundry offices that it looked like this summer would be a *real* summer, and the weather would hold.

Penny wore an emerald-green Jean Patou vintage shirtdress that went very well with her red hair. The dress stopped midthigh and showed her model long sleek legs as they ended in emerald-green fringed suede Aquazzura sandals. She accentuated her slender waist with a black Dior belt. Harry thought that the Dior didn't match the Patou, but then maybe it wasn't supposed to, and what did he know about fashion compared to a fashion designer.

"Harry," she said, and he rose to air-kiss her, once on each cheek. She smelled of something spicy and exotic.

No, Harry thought. *No, no, no.*

"I'm sorry I'm late," she said, a little breathless, as if she had run all the way from her boutique on Strøget to Café Victor. "Crown Princess Mary was in the store, buying a dress for the opening night of *Giselle* at the opera house. Mary wanted something red, *Giselle*-like. So it took some time. But at least it was Mary; Princess Marie is a lot pickier because she's French."

"I'm sure you had just the dress for her," Harry said politely.

The waiter stood discreetly to the side of their table, waiting for the gentleman and the lady to address him.

"A glass of champagne, please," Penny said.

Harry didn't raise an eyebrow even though he wanted to. Europeans had a lax attitude about wine. He would never order alcohol for lunch on a weekday. He had to go back to work after this little encounter.

"Water, please. And a café latte." Harry allowed himself one cup of coffee during the day; otherwise, he stuck to water. The body, after all, was a temple.

"I love champagne," Penny said. "If it wasn't so decadent, I would have it for breakfast."

"As Fitzgerald said, too much of anything is bad, but too much champagne is just right."

"Already quoting Fitzgerald," Penny said, her voice husky and, Harry had to admit, really sexy with that Danish plus British accent. "You must be wondering why I invited you for lunch."

Harry smiled, his eyes sparkling with anticipation. The chase was always fun. Except with Sanya. He hadn't wanted to chase as much as possess. One of his paramours had once criticized Sanya as *average*, but Sanya was a woman who challenged him. She knew how to trigger Harry's intellect. Not many women or men did that. Had he always known this, or was he just discovering these truths since Sanya was no longer the wife he knew from a few months ago?

Penny ordered the terrine of foie gras, while Harry ordered the smoked salmon from Fanø, an island off the coast of southwestern Denmark.

"Ravn has the most amazing summer house in Fanø," Penny said. "Did you ever see that movie by Polanski called *The Ghost Writer*?"

Harry nodded. "The one with Pierce Brosnan."

"Yes. The house where the movie takes place? That's Ravn's summer house. They shot the movie on Fanø. With that rape charge, Polanski obviously could not go to New England to shoot the film. The editor on the film is a good friend of mine so I hooked them up with Ravn's summer house," Penny said.

Harry alternated between drinking his water and his café latte and waited for Penny to get to her point.

"I really like your wife," she said, stalling.

"Thank you, I like her, too," Harry said.

"And because I like her, this is a bit strange," Penny said and smiled, a girlish smile. "Well . . . you know . . . we Danes are actually quite nonconfrontational. But I'm not entirely Danish anymore, not after the global life I have lived." She paused for a long time.

"We're already here, and it would be a pity if you talked around what you want to say," Harry said.

Penny emptied her glass of champagne to show that she needed its support.

"I got the feeling at the dinner at the ambassador's house that you were interested in me," Penny said, paused, probably to measure the effect on Harry, and then continued, "And I wanted to ask you if you would like to have an affair with me. A sexual one, of course. We're both married."

Harry had been propositioned more than once. A man who looked like him had that pleasure. But never like this. Never balls out *have sex with me.* Harry couldn't help it. He smiled broadly, not in invitation as she unfortunately perceived but in utter amusement. He'd heard that Scandinavian society was egalitarian and that Scandinavians were open when it came to sex, and Harry, the eternal feminist in matters of sex, was thrilled to be at the receiving end of this suggestion.

"I keep an apartment in the city," Penny continued. "And I'd very much like to share your company there when we both have the desire and of course the time."

He had lost fifty dollars to Lucky, and he'd have to pick up the check for lunch. He was bemused and more than a little flattered. This woman was an ex-supermodel *who walked for all the big houses.*

Before Harry could conjure up a polite answer, the waiter brought their food. As the waiter described the contents of their respective dishes, the heat inside Harry's chest subsided.

Penny Barrett was a gorgeous woman. However, she was too close to home. He was planning on being a good, loyal husband. He wasn't interested in Penny's desperate ploy to milk him for information on her husband's corrupt dealings as reported by the papers. Because he was certain that was why she had asked him to lunch.

"Well, don't keep me waiting. Say something," Penny said.

Harry smiled. He took Penny's left hand, which lay on the side of her plate, into both of his. He knew how to let a woman down.

"You're a very beautiful woman," Harry said. "But I really can't. I'm a married man, and you're Ravn's cousin. I'm afraid it won't be prudent to accept your offer, though it is very tempting."

"So you're resisting me out of some sense of loyalty to your wife or loyalty to Ravn? Because Ravn has nothing to do with me and my life," Penny said in an icy tone.

Harry let go of her hand. "Be that as it may, Sanya is my wife, and it's not *some* sense of loyalty; it's all my senses. Should we enjoy the rest of our lunch, and you can tell me about this article I read in the paper today?"

He started with gusto to attack his salmon while Penny didn't touch her foie gras. She looked a little shell-shocked, like she was not used to being rejected.

She nodded carefully. "It's nothing—the article, I mean. It must've been a slow news day. But tell me, how is the due diligence on IT Foundry going? Have you found anything off-kilter with Ravn's books?" She added the last part in as a joke. It came out flat.

"It's work in progress. You know how it is. We have to take reasonable steps to satisfy all the legal requirements of such a purchase. So we first spend time looking at everything, and then we spend time looking at everything again—that's why they call it due diligence," Harry said. "Would you like another glass of champagne?"

Chapter 10

A Most Casual Barbecue

When the Americans arrived, the impact of Mandy's home was just as she had intended: it blew their mind.

Lucky whispered to Harry, "Holy fuck, it's a mansion."

Harry had nodded, but Sanya could see his competitive muscles tense. "Well, they have a lot of money, and looks like Mandy has good taste," he said.

Now it was Sanya's turn to feel a pinch of envy. This was the kind of woman Ravn had married, and this was what he liked and wanted in his life. Not Sanya with her Excel sheets—and not even that anymore. The envy only compounded when she saw Mandy was wearing a sexy dark-blue silk jumpsuit that showed a perky bust and a slim body. She had done her hair so it was curled like a delicate golden halo around her faultlessly made-up face. Sanya was wearing a pair of ankle jeans, Skechers, a white T-shirt, and a gray sweater. She had wanted to dress up, but this was a barbecue and she didn't want to be too obvious about wanting to impress Ravn. Now she wished she'd known what people in Hellerup wore to barbecues.

Mandy served champagne on the wraparound deck where polished Trip-Trap (another old Danish brand) wooden furniture invited them to relax atop colorful cushions. The patio led into a fenced garden well populated with flowers.

"The Charlottenlund forest is right there," Mandy told them. "Ravn goes for a run every day down to the pier, and then he winter bathes."

"Winter bathing?" Sanya asked.

Mandy pointed to the expansive view of Øresund, the sound between Sweden and Denmark where colorful sailboats were kissing the impossibly blue and silky waters.

"It's very popular with Scandinavians. They bathe in the water and then go into the sauna—you're supposed to do it three times. It's very relaxing. I do it in the winter only, but Ravn, he does it every day," Penny said.

"I've started going as well," Mandy said. "And it's very refreshing. Of course, Danes are all naked, but I put on a bikini; I don't have their courage."

"Maybe I should try it," Harry said.

"I'd love to take you," Penny said. "You have to be a member of the sauna, and there's a long line for it. But I can take guests."

Sanya saw Lucky glare at Harry, and he was about to say something when his phone rang, and he walked down the stairs from the patio to the garden as he spoke.

Penny is almost purring, Sanya thought, perturbed. Was she hitting on Harry right in front of her? Sanya wondered if she should say or do something but then decided it was too much trouble. Mandy, on the other hand, Sanya noticed, was uncomfortable and smiled broadly. It was such a big smile that if she stretched any more, her face would crack; Sanya was sure of it.

"This is such a beautiful area," Harry said, also aware of the tension that Penny's suggestive behavior had provoked.

"It's *the* place to live," Penny said. "Like you have *Beverly Hills 90210*, we used to have a show here called *2900 Happiness*. Different countries, same scandals."

"Oh, Penny, Hellerup is nothing like that," Mandy said. "There are decent people who live here. You know, Harry, I'm going to pick out some wine; would you like a tour of the wine cellar? Ravn loves wine, so we buy everywhere we go. With your interest in Napa, I think you'll enjoy it."

As she led him inside, Penny focused on Sanya with such intensity that Sanya wanted to get away from the other woman.

"Do Harry and Lucky always work together?" she asked Sanya, while she watched Lucky talking on the phone. "They probably know a lot about each other's work, right?"

Sanya looked pointedly at Penny and then Lucky. "Huh?"

Penny smiled. "They seem very close."

Sanya ignored her and allowed Knud, Mandy's helper, to fill her glass of champagne. Since Ravn was delayed at yet another meeting, Sanya decided she might as well drink while she waited.

Lucky finished his phone call and came to stand by Sanya. He eyed her champagne glass accusatorily.

"It's fine," Sanya said, because she knew he was thinking how anti-depressants and alcohol didn't mix well. But she was feeling discombobulated, what with these new and sexually charged emotions that she hadn't had since she'd met Harry, and being in a new country with new people. It was all too much. A little champagne was definitely warranted.

Penny lost interest in Sanya and went for Lucky, which helped Sanya make her escape. She stood at a distance, leaning against the deck's balustrade, and watched Knud walk around filling glasses. Mandy was back from the wine cellar talking to Harry as she offered him a plate of hors d'oeuvres, phyllo-dough pastries stuffed with spinach and goat cheese. He politely took a roll and nursed his glass of champagne. His eyes were furtively searching. Sanya smiled. She wasn't the only one waiting for Ravn.

"Mom said you have a daughter my age," said a young woman, approaching Sanya from behind.

She was *his* daughter. Even though she had Mandy's blond hair and light porcelain skin, her aggressive facial expressions were all his. Sanya just knew.

She introduced herself as Katrine Ravn.

"Sara is eighteen," Sanya said. "She's studying at UCLA."

"Can I tell you something? You don't look like someone who has a daughter my age. I mean, my mother, despite all the *this* and the *that*"—Katrine moved her hand around her face to denote, Sanya presumed, makeup or cosmetic surgery—"she still looks like a mother. Don't tell her I said so. She'll be dieting for days to come."

"I won't," Sanya said. She was her father's daughter because she tempered her aggression, as he did, with charm.

"How do you like living in Denmark? Do you feel settled, or still like a tourist?" Katrine asked.

"Oh, definitely not settled, it's not been very long," Sanya said.

"I've always lived in Denmark, and I probably will never leave," Katrine said. "I have traveled a lot, but I can't imagine making my home anywhere but here for any real length of time."

Sanya responded without artifice, letting the truth tumble out of her: "Home is a construct, involving the people who live there and its geographic and emotional placement. For me, home has always been where Harry and Sara were—but now Harry lives in Copenhagen and Sara lives in LA—and I'm not sure where home is anymore."

They were silent for a moment after that, and then Katrine said with a smile, "I'm sorry my father is late, though he's never late for school meetings or to spend time with my brother, Jonas, or me."

"He prioritizes you over his work, and he doesn't prioritize a barbecue over his work," Sanya said.

"Exactly," Katrine said. "Mom doesn't understand that. She doesn't complain when people are around, but when they're not, she's . . . she doesn't like it."

Maybe because she realizes that he doesn't prioritize her, Sanya thought, and felt a little burst of happiness because of it.

Mark Barrett arrived then with his two daughters, who primly introduced themselves as Sophia and Annabelle and shook hands with everyone. They wore pink and white dresses, and pink and white head-bands atop their long blond hair.

They sat in a corner with their au pair, Jinny, who smiled in the same doll-like way as her charges. Sanya noticed that her eyes followed Mark and then, as if realizing that she was staring, dropped down to her lap.

"Sophia and Annabelle speak Filipino," Katrine whispered to Sanya. "And they're not the only ones. So many children in Hellerup . . . you know about Hellerup, don't you?"

Sanya shook her head.

Katrine grinned and settled in to dish the dirt. "A standard Hellerup wife worries about how she looks, so she spends a lot of time in the gym and taking care of herself, while the Hellerup man is busy making money. They let their Filipino nanny raise their children bilingually—Filipino and Danish, with their Danish needing work when they start school because their parents haven't spoken to them enough."

And then, as if on cue, she added with pride, "We never had an au pair; Mom raised us. And I mean *she* raised us—she was one tough mama."

Lucky and Penny wandered up to where Sanya and Katrine were. Quick introductions were made between Katrine and Lucky, who was holding three little foie gras puffs on his plate, hors d'oeuvres that Knud had just started making the rounds with.

"Have you tried the foie gras? It's really good," Lucky said.

"I'm morally against foie gras. I've tried to get Mom to stop serving it, but she doesn't listen," Katrine said.

"Sara, Harry's daughter, is vegan," Lucky said. "What's up with you kids? You don't like food?"

Katrine shook her head. "I'm not vegan. I eat meat—organic and free range, of course—but I'm against the force-feeding of geese to make foie gras. It's barbaric."

Penny sighed. "You're so melodramatic, Katrine."

Sanya zoned them all out. She didn't care. Harry came and stood next to her, his arm around her, and she wanted to shrug it off because she was uncomfortable in her skin. She was waiting for Ravn, and it was starting to bother her, this obsession for the man, napalm-hot and burning in a way that she couldn't remember ever feeling, not since she was a teenager.

And then it struck Sanya: *I have a teenage daughter and I'm behaving like one.* She let the humiliation of that run through her, and as she did she allowed herself to lean into Harry's embrace.

"So I hear you'll be entering Copenhagen Business School. I recently met a marketing professor of yours, Thomas Ritter, at a marketing seminar in the city," Harry said to Katrine, his arm still around Sanya.

"Oh, he's a marketing genius, and he's got such a great sense of humor," Katrine said, flushing at his attention. Harry might be as old as her father, but he still made her eyes flutter. Sanya had seen it before, many times.

"He looks like something someone has sculpted," Mira once told her when she and Vinay were visiting them in California and they had gone to the beach. Harry had gone for a swim, and when he came out of the water, she had watched openmouthed and said, "I can see why you married him even though he's not a doctor."

Sanya felt smug that she was one up on Mira in the husband attractiveness department. Vinay had already lost his hair and was sporting the bald Bruce Willis look.

Just a year or so ago, Mira had again mentioned Harry's looks when she had seen a profile of his company in the *Chronicle*. He outshone the other four partners in the firm with ease.

"How can he still look like this at his age? How can you stand this beauty?" she asked.

Because I don't see it anymore, Sanya had thought, though she hadn't said it. After two decades of waking up with this man, he had become normal, no more stunning Greek god, just Harry. Familiarity did that. Everything that was special and unique became rote, mundane. He probably felt the same about Sanya. When they had met he found her beautiful, attractive, even exotic. In those early days he'd watch her sleep, and when she would awaken, he would say, "My god, you're like an Indian princess. I love looking at you."

He didn't say such things to her anymore. But, twenty times a day, he asked her if she was okay.

❖   ❖   ❖

Katrine took Sanya away from the others to show her the azaleas she had planted at the end of the garden.

"I love gardening," Katrine told Sanya. "I want to have an apartment in the city because I love living in the city; and then I want a nice *kolonihave*. Do you know what those are?" she asked, and when Sanya shook her head, she explained how many Danes who lived in the city would purchase a piece of land in a "garden colony" where they'd have a small shed and a garden. The first *kolonihave* allotments were made all the way back in 1814 in Jutland so city dwellers would have access to their own gardens. "And in my *kolonihave*, I'm going to have a greenhouse and grow all kinds of flowers."

"That sounds lovely," Sanya said.

Katrine shrugged. "But I don't know how it all fits. I start business school this September at the Copenhagen Business School. I mean, someday Daddy's business or part of his business will be mine. Jonas isn't interested. And even though Daddy is selling IT Foundry, he'll still be on the board of the company and he'll still have shares. They'll come to me."

Katrine was so sure of what her future held. Sara was interested in not knowing, in enjoying the adventure of uncertainty. She never thought of Harry's business as having anything to do with her, and it didn't. He was a partner, and when he left someone would buy him out. There would be money and some assets, yes, but Sara wasn't interested in any of it. She never talked about her future in terms of Sanya and Harry. Her future was her own. Maybe this was the difference between dynasties and regular people.

"But I can have a garden and a business, can't I?" Katrine said. "Nowadays women can have everything."

"Yes," Sanya said. She felt a rush of affection for her, probably stemming from her attraction for her father.

"But I'm just nineteen," Katrine said. "What do I know? Right?"

"Just because you're nineteen doesn't mean that you can't know yourself," Sanya said.

And that was when *he* came.

Ravn walked up to them brusquely, like he wanted to run but was controlling himself to walk. He did the Danish thing, or was it the French thing, of leaning into Sanya and kissing her on one cheek and then the other. She felt his lips, cool and firm, and the smell of his cologne and the brush of his stubble. It was only for a small moment, but just like in the movies, time stood still and they both closed their eyes to savor it fully and drench their senses in that touch.

Time moved at its own pace when he moved away to put an arm around his daughter and kiss her forehead.

"My daughter loves gardening," he said.

"So I hear," Sanya said.

Mandy then, opportunely, called out for Katrine, and they were alone.

"How are you?" he asked, their eyes holding each other, and they were both smiling widely, happiness a *real* and *tangible* emotion.

"Good," Sanya whispered.

"Really? Since when?" he asked. "Because I started to feel good *just now*, right this moment . . . since I saw you." He spoke with such feeling that Sanya's breath came out in a whoosh.

I'm not ready for this, for him, she thought. He was unreal with his intensity and his focus, with passion that oozed out of him. *Or I'm imagining all of this, and he's just a scumbag who is hitting on a woman in front of his wife.*

"I'm reading a feminist novel that my daughter got me from a secondhand bookstore in Paris," she said without thinking, to break the connection, to quash the rise of emotion.

"Is it a good book?" he asked without breaking stride, without seeming surprised at the change in the emotional weather around them.

"I don't know," Sanya said. "I'm struggling with it and can't seem to get into it. I used to read a lot; now it's like a giant step."

"I'm reading a book as well," Ravn said. "It's a biography of Caesar."

"Tell me something about it," she asked.

"There is this quote from Caesar that speaks to me," he said, and then, looking into Sanya's eyes, he said softly, "What we wish, we readily believe, and what we ourselves think, we imagine others think also."

"What are you both discussing so intently?" someone asked. It took Sanya a moment to realize that Lucky had walked up to them, breaking the enchantment.

Ravn looked at Lucky in bewilderment, as if asking, *Why are you here?*

Instead of answering him, Ravn only smiled. "I think dinner is ready," he said, and ushered them back to the patio where a large dining table was set with place cards.

Sanya did not sit next to Ravn.

❖   ❖   ❖

Everyone appreciated the food. Apparently Mandy was a great cook. Maybe it was the Indian genes, but Sanya needed a little more flavor— some heat. She had a craving for a spicy curry as she ate only a quarter of her bland salmon.

"When Mandy cooks, we all just skip lunch and breakfast," Penny said. "She's amazing. And she's such a great mother, too. You know how everyone we know has an au pair. I mean we'd be lost without Jinny. But Mandy never had help."

"Not to raise my children," Mandy said proudly. "But, Penny, I didn't work. You are a career woman." She might have put it as if she were rationalizing giving Penny a reason for why Jinny was the one helping her children eat instead of their mother, but it was evident that Mandy didn't think highly of career women.

"We never had an au pair," Harry said. "Sanya managed everything on her own. And sometimes when I look back I'm not quite sure how she did it. She worked just as hard as I did at her career, and she still took Sara to her soccer games and whatnot. She went to all the parent-teacher meetings, even baked cookies for school."

"I bought the cookies at Whole Foods," Sanya said flatly. *What is Harry up to now?*

Harry never talked about Sanya like this. Never even told her that he appreciated what she had done, the work she had done to raise their child so he could be who he wanted to be professionally. This was all part of the *Sanya is crazy so let's be nice to her* routine.

If she could have thrown up, she would have, and after all that champagne, it wouldn't have been difficult. She felt irritation simmer inside her, replacing the emptiness that had become a familiar companion for months and erasing the surge of lust and passion for Ravn.

"Sanya used to be a successful management consultant," Lucky piped in. Now it was his turn to unruffle the feathers. "And Sara is an excellent person as well, all thanks to Sanya. If Harry had raised that girl, she'd have turned out to be something else."

He said it jokingly, but Sanya knew he believed it and so did Harry, just as her parents and sister did. Sara was not ambitious because Sanya raised her. If Harry had raised her, she'd be so much more ambitious.

"I think it's great that Katrine wants to go to business school and play an active role in your business," Harry said to Ravn. "Sara, our daughter, she's . . . much more interested in yoga."

Sanya shut the noise out. She was getting tired again.

Her therapist had told her that she shouldn't hear everything Harry said about Sara or their lives as a judgment on Sanya as a mother and wife. She sometimes felt like one of those rats in a cage, running and running and running with nothing happening. It was like sitting on an exercise bicycle. You pedaled and pedaled and pedaled and were still where you started.

There were too many people here, she thought. *Too many people.* Her vision was getting blurry. So blurry that she couldn't even see the man with a scar on his cheek, and if she couldn't see him, she couldn't use him as a crutch as she had the past few weeks. She looked around and felt hysteria bubble through her. It was too soon. All this was too soon. She shouldn't have come tonight. It was too soon to have a crush. Too soon to drink champagne. It was all too soon.

She wanted to leave. She wanted to lie down. She wanted to hide under the covers and stay there. She didn't have the energy to eat the poached pears that Mandy had promised were divine and that would be served for dessert with a crème anglaise. It was just all too soon.

Her heart started to beat fast. She felt the garden swim around her, and she held on to the arm of her chair. It would pass. She knew it would. She just had to breathe. *Just breathe and it will be all right.*

"You look pale." Ravn's voice came to her through the merry-go-round the world had become. He was standing behind her pouring water into her glass.

Sanya couldn't speak. The voice was locked in her throat.

She gripped the arm of her chair even more tightly so that the world would stop spinning. And she turned to stare into the black eyes of the man with a scar on his cheek. Harry and Lucky and the others were far away, holding on to plates with bloodred pears.

Ravn held a glass of water near her face. "Drink," he said.

She drank, and as she did, the world stopped spinning, and when she was done she whispered softly, "Thank you."

❖   ❖   ❖

On their way home Sanya interrupted Harry as he spoke about how different the lives of their hosts were to theirs and asked him, "Why did you marry me?"

Harry braked smoothly, not because of her question but because there was a red light. He turned to look at Sanya. She watched the glittering red streetlight.

"What kind of question is that?" he asked.

She didn't say anything but waited for him to respond.

"I married you because I fell in love with you, head over heels," he said as the light turned green and he accelerated.

"Are you still in love with me? Head over heels?" she asked.

"I'm still in love with you," he said without waiting a beat. "I fell in love with you because you were positive and full of energy, you believed in the universe the way I never had. You were close to your family even though they drove you out of your mind. I've never been close to mine; I feel nothing for them. I loved that you took care of everyone. I loved that every time you looked at me, your eyes went wide like you'd found a treasure at the end of a rainbow."

"But what if I'm not any of those things anymore?" Sanya whispered. "I'm not that positive person . . . I never was. I was faking it the entire time."

"You've not changed as much as you think you have," Harry said.

"And maybe you're just fooling yourself," Sanya said.

"I know you better than you think I do," he said.

He had driven up to their street and was now looking for a parking spot. He found one remarkably quickly for a Friday night and angled the car to parallel park.

She waited for him at the door of the apartment building because he had the key. He paused before opening the door and put his hands on her shoulders and looked her in the eyes. "I'm not fooling myself, not about you. You are and have always been the light in the darkness. You brought color into my life. What I'm scared about is that I have taken and not given and that you don't love me anymore."

Sanya took a deep breath and nodded. She knew he wanted her to say, *Don't worry, I love you, I still love you, and I always will.* But she wasn't Old Sanya anymore. She didn't say things just because they were the right things to say.

"I need time," Sanya said.

He smiled and kissed her lightly on the lips. His lips were different from Ravn's. They were warm and soft, indulgent . . . and hers.

"I know. I have faith that we will work through this," he said.

Sanya felt a pang of loss. Their roles had really reversed. Now he had faith in the universe and she was the pessimist.

Chapter 11

The Swedish Summer House Plan

Penny invited Mandy for coffee at Café Plateau on Strandvejen the day after the casual barbecue. And even though Mandy had protested—she had just finished with her personal trainer at the gym and was sweaty and messy—she arrived with coiffed hair and in a DVF wraparound dress and Gucci sandals that showed her properly pedicured toes.

For Penny, there was no one else to go to but Mandy during a crisis, and as crises went, this was right up there with a zit on her forehead the first time she had walked for YSL at Paris Fashion Week. Even then Penny had called Mandy, who had walked her away from the ledge and sent her packing to makeup.

Penny ordered a café latte for Mandy, while Penny was on her second glass of Malbec, the house wine for the day.

Café Plateau had opened a few months ago and was just what Strandvejen needed. It was like a little piece of Parisian heaven in the heart of Hellerup. The café could seat twenty and served a limited breakfast and lunch menu, cocktails and wine for the after-work crowd, and, at all hours, the usual range of café lattes, cortados, and chai lattes. All drink orders came with a bowl of nuts—usually toasted almonds or, with wine, green olives.

Mandy sat down and wrinkled her nose as she held the latte glass with both hands. She turned around and smiled at the young man at the counter. "Could you make me another one? Hot, hot. Please."

"I can just microwave that one for you. It's just been there for like two minutes," the young man suggested.

Mandy smiled all teeth and said, "I'd like a fresh one, please." Then she took the warm glass of latte and placed it on the counter, her smile intact, and put down a fifty-kroner note next to the glass and came back to sit with Penny.

"I'm worried, Mandy. I'm really worried about this whole tax thing, and I think IT Foundry is involved somehow. I don't know how, but Mark and Ravn have been up to something together," Penny said.

"Ravn won't tell me anything," Mandy said in a hushed voice, because this was Hellerup, and you never knew who was listening.

"He doesn't tell anyone anything if there's trouble, only if there's good news," Penny said irritably. "Did you see him yesterday at the barbecue? He was so serious. Something is up, Mandy."

Mandy believed, truly believed in the man of the house being the man of the house. She had grown up in a tiny town in Oregon, or what movies liked to call Small-Town America. Her father had worked in a bank, and her mother had been a homemaker. She had two older brothers, and both of them still lived in Cedar Hills, with a population of just over ten thousand. One of her brothers had a clothing store at the Cedar Hills Shopping Center, while her oldest brother worked at the same bank her father had retired from. They were married and had two children each. She hardly ever saw her brothers, especially since her mother had passed away a few years ago and her father lived in a retirement home. Her brothers' lives today were no different than their lives had been growing up in Cedar Hills.

Going to school in that small town she had dreamed of Prince Charming. A gallant prince on a white horse who would get her out of her miserable life, but she had not expected to find him. It was a fairy tale, and she knew that fairy tales did not come true.

She met Ravn in San Francisco, where she had gone for a July Fourth weekend with her friends. She had been studying at a community college in Beaverton. She was a sophomore with no idea as to what she was going to do with her life. She knew she would have to get married, and she was hoping it would not be to Rick Briscoe, her on-again, off-again boyfriend, to whom she'd lost her virginity. Rick had never even talked about going to college, and right after high school he had started working in his father's Italian restaurant, Bella Italia in Cedar Hills. She'd had her fill of eggplant parmigiana.

But Mandy had something that neither her friends nor her brothers possessed. Mandy was beautiful. With her blond hair and delicate features, Mandy was an intense mixture of innocence and sensuality all bundled into one. Her town's Marilyn Monroe with slimmer hips. For a while she had wondered about going to Los Angeles and trying her luck at the movies, but, thank heavens, she'd met the love of her life before she could do something that foolish.

Ravn had been *perfect*. With his accent, his money, and even with that hideous scar on his cheek, he had been a breath of fresh air. They had met at Fisherman's Wharf, and it had been love at first sight. People joked about it and mocked it, but for Mandy it was the truth. One look and she was deeply and madly in love, and not only because she knew how much the Omega watch he wore cost.

Just six months after that meeting at Fisherman's Wharf, Ravn and Mandy were married.

Ravn came to Cedar Hills and met Mandy's family before he whisked her off to Denmark, where he made her part of his family. His family didn't mind that she wasn't Danish and didn't come from money. They came from money. They felt they had enough.

Mandy could see that even though Ravn and she lived in a small apartment in the city when they were first married (he was working his way up, he told her), the family money wasn't going anywhere. It would come to the only son. It would come to Ravn. And then when it had, he had invested in IT Foundry and made it the grand success it was.

For her part, Mandy had had to learn how to eat, how to talk, how to walk, and how to dress. It had been her personal *Pygmalion*.

She worked hard to fit in. She became friends with Penny and Ravn's parents, whom she hardly ever saw now, because his father was busy with his life in France and his mother had moved with her second husband to New York, where she lived on Fifth Avenue. They weren't the nicest people Mandy knew, but they weren't the worst, either. Now she saw them some years for Christmas, but mostly they were part of neither her nor Ravn's life.

As Mandy had lived longer and longer with Ravn, she started to realize that she was now part of a *very* wealthy family, and she had money and influence. When the children were little, she slowly started to better herself with nicer clothes, shoes, and jewelry. She kept waiting for her husband to say something about how she spent money, but he never did. He never said that this was too much or that was too expensive.

Now, after twenty-five years, she knew she could buy whatever she wanted and she did. She went to Paris and bought a Kelly bag *and* a Birkin bag. She went to Milan to shop for the latest fashions. She had a close relationship with all the fashion houses in Copenhagen, and when Gucci had a sale, they called her so she could have first choice because she bought handsomely even when there wasn't a sale. It had not been difficult to get used to having money. It had not been easy to become someone who looked like someone who had money. The ease of it—the way the other Hellerup wives just relaxed in their wealth—that had been hard.

It had taken practice to be nonchalant about spending a thousand dollars on Lise Charmel lingerie at BeeLee on Strandvejen. It had taken practice to not balk when she bought her first Chanel pearl necklace with a diamond-studded Chanel logo clasp for ten thousand Euros. It had taken practice to book first-class tickets for the family to travel to Bali to celebrate her and Ravn's fifteenth wedding anniversary.

Now she was experienced. All that hard work had paid off. She was a bona fide Hellerup wife. She worked out at Well-come at the Waterfront Mall, went to Gun-Britt Coiffure to get her hair done, had her facials at Amazing Space at Hotel d'Angleterre, and took care of nails, waxing, and massage at Evani on Strandvejen.

She had come a long way from having her hair cut at Great Clips in Cedar Hills and buying her underwear at Wal-Mart (because it's not lingerie when you buy it at a supermarket).

She knew she couldn't have done it without Penny, who had booked Mandy's first hair and facial appointments, had taken her shopping, and had taught her how best to mingle with these crowds. And Mandy had been there for Penny whenever she'd needed her. When her super-model career crashed around her ears because she was photographed in Bulgaria snorting cocaine, Mandy and Ravn had flown to Bulgaria to support Penny. She had been there when Penny's Parisian billion-aire boyfriend Serge Arnault had had a very public engagement with a Parisian socialite *before* he dumped Penny. *Wonderful* Serge hadn't understood why Penny was upset because she should've known that he wouldn't marry a model, not when he was an Arnault. Mandy had been there, letting Penny weep all over Mandy's new five-thousand-kroner Missoni dress in her and Ravn's suite at the Ritz.

Oh yes, they had been together through thick and thin, and even though Mandy thought that Penny had had it easy despite the cocaine incident, which only served to give Penny more publicity, and Mandy suspected Penny felt that Mandy had fallen into a pot of gold because of nothing but her looks, they were family, and blood was thicker than water.

"How could you say that to him?" Mandy groaned when Penny told her how she had propositioned Harry. "He's got a wife."

"He's not the loyal type," Penny said. "That's obvious."

"Is Ravn the loyal type?" Mandy asked shrewdly.

"Do you really want to know?" Penny asked.

Mandy licked her lips and shook her head. No, she didn't want to know. Why stir up a hornet's nest over nothing? If Ravn was sleeping around, then he was; there wasn't anything she could do about it, and there was nothing she wanted to do about it. A woman in her position couldn't afford to have a hissy fit over infidelity. And what if he did sleep around? It didn't change anything. Her husband was devoted to her. Even after so many years together, they religiously made love every Sunday. It wasn't as explosive as it used to be, but it was pleasant. She always came and he always came, and it lasted maybe fifteen minutes or so . . . it was nice.

If Mandy was honest, and she never would be about this, she would admit that she actually didn't like to have sex with her husband anymore. She did have sex, and she had an orgasm and everything, but she thought sex should be dirty, a little filthy, for it to be fun. It was strictly missionary all the way for her and Ravn. No kinky stuff. *But* they were happy. He loved her and she loved him, and she kept a lovely home for him and raised his children and let him have sex with her every Sunday. What more could he ask for?

"And the wife . . . good god, what's up with her?" Penny asked.

"Did you see her hair? If anyone needs a makeover, she does," Mandy said. "All those grays, and she's got that dark hair so it ages her. And why does she dress like a bag lady? She looked okay at the ambassador's dinner, partly because Lilly took her to Birgitte Green, but yesterday? I mean, what was that she was wearing?"

Penny shook her head. "I thought everyone in America wore jeans and T-shirts for barbecues."

Mandy snorted. "I'm American, Penny, so I know about America. And yes, a barbecue is casual but . . . this is Hellerup, and she should've known better. And she wore Skechers? Really? I mean a pair of heels would have really helped her look—not saved it, mind you, but it would've certainly helped."

If Mandy admitted it to herself, which she wouldn't do, she made Harry's Indian wife seem ugly because she had seen an exchange between her husband and *that* woman by Katrine's azaleas that made her uncomfortable. She had even grilled Katrine without being too obvious, but her daughter didn't seem to notice anything at all. It was nothing, really . . . but there was an intimacy to the way in which he had leaned into her as he gave her a glass of water, which meant nothing because it was innocuous . . . there was just *something* there. But Mandy was too busy denying that her husband was a philanderer, so she refused to acknowledge that Harry's Indian wife, who seemed to look good even without makeup at her age, despite the grays and the outfit, was going to be a problem for her.

"I think I'm going to try Lucky next," Penny said.

"Why not just *ask* Harry what's going on instead of trying to get into his pants?" Mandy suggested. "Or you know what, let's take that Indian wife of his out to lunch and see what she knows."

"It's not just the looks and clothes, Mandy; that woman looks like she's half dead," Penny said. "She's weird. You talk to her, and one minute she's talking to you and another she's tuned you out. I don't think all the circuits in her brain are in order. I don't think she knows anything, and by that I mean *anything*."

Mandy sighed. "I still think instead of hitting on men you should ask your husband and I'll ask mine. We can just *ask* our men what's going on."

Penny shook her head and bit her trembling bottom lip. "Come on, Mandy, that was the first thing I did. I have asked Mark and Ravn; and they both patted me on my head and told me it would be all right. They're telling me nothing, and I can't go to jail, Mandy. I didn't do anything wrong."

Mandy patted Penny's shoulder. "Darling, we'll figure it out. I promise. Okay, I have an idea. How about we go away for a weekend to the summer house in Sweden?"

Penny lit up. "You mean like an overnight thing?"

Mandy sighed. "It doesn't mean you end up in Lucky's bedroom. He's . . . I don't know . . . suspect."

"He's Italian American," Penny said. "And yes, he's not Harry, but he's okay. I've done worse."

"Not since you've been married," Mandy said.

Penny made a face. "You don't want to know, Mandy. You're so naïve at times. It is sweet, don't get me wrong, but you're an innocent. And I love you for it."

Mandy wasn't sure how naïve she was. She knew what was what. She hadn't lived her life under a stone. Hadn't she managed to fool all of Danish high society into accepting her as one of their own? A stupid person couldn't achieve something like that. She was savvy, and she was known as the perfect hostess in their circles. When she threw a fundraiser, money was raised. When she invited people for a party, everyone had a great time. She knew her wine, she knew her bags, and she knew her people. She wasn't naïve, but she didn't mind that people thought she was. She had cashed in on her dumb blonde looks for years, and it was an advantage that she fully exploited.

"So, who should we invite?" Mandy asked, pulling out her iPad from her new brown Prada hobo bag, recently purchased at Birgitte Green, to make a list of the invitees.

"Well, the Americans obviously, and us . . . and then a few others just so it seems like a natural thing," Penny said.

"How about Bjarke and Leah?" Mandy asked.

Penny nodded. "They *are* nice. And maybe we can find out from Bjarke what his newspaper is doing reporting on my taxes."

Bjarke was the editor-in-chief of *Børsen*, the top financial newspaper in Denmark that had broken the Mark and Penny tax investigation story. Leah, his wife, worked with handicapped adults. They were a down-to-earth couple who had known Mandy for as long as she had lived in Denmark. She didn't confide in Leah as she did in Penny, and Leah didn't confide in Mandy, but they were friends. They went to Zumba class together on Saturday mornings at Well-come Spa.

"How about the children?" Mandy asked.

"No children," Penny said. "Let's keep it child free. Nothing cramps my style more than having Jinny and the kids around. I love them, Mandy, but now is not the time to bond with them. I need to make sure I can bond with them in the next five years, which will be hard to do from jail."

"Ravn will never let that happen," Mandy said emphatically.

❖　❖　❖

That evening, when they were in bed, Mandy told Ravn about the weekend she was planning, and as was the norm between them, he put it on his calendar without asking any questions. She in turn didn't ask him to "please be on time" as a nagging wife would, especially when he was never on time.

"Penny is so worried," Mandy told him. "She thinks she's going to end up in jail."

Ravn, who was reading through something on his iPad, snapped his head up. "I'll never let that happen."

"That's what I told her," Mandy said, delighted with herself for knowing her husband so well. "But what about Mark?"

"What about Mark?" he said, his focus back on his iPad.

Mandy sighed. She knew that tone of voice. It was the *this discussion is over* tone of voice.

"The Americans, do you think they'll come for a weekend like this?" Mandy asked, carefully moving along with the items on her nighttime conversation agenda.

"Sure," he said, and then, as if realizing he was being short, he added, "They know no one here. It's nice of you to invite them. And more Americans are joining them; they have a team in the United States working on the IT Foundry acquisition as well, and some of them are coming next week to Denmark. Why not invite them, too? We have enough bedrooms at the house."

Mandy turned on her iPad and looked through her invite list. "How many more people did you say?"

"I don't know. Why don't you give Lucky a call? He arranges these things for Harry," he said. "And ask that Vietnamese guy, what's his name? Phan? Ask him to come so he can cook. I don't want you cooking for all these people. He can shop and take a car and set up there. Last time was a disaster with all of us chopping and cleaning in the kitchen."

"I thought it was cozy," Mandy said, as she added a note to tell Phan to keep the weekend free. She didn't use him all the time, but lately he had started to cook for them once in a while, especially when they were having guests. Mandy took too much pride in her cooking to outsource it, but this is what the wealthy did; they invited a cook along to weekend parties.

"It *was* cozy, *skat*," Ravn said, turning to look at his wife. "I just don't want you to stress out when we're going to be so many people."

Mandy smiled. "Oh, you're always so considerate," she said, and went back to making plans for a weekend party.

Yes, they would have Vietnamese rolls as appetizers on day one; they were Ravn's favorite, after all, and then for the main course . . .

Chapter 12

Ravn's Ballerinas

"I'd like to take you out to lunch," Sanya heard Ravn say when she picked up her cell phone to a strange Danish number.

How did he get my number? she wondered. *I can barely remember it.* "Where?"

"Café Around the World," he said, and added in Danish, "Café Jorden Rundt."

"I don't know if I want to go around the world with you," Sanya said.

"I'll pick you up in ten minutes. Can you be outside your apartment?" he asked.

"But I won't go around the world with you," she said.

"Have a salad instead," he suggested.

He hung up.

Sanya was still in one of Harry's white undershirts. He kept a stack of old soft ones just for her. And then, when the ones she wore got holes in them, he would just transfer more to her closet. It wasn't flowers or small blue boxes of precious items, but it was his way of showing love. It was making sure for nearly two decades that Sanya always had what she needed to sleep in.

Maybe she took the shirts for granted and he took . . . no, used to take Sanya for granted. Sanya wasn't sure how Harry felt about her anymore. Since the implosion, Sanya certainly had trouble sorting her emotions, but she had more trouble than usual gauging Harry.

A few years ago she had asked Harry, if he could change anything about her, what would he like to change?

His response had been immediate: "Nothing."

She should've been flattered, but she wasn't, because she knew he answered the way he did because he didn't know Sanya. If he knew her, he would've said, "I would like for you to be authentic, not this carica-ture you've made yourself into to make the world happy." If he really knew his wife, he would've said, "Sanya, I wish you still loved me."

Sanya refused to feel guilty as she discarded the soft white nightshirt and changed into a pair of jeans and a white T-shirt. She took a black sweater along just in case she got cold and then for safety wrapped around her neck a black-and-white silk scarf. She was nailing this whole layering thing.

❖   ❖   ❖

Ultimately, Ravn didn't take Sanya around the world; instead he took her to the New Carlsberg Glyptotek, a museum with a café in the atrium.

"I changed my mind," he said. "My wife said she was meeting my cousin there after her workout. She goes to the gym every day."

"Of course she does," Sanya said.

"I run. Do you run?" he asked.

"All the time, and away from lots of things," she said.

"I have a wife," he said.

"I have a husband, and at our age, people usually tend to have bag-gage," she said when they entered the museum. "And how do you know that you won't bump into someone you know here?"

"Copenhagen is a village; I can absolutely bump into someone I know here," he said. "I just don't care to *bump into*, as you put it, my wife."

"Would she mind you having lunch with me?" she asked.

"I have no idea," he said.

"What if Harry asked your wife out to lunch?" Sanya prodded.

"I seriously don't give a fuck who Harry has lunch with . . . even my wife," he said.

They stood in the atrium of the museum, at a crossroads. In one direction was the museum entrance. Another path led to the café, one to the house of sculptures, one to specifically Rodin, and the last straight ahead to the impressionist art collection. They walked straight ahead.

"This museum was built by Carl Jacobsen, the son of the guy who built the Carlsberg breweries. Cees 't Hart, the CEO of Carlsberg, is a friend of mine. Nice Dutch guy," Ravn said. "They could have just called it Glyptotek—*glypto* is Greek for *glyphein*, which means 'carvings' or some such thing, and *theke* means 'a place of storage'—but since everyone has an ego the museum is called the New Carlsberg Glyptotek."

"A warehouse for carvings," Sanya mused.

They walked through the hallways, a few tourists scattered around. No one paid them attention. A man with a scar on his cheek and a damaged woman holding herself together. Nothing to see.

"Are you into impressionistic art?" he asked.

Sanya shrugged. "I don't know much about art. I like that Munch guy with the screaming man."

"That painting was stolen from the Norwegian Art Museum in Oslo a few years ago in broad daylight," he said.

"I read about it. It must've taken balls to steal something so important in broad daylight," Sanya said.

They stepped into the first room, where beauty dripped from the walls in the form of oil paintings, some old and some new. Curators said it took oil paintings that are layered, glaze over varnish over paint over paint, years to dry. Some of the old masterpieces were still not completely dried. Sanya liked the idea of that. Something this time-worn was still in the process of firming itself, finding itself, letting the fluid amalgamate and harden into something that could last an eternity, stolen or otherwise.

"The French collection is the most impressive, with Monet, Pissarro, Renoir, Degas, and Cézanne," Ravn said.

Sanya had heard these names before, and she knew Monet made that painting with haystacks and water lilies, and wasn't Degas the dude with the ballerinas? The rest were just names.

"Which one is your favorite?" she asked.

He took her to a Degas painting in shades of gray, lacking color. There were several dancers in white ballet outfits. There were ballerinas in motion, fluid, arms aloft, their bodies held in accordance with the music that almost vibrated from the canvas—while in contrast other ballerinas were static, waiting to perform.

"This is one of my favorites," he said. "*Répétition d'un ballet sur la scène*, 'Ballet Rehearsal on Stage.' It's on loan from the Musée d'Orsay in Paris."

"Why this painting?"

"Degas was supposed to be a tough guy, but his portrayals of women, especially in his ballerina series, are always so gentle, soft, and delicate," Ravn said. "Many critics actually say this is not a painting but a drawing. So many things are happening here. The dancers in action. The dancers in waiting. The man sitting on the chair in the back. It's brilliant. I have a Degas in my office at home, an original. It has just one ballerina, leaning against a barre; her face is almost hidden, but there is this coiled energy inside her ready to be released. If the house was burning down, that's the one thing I'd save."

They stood in front of the Degas for a while and watched the dancers practice their pliés. He put his hand on the small of Sanya's back to hold her because she had suddenly started to sway. The museum was warm, and the sweater she had worn over her T-shirt because it was cool on this summer day was now constricting her. The waistband of her jeans wrapped clammily around her middle. She turned to look at him and weaved on her feet.

"I have another favorite," he said softly. "Would you like to see?"

She nodded and then removed her sweater. He took the sweater from her and held it in his hand.

As they walked he said, "The sculptures are also very good. The most prized is the series of dancers by Degas, and they're very good. But I like his paintings."

Sanya shook her head, nausea building inside her.

I should not have left home, she thought.

It was one thing to go to a café down the street and quite another to go on a clandestine rendezvous to a museum with a potential lover. This was *not* who she was. She didn't do this kind of thing. She was the good wife. The good mother. She was the happy woman who had a great life and a closet full of white cotton undershirts that her husband had lovingly discarded for her.

And just as she was about to run, he brought her in front of a Monet, *Shadows on the Sea*. Sanya stared at the painting and felt, just as Ravn must have intended, a sense of calm spread through her.

"The series is called *The Cliffs at Pourville*," he said in a low voice. "After seeing these paintings for the first time, I went to Normandy to experience the view."

The shadows on the sea, the jutting cliffs, a scene indecipherable at close range. The viewer had to stand at a distance to see the fine points clearly, to feel the peace. Sometimes life was like that, wasn't it?

They stood in silence for nearly fifteen minutes, both of them staring at Monet's sea, Ravn's hand still on the small of her back, now not supporting her but purporting intimacy. She didn't move away from it. She let the sunlight and clouds that soared over the cliffs of Pourville spread through her, and she breathed in and out slowly and deeply, putting the broken pieces together . . . again.

They walked back to the atrium and went to the café. A waiter took them to an empty table and handed them menus.

When they were seated, Ravn took her hand in his, forcing her attention. His blue eyes were intense with feeling. "People think depression is being sad. People don't know shit."

"Is that what you think I am, depressed?" she asked as she pulled her hand away.

"One damaged person can see another, Sanya," he said. "When I was eighteen, my grandmother died of cancer the same week my girlfriend overdosed and ended up in a coma. A week later she died as well. My father had checked out years before that, he was living in Provence then with his new French wife, still does. My mother was traveling, I think, I don't know where. My grandmother raised me. After the funerals I tried to commit suicide."

There was really no proper response to a statement like he'd just made. There was no asking, *So, how did you try to commit suicide? Did you slit your wrists? Take pills? What did you do, Ravn?* She couldn't ask because his darkness had obviously been much darker than hers. Sanya couldn't compete with a beloved dead grandmother and a girlfriend.

Sanya had told Alec after she had come back from the hospital and started therapy that she felt like a fraud because she didn't really have any reason to be depressed. People struggling to make a living or dealing with abuse or living through a war, these people had the right. Not Sanya who lived in a three-thousand-square-foot house in Los Gatos with a swimming pool.

"Only the hen that lays the egg knows the ass burn it takes to pass it. Everyone's pain is their own personal hell. You *cannot* compare notes. You *cannot* say your hell burns less hot than mine," Alec said. "Your pain is real to you, and that's reason enough."

The waiter came and they ordered drinks. They both were having coffee with milk and sparkling Carlsberg water.

"So you don't usually go to museums?" Ravn asked. "MOMA in San Francisco is very special."

"I've been there with a client—but there just hasn't been time between work and life to indulge . . ." She trailed off, because it sounded like a cliché. *I've been too busy working and not living.*

"There's something about walking around a museum and seeing the different nuances between the various works of art," Ravn said, and raised his hand as if holding a paintbrush. "We can stand in front of the canvas just as the artist did and experience a little bit of that magic. Would you like that? To experience that magic with me?"

He was *obviously* asking about more than museums. She didn't hesitate, well, not for long. New Sanya wanted to fly into the unknown.

"I'd love to walk through a museum or two with you," she said. "I'd love to learn to see art."

"I know nothing about painting styles and eras and . . . all of that. Specific art turns me on," he said.

"And I don't even have sexy lingerie," Sanya said.

He laughed out loud. "You're more complicated, nuanced, and layered than a Monet, aren't you?"

Harry used to call her his Indian princess, when their relationship was still new and fresh, but no one had *ever* called her a Monet. Was this just a line to this man? Or did he really think she was this deep and interesting woman? Sanya decided to, for once, take what Ravn said at face value, and she liked the idea, very much, of being compared to a painting.

They ordered after that. She had a caprese sandwich, and he ordered a steak, medium rare, with new potatoes and béarnaise sauce.

"I've been here before," he said in between sips of his water.

Sanya smiled. He wasn't talking about the museum. "I've *never* been here before," she confessed. "How many times have you been here?"

"Three and a half times," he said. "I say half because I only came to the doorstep one time and returned. But I think it still counts."

"Why did you return?"

"There was a storm approaching, and it was going to be a rough one," he said.

"And three and a half times is what percentage of your marriage?" she asked.

"I've been married for twenty years now. Each lasted somewhere between a year and three," he said.

"That's almost half your marriage . . . give or take," she said.

He nodded as he silently counted. "More or less. I never thought about it that way."

"Did you fall in love?"

"Every time," he said.

"You fall in love easily." She should've felt disappointed that this was not special, she was not special, he did this all the time—but she didn't. Instead, she felt relieved that she was not his first indiscretion and probably not his last. It made this lunch much easier to swallow.

"Not easily," he said, "but definitively."

"I'm sure I fell in love with Harry, a long time ago. I just can't remember anymore," she said.

"We'll make sure you remember *this* time," he said, and grinned broadly, inviting her to jump, to take that leap into space.

Where had this come from? Sanya thought. *This feeling of abandon, this feeling that maybe, yes, yes, why not, why shouldn't I jump? Has this always been inside me, and has it come out because of the implosion?* Where had this recklessness, this affinity for disorder, come from?

In South India, after the 2004 tsunami, lost temples at Mahabalipuram had emerged, rising from the ocean. A big earthquake had to happen for this revelation to be forced out from the belly of the water. *Maybe that was what happened with me.*

"It's not easy for me," she said.

He smiled. "Hell, Sanya, it's not easy for anyone. Falling in love is exhilarating, exhausting, confusing, and maddening . . . but it's never easy. Why should it be? People confuse being in love with being happy. Love has nothing to do with happiness. It's about being *alive*. And right now you're depressed. When you're depressed you love no one, not even yourself."

I'm not ready, Sanya wanted to scream. And wasn't she unbalanced enough without falling in love?

"You don't have to jump off the mountain right away," he said. "Why don't we keep it simple and eat lunch?"

He put his hand on hers again, and this time Sanya didn't pull away. She laughed softly and fell in love with him a little in that moment, because this stranger seemed to have his finger on her pulse and could see her as she wanted . . . no, as she needed to be seen.

Chapter 13

Penny and Mandy Take Sanya Around the World

The day after Sanya had lunch with Ravn, Mandy, who didn't know about *that* lunch, invited Sanya for lunch at Café Jorden Rundt, Café Around the World, in Charlottenlund on Strandvejen, where she was going to meet Penny after her run.

She had deliberately chosen a place that was as casual and inexpensive as this because it was unpretentious and uncomplicated. You stood in line and ordered and paid for your food and drinks and then found a place to sit down. This way everyone paid for her own order and there was no unnecessary credit card wrangling at the end of the meal. Not that Mandy minded paying—she loved doing it, but she wasn't sure what type Sanya was. And it was a beautiful day in June with the sun shining, and the café had such a brilliant view of Øresund and the people swimming in it alongside sailboats and kite surfers. The beach was already packed with beach umbrellas, screaming kids, and sand castles. This year it appeared that it would be a good summer, unlike the past two years, when it had rained through the end of July and the flights out of Kastrup Airport were full of Danes getting to Southern Europe and sunshine.

Penny and Mandy got there a half hour early to discuss how to approach the matter and the American's *brown* wife. They would start with the weekend at the Swedish summer house, obviously, but then how to move into matters of business?

"Why not just ask her how Harry is doing and how the work is coming along? They're supposed to be done by August or so with Harry becoming the CEO," Penny said.

Mandy wasn't sure. "She'll just say it's going well, and we'll find out nothing."

"Mark is singing his *everything will be okay* song and keeps telling me to calm the hell down," Penny said. "I have a migraine building. I asked Mark last night if we should divest from each other's companies, and you won't believe what he said. He said that I could do what I wanted, but he wanted me to *buy him out* because my company was worth more than his. He's such a mercenary asshole."

Mandy nodded and patted Penny's hand to comfort her.

"And something odd is going on. I think Jinny is wearing my lingerie," Penny said.

"She's stealing from you?" Mandy asked. It wasn't uncommon or special; it happened all the time. This was why Mandy never had an au pair; she couldn't stand the idea of having a stranger lurking around the house. It was one thing to have cleaners and gardeners; they came and left and were under her supervision, but an au pair lived in the house with you, and you couldn't keep an eye on her all the time.

Penny shook her head and rubbed her temples. "I saw an Aimer negligee in her room. I think. I told Mark about it, and he says how can that even be possible and why was I spying on Jinny. I wasn't spying; I was just walking by her room and the door was open. But then I checked my closet, and the negligee was there. So I don't know what to think."

"Maybe she's sleeping with some Hellerup type who gave it as a present," Mandy suggested. This also happened often enough in

Hellerup—au pairs would sometimes carry on with men they met through their employers.

"I said the same thing to Mark, but he couldn't see how it was possible, and he has a point. She's working in our house all the time, so I don't think she has time to have a liaison with some rich Hellerup bloke," Penny said. "And who cares what Jinny is up to when my world is crashing around me?"

"So Mark is not worried about this tax audit?" Mandy asked.

"He says that the government will back off soon," Penny said, and tears welled in her eyes that she dabbed with her napkin. "It's all such a mess, Mandy."

Penny went from being teary to being agitated and pulled out a cigarette. She lit it with shaking hands.

"If you don't look calmer, she's going to suspect something is wrong," Mandy said.

"How can I be calm?" Penny asked. "I talked to my lawyer. He knows everything about tax fraud, and he said that if the government is looking into Mark's books, then they have very good reason to do so. He said that the government doesn't screw around."

"But what has Mark's business got to do with Ravn and IT Foundry?" Mandy asked, feeling a slight flutter of panic.

"I wish I knew what those two have been up to," Penny said.

Sanya came in a taxi, wearing a pair of jeans and a ratty T-shirt, a dull gray sweater on her arm. Her hair was a mess piled up around her head. She had good hair, Mandy accepted grudgingly. It needed a cut, badly. And she had to do something about all those white roots. She looked like a beaver with the springy white curls clamoring around her wavy black hair. How could a woman be so negligent about her appearance?

"We're so glad you could come," Mandy said, and leaned over to air-kiss Sanya. Penny did the same.

No makeup, either, Mandy noticed. But she had good skin. She could get away with it. A little makeup wouldn't hurt, though. A light foundation would smooth the edges and . . . the T-shirt had to go. Was that Hennes & Mauritz? My god, where did this woman go shopping? No one shopped at H&M these days. At least Zara or Massimo Dutti would have some dignity. And her husband had money. Couldn't he afford better clothes for his wife?

Sanya sat down next to Penny and across from Mandy. She was wearing sunglasses. Dior, at least that was decent enough, though very last season with the steel frame. It was all about the big round ones this season. Well, she was a career woman, and maybe that's why she didn't spend time taking care of herself. Mandy knew that career women dressed like men and behaved like men to compete with men in the corporate world. Ravn's chief information officer, a woman, always wore shapeless black pantsuits and had her hair cut short. She looked like a man, talked like a man, and walked like a man. Maybe Sanya was like that as well. Mandy smiled at the thought, because there was no way Anders Ravn would be interested in a woman like Sanya. She was certain of it.

"How are you settling into Copenhagen?" Mandy asked when they were seated inside the café.

"Fine," Sanya said. "It's nice. I went to the Glyptotek yesterday and had lunch."

Penny raised an eyebrow. "Did you now? Lunch at the café?"

"Yes," Sanya said pleasantly. "I really liked the impressionist art collection."

"Which painting did you like the best?" Penny asked.

"Oh, this Degas, with ballerinas . . . um . . . in rehearsal? And one by Monet of these hills in Normandy," Sanya said.

Penny nodded and then smiled. Mandy wasn't sure what was going on. Why was Penny asking about stupid art?

"How is Harry doing?" Mandy asked then. "All set to sign on the dotted line?"

As Mandy predicted, Sanya didn't have much to tell them about Harry's work. She seemed distracted the entire time she was there. She refused lunch and only had a latte, so Mandy and Penny didn't order any food, either. It wouldn't do to be chewing while asking questions if Sanya wasn't going to eat.

"So this is Café Around the World," Sanya said in wonder.

The café was round with glass walls on one side and mirrors on the other, so no matter where you sat you had a charming view of the sparkling Øresund. The sun was shining and the sky was blue, and there was just about enough wind that the sailboats were masts up in a rainbow of colors, crisp and beautiful against the satin length of the blue waters.

"It isn't the fanciest place in the world, but I get my latte here after my run. I go to the gym three times a week, and other days I run. Do you run?" Mandy asked.

Sanya looked amused at the question, in an aloof manner. Mandy was sure that the woman was a can . . . no, several cans short of a six-pack, as they said back home. She had these big brown doe eyes with a *deer caught in the headlights* expression.

"I don't run," Sanya said, but she was smiling. "I used to do Pilates, a long time ago, and some yoga. I do neither these days."

"You should join Well-come Fitness," Penny said. "It's a great place with excellent equipment, personal trainers, and classes. You can take yoga or Pilates or anything else you like. They have a lovely pool, steam room, sauna, and all the works. I go there three to four times a week. We all go there—Mandy . . . Ravn, all of us. I even get my facials and waxes there. It's very convenient."

"Yes," Mandy said. "Ravn is friends with the owner. We have to support the local businesses, you know."

"Christ, I haven't waxed in a million years," Sanya said. "It must be a jungle down there."

She wasn't cracking a joke, but since it would be rude to not think it was a joke, Mandy laughed awkwardly. *And she was unshaved?* No, Anders Ravn would simply not be interested.

Mandy was never late for waxes, because of a story that Penny had told her when she had first suggested Brazilian waxing to her many years ago. Penny's first lover had been a Lothario, an ex-soccer player who liked young girls. He wasn't that old, just thirty or so, but when Penny had been sixteen, thirty had been practically ancient and experienced. But he had been one of those enlightened men that Penny discovered there weren't that many of. He was interested in *her* orgasm. Penny had thought that was how all men were, but as she told Mandy, "Lovers numbers two to ten proved otherwise. They were complete duds."

Penny's first lover had looked at her considerable bush and said, "Babe, I want to eat you, not floss."

Penny had immediately gotten a full Brazilian bikini wax and had never gone back; and after hearing that story, neither had Mandy.

Apparently, no one had told Sanya that down under had to be mowed on a regular basis. How did she keep a man like Harry Kessler? Did she give good head? What did she do?

Seeing that the conversation was not moving at all and soon they'd start talking about the weather, Mandy took charge.

"We wanted to tell you about our plans for a weekend party," Mandy said. "I have talked to Lucky, and it looks like we can make it happen in a couple of weekends when your other American friends are also here."

"How wonderful," Sanya said pleasantly.

Mandy realized that Sanya wasn't curious in the least about her weekend party plans.

"It's going to be us, of course, and you. Also, we have invited our dear friends Bjarke and Leah. Bjarke is editor-in-chief of the most important financial newspaper in Denmark, *Børsen*," Mandy said, trying to impress Sanya.

Sanya nodded and sipped her latte. She didn't look impressed.

The woman was unsocial, Mandy concluded, just like the Danes. Since she had moved to Denmark, Mandy had faced all the unsocial people one could tolerate. It wasn't that Danes were not friendly . . . actually, they *were* unfriendly, and rude, and they didn't like including new people in their circles. They weren't curious about people and they didn't try to befriend them. Even after so many years, Mandy had very few Danish friends, and the ones she did have were usually the Danes who were married to foreigners, like herself. The culture shock of people not trying to get to know you had been quite a shift for Mandy, who was warm and friendly, the things Ravn loved about her.

So Mandy used her natural talents and became the de facto "mother" for all the women who came to Denmark as "love slaves." These non-Danish women married Danes and ended up in this cold, gray country where the summers were short and sometimes nonexistent, and the people, just like the weather, didn't welcome you. But her task was usually easy. These women were dying for some company, and when the wife of a wealthy man invited them home and into her life, they were super grateful. Sanya didn't seem interested. Didn't she miss human contact? Wasn't she feeling lonely? She knew no one in Copenhagen, and she wasn't even trying to get to know Penny and Mandy so that her life would have some companionship outside of Harry, who, Mandy guessed, probably worked all hours of the day like Ravn.

"The summer house is in Sweden," Mandy continued. "It's just two hours away from here. It's gorgeous there, and if the weather is nice, we can swim in the lake. Of course, we have a heated indoor pool for the long winters. You'll love it."

"I'm sure," Sanya said, and then, looking around the café, continued, "So is this café called Around the World because you can see out of all the windows?"

Mandy took a deep breath because Sanya was trying her patience.

"I think so," Mandy said. "It's a Hellerup standard. Everyone goes here at some point or another. The menu is simple and never ever changes."

"We don't have cafés like this in the states," Sanya said, as if trying to explain her fascination.

"American cities lack character," Penny said. "Except New York, but then New York City isn't really America, is it?"

"I don't know," Mandy said, immediately defensive about her country. "San Francisco, Chicago, Los Angeles . . . Atlanta, New Orleans—America has many flavors."

"And they are all drenched in ketchup," Penny said with a laugh. "All Americans eat *everything* with ketchup. They have no sense of cuisine."

Mandy felt her temperature rise. She was a better cook than Penny could ever dream of being. The bitch.

"I hear that the world's best restaurant is in Copenhagen," Sanya said.

The women talked about restaurants for a while, and Sanya nodded eagerly.

Yes, yes, she absolutely wanted to go to Noma. Era Ora? Italian. Kiin Kiin, the only Thai restaurant with a Michelin star. *Sounds fascinating.* Certainly, she would tell Harry to book a table right away. Apparently Anders Ravn had enough connections that he could make any dinner reservation possible. And everyone wanted to eat at Noma, one of the best restaurants in the world.

"I thought the food was *okay*," Mandy said. "Ravn took me there for our twentieth wedding anniversary, and I don't think it lived up to the hype."

"You Americans just don't appreciate good food. I thought it was the food of the gods," Penny said, and then turned to Sanya to get down to business. "Well, Sanya, how is Harry doing? Is he very busy?"

Sanya looked at Penny vaguely. "I don't see him much around the apartment, and when he's there, it's usually with Lucky. I hope he's working . . . but who knows? He may have found a mistress or two."

"Oh, I'm sure he hasn't," Penny said self-consciously. "So how is the due diligence coming along?"

Mandy kicked Penny under the table. She had just asked, and Penny was giving them away with her persistence.

"I really can't say," Sanya said. "But they have Raymond Otto coming over . . . he's their accounting guru. I really don't know much of what is happening."

"And once it's all done, Harry takes over as CEO," Mandy said with a bright smile. "You must be excited for him to have such a great opportunity."

Sanya shrugged.

"Oh, come on, it's a big deal. When Ravn took over as the CEO of IT Foundry, we had so many parties to celebrate. I was so proud to be his wife," Mandy said. "It's a big accomplishment."

"It's temporary and it's his accomplishment," Sanya said absently. "He's just going to run it for a while. We're only here for a year."

"I've heard that before," Mandy said. "This couple I know, they came here for six months, and that was ten years ago. She's American and he's Italian and they're still here."

"That could happen," Sanya said. "But I wouldn't be able to stay. I'll eventually have to get back to work, and I don't speak Danish, so working here would be difficult."

"But why would you want to work?" Mandy asked, confused. "If your husband is a CEO, you don't have to work, not for financial reasons, at least."

Sanya looked baffled.

"Mandy is a housewife," Penny said snidely. "She doesn't understand us career women."

"I understand career women just fine," Mandy snapped back. "I may not have an official job, Penny, but unofficially I'm busier than you."

"Oh, come on, Mandy, you're not busy—busy is not picking out the right décor for Ravn's boat; it's keeping a store running and making sure that the designs are . . ." Penny stopped midsentence when Sanya giggled.

The women looked at her curiously.

She waved a hand. "I'm sorry," she said.

"I didn't know what we said was so funny," Penny said, insulted.

Sanya shook her head, controlling her amusement. She left shortly thereafter, saying she wasn't feeling very well. She insisted on walking down Strandvejen instead of calling for a taxi, saying she needed some fresh air.

"She's nuts," Penny said once Sanya left.

"Forget about her; can you explain to me why you were being so bitchy? You were insulting America and me," Mandy said, standing up, her wine-colored Bottega Veneta bag in hand.

"Oh, come on, Mandy, you take things too seriously," Penny said. "I was just making conversation. But did you hear? Lucky knows as much as Harry does about everything. I think he might be the weaker link. He's single, probably desperate. I think he might be the one I need to approach."

"You don't have to prostitute yourself, Penny," Mandy said, aghast.

Penny laughed. "We're all whores, babe, it's just the degrees that vary."

❖　❖　❖

That night, when they were in bed, Mandy talked to Ravn about her lunch with Sanya.

"She suddenly started laughing and then left. Said she wasn't feeling well," Mandy said. "Something is wrong with *that* woman."

"Then don't invite her for lunch again," Ravn said, not looking up from his laptop.

"You know I can't do that, darling," Mandy said. "She must be lonely—I know how hard it can be."

Ravn stopped typing and turned to look at Mandy. "You don't have to save everyone."

Mandy smiled sweetly. "I *have* to try. And who knows? Maybe I can drill some fashion sense into her. If anyone is in need of a makeover, it certainly is her."

Ravn seemed to pause for a moment. "Makeover?"

Mandy laughed. "Bless your heart, darling, for not even noticing. She dresses like a . . . well, like a delinquent, with just one outfit. Her T-shirts are ratty. H&M. Her jeans . . . I think she has only one pair that she wears all the time. Her hair . . . well . . . where do I start with that?"

"Not everyone needs to look like a Barbie doll, Mandy," Ravn said. "Leave her alone. You don't like her. You don't have to deal with her."

"I don't dislike her—I just need to get to know her better," Mandy said.

He looked like he was going to say something, but then he decided not to. Instead he said, "You'll do what you think is best," and went back to his laptop.

Mandy didn't like how he asked her to leave Harry's wife alone. No, she didn't like it at all. But instead of dwelling on it, she impatiently flitted through pages of a book on her iPad. She had just downloaded a novel touted to be female erotica with a sprinkle of S&M. Mandy would never admit it, and would talk about the Salman Rushdie or Joyce Carol Oates book she had skimmed through and not really read, but she was a closet erotica and romance novel reader. Thank god for her Kindle, because now she was able to indulge without worrying about the cover of the book giving her away.

Mandy liked reading romance novels because they made her happy with their positive and love-will-conquer stories; and they made her horny. She had noticed that she was extra amorous after reading a sexy novel. And since they had missed having sex the previous Sunday, Mandy felt she needed to fix the situation by getting into the mood and convincing Ravn to get into the mood as well, even though it was in the middle of the week. Fact was that if she was willing, he was always willing. He never put pressure on her, and he never cajoled her . . . not anymore . . . to have sex with him, but if there was that mutual time when they both kissed a little and it could advance into sex, he took the opportunity. But if she said good night immediately after kissing him, he stayed with his work.

"We haven't been making love," Mandy said to him after she read the first paragraph of the novel.

Ravn looked up from his computer. Mandy was surprised at her boldness. They never really talked about sex. It was something you did. Not something you discussed.

"We've been busy," he said. "Would you like to make love tonight?"

Mandy licked her lips. There was just something about him that was distant. She had seen this before and had wondered if he was seeing a woman. But she had shut that line of thought immediately. She didn't want to know.

"Yes, please," Mandy said, and put her iPad away. She always wore sexy lingerie to bed. A woman had to dress like a woman, and she never understood women who didn't put the same effort into their appearance in bed as they did when they went outside. It was all a performance anyway, wasn't it?

She kissed him ardently, usually step one to sex. And then they made love as they always did. He used his fingers to make her ready and then he came inside. She orgasmed quickly and so did he. It was mutually satisfying.

But the sense of unease refused to leave her. It didn't help that when he rolled off her, he didn't say what he always did after they made love. He didn't say, "I love you, *skat.*"

He went to sleep while Mandy lay awake, dreading the next weeks, months, years. Yes, sometimes it had been years when he had been distracted and distant. It was always—*yes, Mandy, you have to admit it*—it was always another woman. She wanted to wake him up and yell at him. How dare he humiliate her like this? Did he sleep with that other woman before he came to her bed?

But she knew she wouldn't do that. She wouldn't ask questions to which she didn't want to know the answers. It was one thing to suspect your husband of having an affair and quite another thing for him to confirm it. Once he confirmed it, once the cat was out of the bag, you had to do something about it. Mandy liked her life. She *loved* her life. She would stand this as she had the other times. She would never let him know she knew, and he would return the courtesy and never make her feel like he had a mistress.

But this time he had forgotten to say, "I love you, *skat.*" This time could be the time when he actually fell in love with the other woman and left Mandy. She had to tread very, very carefully with Ravn.

A few years ago, when one of her brothers had come to visit them in Copenhagen, his wife had stood in awe of their house, their cars, and their life. "You've really made something of yourself, Mandy," her sister-in-law said. "I mean, look at you. You're living the fairy tale. You're a real-life princess."

And real-life princesses took care to not let the tiara fall off their heads.

Chapter 14

Can the Blind Lead the Blind?

Sanya hadn't seen Harry for nearly a day and a half. The day before, she had come back home tired from lunch with Mandy and Penny at Café Jorden Rundt, where she was certain they were pumping her for information, and she was mildly curious as to why, but overall she really didn't care one way or the other. She did, however, want to ask Harry how things were progressing with the IT Foundry purchase. There were too many late-night conference calls, Lucky seemed agitated most of the time, and now they were having some more people come over from the California office. But by the time she woke up late the next morning, Harry had already left.

That night Sanya's sleep was inundated with confusing dreams that she couldn't remember but could only feel remnants of, clinging to her subconscious like grains of beach sand, making her stay in bed and under the covers.

❖   ❖   ❖

In the afternoon, Ravn sent her a text message: How are you?

Sanya felt a weight lift, and she sat up on the bed and typed her response. I Went Around the World with your wife and your cousin.

He called then and asked, "How was lunch?"

"I didn't eat anything and neither did they," she said. "I left because I was being rude by laughing."

"I heard. What was so funny?"

"I'm going to sound terrible saying this. But your wife doesn't work for a living and your cousin, well . . ."

"Doesn't really work for a living, yes, I know," Ravn said.

"These two women were discussing who is busier, whose life has more value," she told him. "And suddenly I felt a burst of hysteria because I realized I was like them. I wasn't busy. I . . . am just as useless. Then I felt worse and I had to leave. I was tired. I came home and slept. You know, I don't think your wife likes me."

"I love my wife, but she measures people by the brand of handbag they carry," he said.

"I don't have a handbag. I have a small wallet," she said. She looked out of the window as she lay in bed, a bright blue sky over the Copenhagen skyline. "Why do you like me?"

"I don't know. But there's something there," he said.

She knew what he meant. Since that first moment in that café on Strandvejen, which seemed like an eternity ago and not just a few weeks, she had known that they had that elusive thing people called chemistry.

"How did you try to kill yourself?" she asked.

He was quiet for a long moment. Old Sanya would have broken the silence and said she was sorry for asking the question. New Sanya waited.

"I indulged in my mother's arsenal of barbiturates and took a few too many," Ravn said.

"But you obviously didn't die," she said.

"It was close. I almost lost kidney function. A friend saved my life," he said.

"Sounds intense."

"Yes, it was. He's a biker in one of the biker gangs in Copenhagen. We were in high school together and remained friends even though he chose a very unusual life. His name is Tandhjul, not his given name obviously because Tandhjul means 'a gear' in Danish. He knew that I was fragile, and he was keeping an eye on me. He took me to the hospital. He took me to see a therapist every week for the next six months. He made sure I took my pills, worked out, went to school, ate . . . he saved me."

"That's a good friend," she said. "My friend Alec did some of that for me. I never tried to kill myself."

"That's good," Ravn said. "That's very good. You keep it that way."

"My therapist told me about triggers. According to him, being criticized by my family, Harry included, which makes me feel small and irrelevant, is a trigger for me; that's what sends me down the rabbit hole," Sanya said.

"Losing people I'm close to is the trigger for me," Ravn said.

"Is that why you're not close to many people?"

"Yes," Ravn said.

"Isn't that lonely?"

"It's better than the dark place."

"Do you go down the slippery slope to the dark place often?" she asked.

"You mean like the inside of a well?"

"Yes," she whispered, and tears started to form in her eyes. One damaged person was asking the other damaged person to show her his wounds so that they both would feel less alone.

"It happens. It never goes away, Sanya. It's always there. An abyss next to you. So you have to be careful, like you're hiking on a narrow trail, or you will fall," he said.

"How careful?"

"The everyday and the all the time kind of careful."

"Ravn, are you attracted to me because I had a nervous breakdown?"

"I don't know."

"Are you attracted to me at all?"

She felt him smile across the line. "Now that's a feminine question if I've ever heard one. Yes, I'm attracted to you. And, no, it's not just because you're damaged like I am—maybe more so because you've survived like I have."

Chapter 15

Imperfections Make Life Interesting

"Why did Ravn take her out to lunch?" Harry asked Lucky as they sat huddled in a small meeting room in the offices of IT Foundry.

"Penny and Mandy also took her to lunch; how is this any different?" Lucky asked. "We have way too many man hours already spent on this and more to come, so can you focus on the business at hand instead of your wife? We have J Yu, Tara, and Otto here."

As part of the acquisition project plan, the team of three people from California had arrived the day before to further delve into IT Foundry's financial health.

J Yu was twenty-nine and a wunderkind, with a bachelor's in finance from Stanford, an MBA in finance from Yale, and a PhD in finance from Harvard.

Tara Hansen, their legal counsel, was thirty-five and brilliant. She knew Scandinavian law well, as she had lived and worked in a Copenhagen law office for three years in her twenties and had met and married a Dane then. Now her husband took care of the kids while Tara went to work.

Tara and Harry had had a sexual relationship, on and off, for years—conducted mostly when they were traveling. But after what happened with Sanya, Harry had put a stop to the on and off. Tara had not been resentful; she had a husband as well.

Raymond Otto was their forensic accountant who was nearing fifty and had always, even in his twenties, had a Yoda-like attitude, wise and even-tempered. Otto was openly gay and in a long-term relationship with an artist, with whom he lived in the Haight in San Francisco, who sold his sculptures to Silicon Valley CEOs.

"He took her to a goddamn museum," Harry said, ignoring Lucky's remark about getting back to work. "He canceled that meeting with us and took her to a museum for lunch. His favorite paintings are a Degas—ballet dancers in rehearsal or some shit like that—and a Monet landscape of some cliff on Brittany or Normandy, which now is apparently Sanya's favorite painting as well."

A beep sounded from Lucky's phone, and he browsed through it as he said, "What can I say, the man has big hairy ones."

"First his cousin propositions me, and then the son of a bitch takes my wife out to lunch," Harry said. He stood up and started to pace the meeting room from one end to another. He was flustered.

"You trust Sanya," Lucky reminded him.

"But it's different now," Harry said. He stopped pacing as he tried to explain the predicament he was in. "Don't you see? Now she has an excuse. I can't blame her for having a fling when she's mentally unstable. If she slept with Ravn, I'd have to forgive her."

"She's not going to sleep with Ravn," Lucky said. "Ravn isn't even good-looking. He's got that scar and . . ."

Harry got even more agitated. "That *fucking* scar."

He knew deep in his gut that it was the scar that appealed to her. She complained often enough about how perfect Harry was. When Old Sanya used to say it, he used to feel proud, but New Sanya, he suspected, liked defects.

"If she was going to sleep with him, she wouldn't have told you she had lunch with him," Lucky said.

"That's the beauty of it, isn't it? She's telling me everything," Harry said. "She's being open. I think she's attracted to him."

Harry had come home last evening and found her on the couch, reading. She had smiled at him, so he'd poured himself a beer and sat down on the couch with her. That was when she said, matter-of-factly, "Oh, I had lunch with Ravn today."

"With Ravn?" he had said almost stupidly.

She had nodded. "He called me and asked me if I wanted to meet. I thought it was nice of him."

Harry drank his beer carefully, aware that what he wanted to say and what he should say were at odds with each other. "Very nice of him. Where did you go?"

"The museum," Sanya said, and Harry could have killed Ravn for making his wife this animated after the past months when nothing Harry had done had made her so much as get out of bed.

She then proceeded to tell him about the paintings she had seen and the ones that were Ravn's favorites. She might as well have been talking about a friend or her sister or her mother, but Harry knew she wasn't. There was a gleam in her eyes. A new gleam in this altered Sanya's eyes. One that wasn't there before . . . ever. Since the nervous breakdown, he knew that Sanya was unstable, and that had led to him being slightly wobbly as well, and this meant that their marriage was also not on firm footing. And here came Ravn, swinging his dick and taking his wife to a museum. It was like watching a documentary about why married women cheat. Degas! Really? At least the son of a bitch was original. Harry would never think of taking a woman to a museum.

"You're turning into a paranoid lunatic. Ravn? Sanya? I don't see it," Lucky said. "She probably thinks he's a *mimbo*, you know, a male bimbo, spoiled brat, child of fortune, that kind of thing. You do know your wife is an intellectual snob? As is that friend of hers, Alec. Stanford professor with a stick up his ass."

"Alec thinks *I'm* the mimbo. So . . . I don't think she's averse to that kind of man. Can't you see? She's attracted to Ravn," Harry said, wringing his hands now. "Damn it, Lucky. I might lose her."

There was a knock on the door. Ravn stood outside looking calm.

"Lunch, gentlemen?" he asked.

Harry let a smile ease his expression. "I hear you took my wife to lunch yesterday. It's very nice of you to make her feel at home in Copenhagen."

Ravn's expression didn't change. "It was my pleasure," he said.

Chapter 16

Dinner at the Almanak

Sanya knew. The minute she saw Tara Hansen, she knew. She'd heard her name before on occasion from Harry or when he was on the phone with her or in meetings, but this was the first time she met her, and as soon as she saw her, she knew.

She told this to Arthur, the new therapist Lucky had found her and booked in record time. When they had first moved Sanya had thought that she would take a break from therapy, just for a while, but after she met Ravn she knew the break was over. She needed to sort through what it meant, this attraction to Ravn. Was this because of her depression, or would this have happened no matter what? And now she also needed to sort out how she felt about Tara and how she felt about Harry having an affair. Did it really not bother her? Did it bother her? It was so hard to peel back the layers of gray that clouded her mind, to understand how she felt.

"Did you see them together? Did you see something happen between them?" Arthur asked when Sanya told him.

"Not at all," she said. "It's just a feeling." She had been sitting still while she had given Arthur her background and her new certainty about her husband's infidelity. But now that the words were out, she relaxed and leaned back on the couch.

She imagined Tara with her glowing long blond hair, naked, entwined with Harry, flesh meeting flesh, the sounds of sex, the gasping, the panting, and the orgasmic moment of release. She imagined it all. It was permission to imagine two other bodies naked and entwined. Hers and the man with the scar.

"Have you suspected anything in the past?" Arthur asked.

Sanya shrugged. "I don't know. Maybe. Of course it has crossed my mind, but I've never dwelled on it. Now I'm certain."

"And how does this make you feel? This certainty you claim to have that he's cheated on you?"

"I'm not upset, if that's what you're asking," she said without hesitation.

"What you need to ask yourself is why you're not upset. You should be indignant. It would be normal behavior. Instead you're almost . . . relieved," Arthur said. "Why are you relieved?"

"Because it makes him imperfect. I didn't, maybe, want to dwell on it earlier because I wanted him to continue to be perfect, so I could continue to be lucky to have him," she said honestly. "Now it allows me to keep having this crush on Ravn without feeling guilty."

Arthur nodded. "Have you decided what you want to do with Ravn?"

Yes, she had decided to not make a decision, because making a decision meant she had to think and feel, and she really didn't want to do either—because looking inside herself was a lot of work, and she didn't know if she was ready to take that upon herself yet.

"Go with the flow," she said uncertainly.

Arthur shook his head. "People who haven't had a mental collapse can go with the flow. People who've had one need to act with caution. So you need to make an active decision."

"I think maybe I already am having an affair. We haven't consummated it, but the dance has begun," she said. "Maybe I have made an unconscious choice."

"I think this—allowing choices to be made without your active participation—this is key," Arthur said. "Let's talk about that."

Sanya sighed. "Do we really have to?"

Arthur nodded. "Let's start with how you feel about your role in your marriage."

"I'm the wife," Sanya said flippantly.

"And . . . ?"

Sanya shrugged. "I used to be the doormat. I used to be accommodating Sanya. Harry came first. I came last. But after the breakdown it was like I had permission to be selfish and not worry about anyone, including myself. There's a payoff in just lying there in bed doing nothing. There's a payoff in doing exactly what I feel like when I feel like it—almost like a belligerent teenager."

"And what is the role of this Sanya in your marriage?"

Sanya let out a laugh. "I was hoping I'd find that out on your couch, because I have no fucking idea."

❖ ❖ ❖

Harry borrowed Ravn's sixty-foot boat, *Amanda*, to take his team and Sanya out for a sail in Øresund and then into the canal through Copenhagen. It was a warm June day, ideal for being at sea. The water was like a silk sari, rustling softly, and glossy under the gaze of the sun.

Sanya could see that Harry loved the boat and was envious. He had always wanted to have a boat because he did like to sail. But he had never bought one because he knew he wouldn't have time to use it.

"This is nice," Sanya heard him tell Tara as they stood next to each other at the helm while Harry steered the boat. "It's a Gunboat 60, spacious, ideal for long-term, live-aboard cruising."

He continued to talk about *Amanda*'s hybrid propulsion system, which Sanya didn't know anything about, and the four staterooms plus a crew cabin. The boat could easily accommodate up to ten people.

Ravn's boat even had customized features, Tara noticed. "Saloon seating, very nice. And it has an extra deep-freeze freezer so you can take her away for a long time."

"I wish I had more time to sail. It's beautiful in the night, isn't it?" Harry said, "When the moon is high, you can sail down the silver highway."

"Remember that time in Kiel?" Tara said.

Sanya watched them like she would a movie that she didn't have much of an opinion about. Or did she? It was difficult to assess her feelings. She had told Arthur she didn't care, but what she was actually saying was that she didn't know if she cared.

"That was a great sailing trip," Harry said, and then he looked at Sanya, who was watching them, and added as if to appease, "and a good business trip."

❖ ❖ ❖

"My husband tells me you're very bright," Sanya said to J Yu, whom she was sitting next to on the deck.

He wasn't exactly shy, but there was a certain reticence about him. He was, Sanya realized, careful about what he said and whom he said it to. He was the weigh-and-speak kind of person.

"I *am* very bright," he said unabashedly.

"Is this your first trip to Copenhagen?" she asked him. It was small talk, but she wanted a distraction from her husband's perceived infidelities.

"No, I've been here before," J Yu said. "I did the whole Eurail thing right out of college. Three months, all of Europe, backpacking and hostels."

"I've never been anywhere," she said. "I've been to Amsterdam, Frankfurt, and London, all for work. Once I was in Amsterdam for meetings and didn't even come puffing distance to a coffee shop. I've never even been to Paris."

"Oh, but you have to. I fell in love with Paris," J Yu said. "Paris is like an outdoor open-air museum. It's breathtaking. Vienna is similar but with a different appeal, and German just doesn't sound as good as French, which I don't speak. I do speak Spanish and spent some time living in Barcelona and Córdoba."

"I only speak English," Sanya said. "I can understand some Hindi because my mother made me watch Bollywood movies while I was growing up. But I think I can only understand it when people speak in movie language. If people spoke normal Hindi, I probably wouldn't comprehend a word."

"Harry speaks French and German," J Yu said.

"And menu-ordering Italian," she added. "He's a superstar."

"He's my idol," J Yu said reverently. "I want to grow up to be like him."

Sanya wanted to snort, but it would have been rude so she didn't. Instead she decided to pursue her investigation into what the hell was going on with IT Foundry.

"Hey, J Yu, why are you all here?" she asked. "Is something wrong?"

J Yu was uncomfortable with the question. "Well . . . it's just standard work for such a purchase."

Sanya didn't correct him that it wasn't. They had already done the bulk of the work even before Sanya and Harry had come to Copenhagen. She *really* had to talk to Harry about this.

❖ ❖ ❖

They sailed past Nyhavn, the "new harbor" (which wasn't new, but over three hundred years old) for dinner and anchored the boat by the old

135

customhouse building, which was now the Standard, home to three restaurants and a jazz club. The customhouse building had a lot of history, and after its time as a tollbooth for ships entering Copenhagen, it had become known for hosting restaurants.

Sanya and her party dined on modern Danish food at the restaurant Almanak.

Ravn couldn't get them a table at the Michelin-starred Studio, even though he was good friends with the jazz musician Niels Lan Doky, part owner of the Standard, but he had managed the Almanak on short notice.

They sat outside under infrared lamps, wrapped in blankets by the canal with a view of the Danish Architecture Centre, the world-famous restaurant Noma, and the opera house.

Sanya sat next to Tara. It was not by design; it just happened. They were not sitting Danish style.

"This is an exquisite boat," Tara told Sanya as she sipped a glass of the mature and rounded 2005 Domaine des Baumard Savennières from the Loire Valley that was served with their first course, fried scallops in creamy hazelnut sauce, browned butter and onions from Søren Wiuff, a Danish farmer famous for delivering fruit and vegetables to all the top restaurants in Copenhagen, including Noma.

"I know nothing about boats," Sanya said, and picked at her scallops. Despite the beautifully plated dish, she couldn't muster the appetite to eat, not while she was sitting next to Harry's lover.

"I love to sail," Tara gushed. "My husband is big on it. He even sailed across the Atlantic once. I love the water. I'm big on dolphins. Not the SeaWorld kind, mind you, because that's disgusting, but my cause of choice is saving the dolphins and all sea life. If I could afford to leave this corporate career, I would work for the Safina Center, Greenpeace, or the Environmental Defense Fund . . . and maybe someday I will."

"I like the aquarium in Monterey," Sanya said, and decided to forgo the scallops and stick to the wine. "We used to take Sara there when she was little . . . actually, I used to take Sara there. Harry was always working."

"So were you, I hear," Tara said. "I'm lucky in many ways. My husband is the primary caregiver for the children in our house. But you did it all. You worked *and* raised your daughter."

"A lot of women do that," Sanya said. "I don't think it is medal worthy. And maybe my job was always less important than Harry's. He's a partner, and I was *just* a consultant even though they gave me that director title."

The waiters came then with the second course, a baked North Sea cod with cabbage from Kiselgården, another organic Danish farm, and blue mussels and dill sauce served with a 2013 Louis Latour Meursault Blanc, another round and rich white wine that the sommelier told them had aromas of apricot kernel and vanilla with a beautiful long finish. Sanya drank the wine and missed all of the nuances he had mentioned because everything tasted like ash in her current mental state.

"Harry says that if you want to know about the financial inner workings of a company, you're the man . . . woman to talk to," Tara said as she attacked her cod and made appropriate sounds to convey her pleasure. "You have a knack, he says, of going into a company and seeing how they work and knowing how to fix it, not based on methodology or only methodology but your gut instinct. It's a rare skill."

Sanya should've been flattered, but it pissed her off that Harry discussed her with Tara. The son of a bitch.

"You know, I'm surprised," Sanya said, and when Tara raised her eyebrows, she added, "I didn't know that Harry even talked about me to his colleagues. I didn't think, you know, I was relevant or interesting enough for discussion."

Tara smiled uncomfortably, as if caught doing something wrong.

Just then a couple was seated at a table across from them. The woman wore a short black lace dress. Her hair was done up, not thrown together, and lay in dark curls around her face. She wore an expensive leather purse and strappy black heels. The man wore sneakers, a pair of torn jeans and a black-and-white AC/DC T-shirt, and a look like he'd spent the day watching a *Game of Thrones* marathon and forgotten to take a shower.

"Why is it that women dress up and men don't?" Sanya said to Tara as they both watched the couple.

Obviously happy to talk about something less controversial, Tara jumped at the opportunity. "I've seen this several times. Women primp while men barely run a comb through their hair. Must be some societal pressure thing, don't you think? Women have to look their best; men just have to be there."

Sanya partly agreed. "Do you think maybe it's because women are more insecure than men? We need to prove we're worthy of the man, while the man knows he's superior to the woman. I think when a man is unsure he dresses up, just as a woman does."

They both looked at Harry, who was wearing a pale blue shirt and dark-blue sailing pants from Nautica with a pair of Ferragamo boat shoes. His hair was groomed, and they both knew he regularly visited a men's salon for manicures and pedicures.

"Maybe you're right," Tara said.

Sanya raised her wineglass to Tara and said, "Cheers."

❖ ❖ ❖

While the others ate dessert, a Danish layer cake with honey and cherry wine, covered with Valrhona chocolate, Otto, who was diabetic, and Sanya, who wasn't hungry, went for a walk. They strolled by the canal to the bicycle and pedestrian bridge that went across from this side of the city to Papirøen, Paper Island, known for its street food, according to Otto, who had done his *Condé Nast Traveler*–style Copenhagen research.

Sanya and Otto had known each other for nearly a decade and were friends. He had even come to visit her at home after the implosion, with self-help books by Deepak Chopra on how to overcome adversity by fixing her chakras.

"How are you settling into life in Scandinavia?" Otto asked.

"Very well, I think," Sanya said. "And it's just for a year. So it's transient."

"Maybe shorter now that we know what we know," Otto said, and then he saw the look of irritation on Sanya's face, and he seemed to realize he had said something he shouldn't have.

"Okay, what is going on?" Sanya asked.

"Nothing," Otto said, and then blew some air out. "I thought he told you, or at least asked your advice. You've seen the files, right?"

"Why would I? Why would he send them to me?"

"Because he always asks you," Otto said.

"Used to," Sanya said. "I haven't looked at a single Excel sheet. And I *used* to give advice on small stuff. ComIT doesn't pay me to support mergers and acquisitions."

Otto nodded, shoving his hands in his pockets. "We don't know enough yet. Maybe it's going to be nothing, and it's all going to come out smelling roses."

"I'm not well enough to start investigating financial procedures, and I don't know anything about Danish regulations," Sanya said in her defense.

"Hey, that's why I'm here, and J Yu. And Tara, who knows Danish corporate law," Otto said.

"And isn't she fabulous," Sanya said with more venom than she'd have liked.

Otto's response, which was to divert to another subject, told her more than a platitude about the state of her marriage would have. She was the last to know. Lucky probably knew as well. Otto obviously knew.

How long had this been going on? How many others had there been? Was Harry like Ravn? Had he for half their marriage been diddling other women? Was Sanya actually attracted to Ravn because he was just as much of a philanderer as her own husband?

"Do you know that Harry feels that part of your mental state is his fault?" Otto said. "The thing with men like Harry is that to become a man like Harry, you have to be selfish; you have to take and not give. Harry never learned to give. And you never asked him to give . . . not until now."

Sanya looked at Otto, puzzled. "I'm not asking him for anything."

Otto smiled. "Aren't you? Maybe not overtly, but your circumstances are demanding that he be present and engaged or he'll lose you. It's a gun to his head, and it's fascinating to see Harry actually worry about losing . . . anything."

Sanya had to admit that it *was* interesting to see Harry squirm, because he was always so confident and sure of himself, so certain of his past, his present, and his future. He showed no fear. One could never smell blood around him. But now . . . now . . . maybe, Sanya wondered as a new idea flitted through her consciousness, could it be possible that Harry had his own implosion after Sanya's, and he was changing as well, going through a reinvention to become a new Harry?

"Do you know that Mærsk Mc-Kinney Møller, the owner of Mærsk, built the opera house?" Sanya told Otto, and continued without waiting for a response as they stood across from the opera house, separated by the canal. "He built it so that the opera house and the royal palace are in the same line, like the Louvre and the Arc de Triomphe in Paris."

"Have you been to the opera house yet?" Otto asked.

"No. I've never been to Paris, either," Sanya said. "You know, Otto, all of a sudden the fact that I've never been to Paris bothers me. I don't know why. Maybe because this is Europe, and everyone who comes to Europe goes to Paris."

"It is the city for lovers," Otto said.

"Why do you think Harry and I have never gone on a romantic *anything* ever?" Sanya asked.

Otto shrugged. "I told you. Harry is selfish."

"And he got his romance elsewhere," Sanya said softly, her eyes shimmering with tears, blurring the bright lights of the opera house. They disappeared as quickly as they came, but Sanya felt a softening inside her, a churning, and a movement like a butterfly that flies past and leaves just a tiny ripple in the air.

Otto put both his hands on Sanya's shoulders. "Harry loves you. He's terrified of losing you."

"Why?"

"Because you're the light in his darkness," he said.

"I have no idea what that means," Sanya said. "He said it once, too, that he didn't want to be without me because he didn't like who he was without me."

Otto seemed surprised that Sanya didn't know how her husband felt, because it apparently was obvious to him. "He wouldn't be human without you. Look at him. He's . . . this . . . I don't know, businessman persona, two-dimensional with no affiliations. *You* give him family— you're his only family. He loses you, what is he left with? Lucky?"

When Sanya nodded he let his hands drop from her shoulders. They went back to looking at the opera house. "I should check the season. If *Tosca* is coming, I'd like to go. I like living here. It's like the city was made for me," Sanya said a little dreamily. "The weather, I know, is unreliable, but it matches my moods. They tell me I'm going to hate the winter. It gets dark by three in the afternoon, and the sun doesn't rise until after eight in the morning. But in June and July it's glorious with the sun shining until midnight. How long are you here for?"

"Just a few weeks," Otto said. "If all works out, I go back and work with the team at home. J Yu will stay a few months to help Lucky and Harry."

"How about Tara?"

Otto was sharp and didn't miss a thing. "You don't have to worry about her. She won't be staying long."

She could have said, "Why should I worry about her?" But it would be disingenuous. They both knew why. And that was how the universe confirmed it. It was one thing to be certain with no proof but quite another to have the proof. She felt her heart constrict and break a little. She decided to ignore it.

"Will you send me the IT Foundry files you think I need to look at?" Sanya asked Otto. "And don't tell Harry."

It was an unusual request, but Otto and Sanya went a long way back and she knew he would do as she asked.

Otto wrinkled his nose. "Why do you want to do this?"

"Because I need to know."

"What?"

"Just how corrupt IT Foundry is," she said.

What she didn't say was that she wanted to know how corrupt Ravn was.

Chapter 17

Improper Fantasies, Sexual and Otherwise

"We should do this more often," Harry said as he collapsed on his side of the bed, still panting. "Why don't we do it more often?"

"Because we've been busy."

He looked puzzled, as if saying, *You've not been busy.*

"I've been busy having a nervous breakdown," Sanya said. "And you've been busy trying to buy a company."

Harry smiled. "But we're both almost on the other side of the tunnel now."

He seemed so hopeful that Sanya didn't have the heart to tell him that she was still in the darkness, still trying to strain her eyes to figure out what the hell was going on around her. Worse, she couldn't even see the light at the end of the tunnel and was sure that if she did, it would be an oncoming train.

"I like living here, Harry," Sanya said. She felt him tense next to her.

"What do you like best about Copenhagen?"

"I like the ease of living here. I like living in a city, *this* city. I feel at peace. You did good by bringing us here," Sanya said. "Do you think we could stay longer than a year? I could find a job. Maybe Ernst & Young in Copenhagen will hire me as a financial consultant even though I don't speak Danish."

"The weather sucks," Harry said, "and once this IT Foundry business is settled, I'll have to go back."

"Then maybe I can stay," Sanya suggested.

"Without me?" he asked, now lifting himself up on one elbow to look at her.

"Why not? You travel so much anyway—and you can come visit," Sanya said, smiling at him.

She waited for Harry to ask what she knew he wanted to. *Do you want to stay because of Ravn?*

Harry lay on his back again, his head hitting the pillow. "I find Danes to be . . . I don't know . . . sexually debauched."

"Sexually debauched? Where did that come from? And you sound like a prude."

"Half their marriages end in divorce, and most of them don't even get married," Harry said.

Sanya laughed. "Really? This is your problem with Denmark? The moral standing of marriage in their society? The United States is no different."

"Did I tell you that Penny propositioned me?"

Sanya sat up then. "What? No, that I would've remembered, slow brain or not."

"She said something about both of us being adults and interested and that she had an apartment that she kept exclusively for extramarital . . . liaisons," Harry said, and Sanya could see he was slightly smug about a beautiful, ex-model type like Penny coming on to him.

"And then she takes me out to lunch," Sanya said in amazement. "So, how did Penny take the rejection?"

"How are you so sure that I rejected her?" Harry asked.

"You wouldn't have told me if you'd gone and fucked her," Sanya said, and then, as if making a decision, she reclined again and stared at the ceiling. "This is an egalitarian society when it comes to sex. It only makes me like this country more."

"All I can say is that moving here has been good for our sex life," Harry said.

Sanya wondered if it was moving to Denmark or Anders Ravn that had contributed to this night of sexual frolic. Was Harry a substitute for Ravn? And, if so, wasn't that a terribly Danish and debauched thing for her to have done?

Chapter 18

The Love Doctor

It was Alec who suggested Kiin Kiin, the Michelin-starred Thai fusion restaurant.

Alec was a foodie, and not just now when it was fashionable, but always. He would come visit them in Copenhagen, he declared, even though he had not been able to get a table at Noma, but he had heard great things about the meatpacking district, Kødbyen, and he was very keen on going to Christiania, a hippie area in the heart of the city where one could buy weed on the main street.

Sanya had asked Alec for tips on what to do when Arthur had given her an exercise to increase intimacy with Harry. Plan a dinner, he suggested. Or go for a walk. Do something that brings you closer *outside* the house.

So Sanya decided that for her and Harry's twenty-first wedding anniversary, in late June, she would book Kiin Kiin and surprise Harry with a world-class meal. She called the restaurant, and when they told her that the next available table was a month away, she phoned Lucky.

"If they don't have a table that evening, then they don't have a table that evening," Lucky said. "Sanya, there are a zillion restaurants in Copenhagen and many with Michelin stars; just book another."

"I want to go here," Sanya said like a stubborn child. "Why can't you help me? Use your influence."

"What influence? I'm not even from Copenhagen. Why is this so important to you?" Lucky was exasperated.

Sanya felt a surge of emotion, and inadvertently her voice choked. "Because I want to do something normal."

There was a long pause from Lucky, as if he were waiting for the other shoe to drop and for Sanya to start crying uncontrollably or do something else remarkable. When she didn't, he sighed. "I'll take care of it," he said. "I'll send you an email with the details."

❖   ❖   ❖

Sanya took pains to dress up for the dinner. She had called Chloe, her British friend she had met at Café Bopa, to help her shop. She didn't want to go to a fancy place, but she wanted a fancy dress, a *va va voom* dress (and not the yellow one with red flowers that Birgitte Green had wanted her to buy for the ambassador's dinner).

"You need more than a new dress, girlfriend," Chloe said as she smoked a cigarette over a cup of coffee at Café Bopa. "Your hair . . . what's with that?"

There was a numbness about appearance after an implosion, a white, blinding silence that took all judgment away. Just like after someone's leg falls asleep and the pins and needles hurt, Sanya had experienced something similar as she stood in front of the mirror that morning and saw herself for the first time in nearly a year.

The hair Chloe had asked about disparagingly had not been tended to. It was frizzy. There were split ends. Her roots were white, a halo around her dark face. Her eyebrows were unruly caterpillars (it was the fashion now, Chloe told her, though they did need a little cleaning)— and then, to her embarrassment, Sanya saw that she had facial hair. Yes, upper lip and sideburns.

Her first reaction was that someone like Ravn would never be interested in a woman like her, and she wondered if Ravn was also doing what Mandy and Penny were doing, digging for information. And what if he was? Did she care?

Otto had sent Sanya some large zip files via secure email. These were IT Foundry financial documents. She still hadn't opened the email. She would, she promised herself, very soon.

"I don't know what to say. I have no defense," Sanya said, touching her hair. "To be clear, I was never a fashion plate, but I did basic maintenance."

"When was the last time you shaved your legs?" Chloe asked, looking at Sanya's jean-clad legs.

Sanya nodded and then sighed.

"We'll start with the hair and work our way down," Chloe said, picking up her phone and pressing a number in her contacts. She looked at Sanya's crotch pointedly.

Sanya smiled weakly. Was she ready for this? But the more important question was, who was she doing this for? Harry or Ravn?

"Wafic," Chloe squealed. "I have an emergency." She paused and then said, "*No, it's an emergency,* and it needs to be now. I'll also book her at DermaBelle for . . . everything else."

She hung up and smiled at Sanya. "He'll see you in twenty minutes. Take a taxi; I'll give you the address. And then you'll go next door to DermaBelle, where Yasmine will take care of you. She's Iranian and is *very* good with body hair. I'll come and get you from DermaBelle after you're waxed and polished, and then we'll buy you a new dress. That will give me time to pick up Caroline from kindergarten and drop her off with Johan's parents, who are babysitting."

Sanya felt like Audrey Hepburn, a much more beaten down version than Eliza Doolittle in *My Fair Lady*. Chloe put her hand on Sanya's shoulder. "This is not a drill, soldier. So let's find you that taxi."

❖　❖　❖

"I am the Love Doctor," Wafic Sileba, Chloe's favorite hairdresser on Kronprinssesegade in the city center, announced. Wafic was from Lebanon, had long, curly hair that he collected in a top bun, and spoke English with an Arabic accent.

Sanya raised her caterpillar eyebrows.

Wafic smiled and showed bright white teeth. "After I cut their hair, women get laid. One client, she comes every week for a wash and blow dry on Fridays because her husband travels during the week. He comes home on Friday evenings, and the hair does the trick."

"Or maybe he's just horny because he's been gone for a week," Sanya suggested.

Wafic laughed. "She's not the only one, *chiquita*. Now, what should we do with you, besides getting rid of the whites?"

"I don't know," she said. "I have no idea what should be done with me."

"We'll go short, take some length off. It'll make you look younger," he said. "And product. You need product. I'll give you a hair mask. Use it once a week and your hair will shine."

A frisson of panic ran through Sanya. She could barely sustain herself through this day, and he was talking about next week? But wasn't she getting better at dealing with her days now? She went out. She showered. She had started to go for walks alone during the day and enjoy the city. There were still times when it was all too much and she got under the comforter . . . but those days were becoming less common.

Still, a makeover was a big step. Thankfully, Sanya realized that she wasn't the first skittish client Wafic had ever had. He winked at her and said, "And whomever it is you want to, you know, have fun with tonight, you can."

Yes, Sanya, she asked herself, *who do you want to have fun with tonight?*

Once her hair was washed and colored, and while they were waiting the mandatory thirty minutes for the color to sink in, he asked, "Do you smoke?"

Sanya shook her head.

"Great, let's step in the back and have a cigarette," he said, and held his hand out to her.

They stood by a giant trash can in the back of the apartment building where Wafic had his salon. Sanya took the cigarette he offered even though it had been years since she'd smoked.

"So, what's your story?" Wafic asked.

She took a tentative puff and exhaled. "I had a nervous breakdown," she found herself telling him.

He nodded appreciatively. "Suicide attempt?" he asked, as if that was a natural follow-up question.

Sanya shook her head.

"That's good," he said. "So . . . now . . . depression?"

She nodded.

He nodded.

She took another puff. She could take up smoking. It would give her something to do with her hands, especially when they were shaking.

"And now, you're stepping out of the darkness with your new hair," he said. "New hair is not just about getting it cut; it's a new way of looking at life, of living life. When you look at the mirror, if your hair is shit, you don't spend time looking at yourself, playing with your hair. But when I'm finished with your hair, you're going to stand in front of the mirror."

Sanya smiled. Yes, she looked forward to looking at herself in a mirror. It had been such a long time since she'd *actually* seen herself.

"And that's when the healing begins," he added, and threw the cigarette on the ground, silencing the fire with a shoe. "When you look in the mirror and look yourself in the eye."

❖ ❖ ❖

The Love Doctor had cut her hair to shoulder length, and it had a bounce in it that it had never had before. Yasmine had waxed, scrubbed, polished, and squeezed dirt out of the pores on Sanya's face. She had also given her a pedicure so her feet were soft and her toenails were painted a lovely pink, same as her fingernails. Between her legs, her skin itched ever so gently despite Yasmine's assurance that *sugaring* was so much better than waxing and Sanya could have sex that night without worrying about an infection.

Sanya's dress was a very light pink with bows on the sides. Chloe had assured Sanya when she tried it on at COS, a store on Strøget, the walking street, that it made her glow. After Sanya had put on the dress, Yasmine had done Sanya's makeup, cut the price tags out, and sprayed her with generous spritzes of Absolutely Irresistible by Givenchy.

While Yasmine had done Sanya's makeup, Chloe had taken Sanya's Dankort and gone to Magasin down the street and bought Sanya a silver clutch with rose undertones to match the dress and dangling Pilgrim brand silver earrings that danced when she walked.

Harry had to pick Sanya up outside the DermaBelle salon because the makeover had taken all day, and they barely made it to the restaurant on time. He had been surprised with how Sanya looked and had responded charmingly.

He kissed Sanya and looked at her in wonder as if thinking, *Where have you been all my life?* It gave Sanya a boost, confidence that had abandoned her for a very long while but was now making a comeback.

"You look like an Indian Audrey Hepburn," he said.

She glowed and basked in the praise. "I was thinking about *My Fair Lady* myself."

Chapter 19

Percy Shelley Strikes at Kiin Kiin

Kiin Kiin was housed in the unpretentious, downright unfancy neigh-borhood of Nørrebro, the north bridge, Sanya had learned, just like she and Harry lived in Østerbro, which was the east bridge. The north bridge was the *other* side of the tracks. This was where the immigrants and the students lived.

"I've read about this place," Harry said as they took the steps down to the restaurant. The entrance was in the basement, which was a kind of lounge area where several guests were scattered, enjoying drinks and small nibbles.

"Welcome to Kiin Kiin," a young Danish waiter said to Harry and Sanya, after serving them a glass of champagne. "We will serve you Thai-style street food now in quick succession. That should take thirty minutes or so, and then you'll be taken to your table upstairs. Are there any allergies you would like me to inform the chef about?"

For someone who had been eating sporadically, this promised seven-course menu was making her stomach churn. Sanya wanted to say, *Yes, I'm allergic to food and people, and I shouldn't mix alcohol with my happy pills. But I'm doing all of it all the time.*

Instead, Harry said, "My wife is allergic to peaches. But aside from that we're okay."

The waiter smiled and then the first dish arrived, a concoction of something fried and baked atop hot black stones. They were quickly served seven small amuse-bouches, and Sanya ate two of them.

"You're sure I can eat yours?" Harry asked each time, and when Sanya nodded he ate his and then hers. "This is awesome. You know what we need to do? We need to go to Noma. I mean, we can't live in Copenhagen and not go there."

"Alec tried and couldn't get reservations," Sanya said. "It's eighteen courses, though, Harry."

Harry put his hand on Sanya's and squeezed. "But you only have to eat one course at a time. Just one sip of champagne at a time. One bite of food at a time."

Sanya nodded weakly. How could she not love this *new* Harry?

And as she smiled warmly at him, love streaming through her insides like fresh, bubbly champagne, the man with the scar walked into her line of vision with his petite blond wife.

"Oh my god," Mandy squealed. "It's . . . *you.*"

Harry turned to look at Ravn and rose to greet them. Ravn smiled broadly and said politely, "What a lovely surprise."

"This is awesome," Mandy said, and air-kissed Harry and then Sanya. "You look . . . amazing."

Sanya knew she looked amazing. Especially in contrast to how she used to look.

Harry put an arm around Sanya as if she needed protection from Mandy's scrutiny. *No,* Sanya wanted to say to him, *not Mandy's but Ravn's.*

As Ravn conferred with the maître d' to arrange for them to sit together for their meal, and while Mandy was looking at the menu and discussing her nut allergy with another waiter, Harry whispered in Sanya's ear.

"I think he planned this," he said. "Lucky got Ravn to book our table. He knew we would be here."

Sanya's heart started to hammer. "But why?"

"I don't know," Harry said. "But with this guy, everything is business. He must have an angle."

Yes, Harry, and I think that angle might be me, Sanya thought.

"Does it matter?" she asked.

"Hell, yes. This is our anniversary dinner," Harry said.

Sanya licked her lips. "I'm going to just step outside to smoke a cigarette," she said, because her hands were starting to shake, and she gripped her silver clutch tightly.

"Since when did you start smoking?" Harry asked, more than a little surprised.

"This afternoon," Sanya said. She had bummed a pack from Chloe, who hadn't questioned why she suddenly wanted to smoke. She accepted that Sanya was at a crossroads, and everyone at a crossroads needed nicotine.

Sanya saw Mandy curl her nose, and Ravn had a look of amusement, like he knew how Sanya felt. And maybe he did. He had been in the hole Sanya was in, he knew how deep it went, and he knew how desperate the clawing to get free initially was, and then the slumber of wanting and craving the darkness of the hole, not wanting to leave, not wanting to live.

"I'll join you," Ravn said.

"You promised you'd stop," Mandy said stiffly.

"I'll just light her cigarette and keep her company," he said.

Sanya knew that Harry would like to join them because he didn't want her to be alone with Ravn, but then Mandy said, "I hate the smell," and Harry had no choice but to stay and keep Ravn's wife company.

❖ ❖ ❖

Ravn lit Sanya's cigarette because her hands were still shaking.

"You look . . . done up," he said.

"Yes," Sanya said. "It's our wedding anniversary. Twenty-one years of marriage."

"I'm sorry for the intrusion," he said, and lit a cigarette for himself even though he'd a minute ago promised his wife he wouldn't smoke.

"No, you're not," Sanya said, and felt a smile form on her lips. If nothing else, *this* was entertaining. When one was deep down in a well, one needed entertainment, especially before starting to claw one's way up again.

"No, I'm not," Ravn said. "You look like a Disney princess with the bows on your dress."

"You prefer the made-over look?" Sanya asked.

"How you look has nothing to do with how I feel," he said. "It has more to do with how you feel. How does it make *you* feel?"

"Like a Disney princess on speed," she said, and started to laugh. Not the crazy, *I'm going to lose my head* laugh, but a genuine, full-throated laugh because she was happy. A small light in the midst of darkness.

❖ ❖ ❖

After the street food, they were taken upstairs to the main restaurant.

"I prefer Studio," Mandy said. "It's also a Michelin-starred restaurant, at the Standard. I heard you and your colleagues went to the Almanak for dinner when you borrowed Ravn's boat. Studio is upstairs in the same building. Niels Lan Doky is one of the owners; his wife is a good friend of mine. She's half Danish and half French Guyanese, lovely lady. They live in Paris now, but I see her often in Paris and here."

The first course was an outlandish concoction of a syringe with noodle paste that they injected into warm broth (which both Harry and Ravn agreed tasted very good).

"This is amazing," Harry said. "What do you think, Sanya?"

"It really is," Sanya said, and looked at Ravn. "What do you think?"

"It's fine," Ravn said. His eyes matched the amusement in Sanya's eyes, so she looked away before her husband could catch the intimacy.

"Studio is so much classier," Mandy continued. "It's the whole Asian thing here, you know, it's . . . so gaudy and lacks sophistication. It's the same when you travel there. I like Asia, but it's so cheesy. Asians are so . . . you know how they are."

Sanya thought the restaurant was chic. The décor was subtle. Yes, there was the big statue of Buddha, but Sanya had read on the restaurant's website that it was an antique from the late nineteenth century, from Mandalay in Burma. The decorative knickknacks and silverware were designed exclusively for Kiin Kiin by Chaovana "Palm" Imocha, a famous Thai jewelry designer, and co-founder and design director of the brand Mafia.

Ravn grinned then. "We have an Asian at the table, Mandy."

"Who?" she asked, and when Ravn tilted his head toward Sanya, she shook her head. "Really?"

"That's okay," Ravn said. "I'm sure you were talking about the *other* Asians."

It was cruel and yet satisfying, because why shouldn't a racist remark be met with cruelty?

"But are you *really* Asian?" Mandy asked.

"Yes, I really am," Sanya said. "I'm ethnically Indian, South Asian."

The conversation meandered after that. Ravn and Mandy discussed the fine meals they'd enjoyed at the many Michelin-starred restaurants in Copenhagen. But Mandy said her favorite place to go was Torvehallerne, an über-gourmet permanent farmer's market where they served the best *confit de canard* sandwiches.

Sanya couldn't eat.

Sanya couldn't drink.

Sanya couldn't focus on the conversation.

She felt suffocated sitting next to Harry and across from Ravn at their small table. She was nervous each time the fabric of Ravn's suit pant grazed her bare legs. She could feel Harry's hand on top of her pink dress on her thigh in a comforting or controlling (she wasn't sure) gesture as each course was served.

It was when they were served the cotton candy dish—a sort of sweet-and-sour minced chicken course with fresh Thai spices and cotton candy that dissolved under the onslaught of a freshly made lime juice sauce with mint—that Mandy brought up IT Foundry.

"Why is it taking so long?" she asked, and when Harry muttered something about how these things take time, she added, "Oh, come on, it can go faster, because I've been promised a month in Tuscany. I mean, it's not like Ravn's cooked the books or anything," she said, and giggled.

Both Ravn and Harry went very still.

"Matters such as these cannot be rushed, *skat*," Ravn said patiently.

"And now you have a team from America here," Mandy said. "I thought it was simple. You know, like buying a bag at Hermès. You go and check it out, and then you negotiate a good price, of course, because they know you'll be back sooner than later for the new season, and then you run the plastic."

"Buying a company is a little more complicated than buying a bag," Sanya said. "You can return the bag, but you can't return a company. I worked some acquisitions, and they can be brutal. Once we worked with this big medical company, and they even announced the purchase to the stock market—but then they found out that the company they were buying had some *huge* compliance issues in how they did their accounting in Africa and Asia. Apparently they had been cooking the books to make the revenues seem more robust than they were. So the big medical company pulled out of the merger, and they're still fighting it out, last I heard. The company that was corrupt is still struggling to get back in the good graces of the stock market. So I understand that

Harry's company wants to be *really* thorough and sure, because once you cross the line, there's no going back—just a lot of court cases."

Ravn focused on Sanya intensely. "ComIT has publicly announced that they'll be buying IT Foundry."

"I'm sure that won't happen here," Sanya said sweetly, and put her hand on Harry's arm. "Right, my love?"

Harry looked like he had been hit by a bulldozer. Sanya knew he was wondering how she knew what she knew. It was a guess and not based on evidence, which Sanya knew was in her inbox in that email from Otto.

Mandy looked poleaxed. She had probably been thinking Sanya was a ditz, and now she was reassessing her competition, *as she should,* Sanya thought smugly.

Ravn was relaxed, like he had this in the bag.

New Sanya wanted to tell him to not be so sure.

❖ ❖ ❖

The text message came during dessert. A banana and sticky rice medley, plated with style. Harry ate Sanya's dessert and Ravn excused himself.

Sanya's phone was lying next to Harry's hand.

She had never had a reason and had never learned to hide her messages or have a passcode on her personal phone. When the message flashed, along with Ravn's number, Sanya grabbed the phone, just as Harry's head turned to look at it.

She looked down so Harry wouldn't see her eyes or her lips as they moved with the words she read in delight.

I have drunken deep of joy, And I will taste no other wine tonight. She was reading the message a second time when Harry asked, his voice low, "Who's that from?"

She pressed the phone to her breast.

"Oh, phones," Mandy said as she browsed her phone at the same time. "I want to be good and never check it when I'm out for dinner, but you know how it is. Especially these days with Penny so upset. She texts me at least fifteen times a day."

Harry didn't even bother to pretend he was listening to Mandy. He was focused on Sanya as she gingerly put the phone on the other side of the banana dessert, away from Harry and facedown.

He'd never asked her before whom a message was from or who called; and she had never hidden it, either. This was a deviation for both of them.

He knew! Sanya realized.

"Mira," she lied without hesitation.

Harry sipped his coffee, which had come with the dessert, and set down the white cup on its white saucer with a clink.

"I thought I saw a Danish phone number," he said. He wasn't even pretending to be nonchalant in his curiosity. He was being blatant.

"It was Mira," Sanya lied again. This time she looked him in the eye.

They sat, staring at each other, at an impasse. He knew she was lying, and she knew he knew she was lying, but she wasn't going to tell him what he wanted to know. They sat for a long moment, conversation buzzing around them. Mandy continued about the pitfalls of phone addiction while she didn't look up at them from her screen.

Harry blinked first.

"Well, say hi to her from me," Harry said, and excused himself to use the restroom. He met Ravn at the top of the stairs. They appeared to square off, but then they walked smoothly past each other, Harry away from Sanya, and Ravn toward their table.

❖　❖　❖

Harry initiated sex that night, as if trying to prove that the message he had almost read wasn't the end of their marriage, wasn't the end of Sanya's fidelity.

"Have you ever cheated on me?" Harry asked her as they lay in the darkness after they'd made love. Sanya hadn't minded making love with him. It felt like an apology for receiving that message from Ravn; it felt like paying for being happy. It was illicit happiness, and no good ever came of illicit happiness.

"Have you?" she asked instead.

"Of course not," Harry said.

"Me neither," she responded, but harshly.

"Have you ever wanted to cheat on me?" Harry asked.

This was a *new* Harry. He was pursuing conflict instead of ignoring it and pretending it didn't exist.

Just the day before, while Sanya was watching aimless television, on some show a woman had said, "Confession might be good for the soul, but it's a hot lead enema for a marriage." It made sense to Sanya, so she told Harry she'd never even had a crush, which was true until Ravn. They didn't need a hot lead enema in their marriage.

"I don't think I could stand it if I lost you," Harry said, his voice shaking just a little when she didn't answer.

"I think you had sex with Tara Hansen," she blurted out suddenly. No way was he going to make her feel guilty by being vulnerable. She had only received a poem by text message; Harry had actually had sex with another woman.

He stopped breathing. If she focused, she thought she could hear his heartbeat, because the tension emanating from him was loud, like that of a little boy caught with his hand in the cookie jar. What a cliché!

"What nonsense," he managed to say, his voice strained.

"Come on, stop this 'what nonsense' routine," Sanya said. "I don't care. I mean . . . I wish you hadn't, but I don't care."

Why had she said that? She kicked herself. Why had she said it? Why? Why? Why? Because she knew. After talking to Tara and Otto, she knew. And then a lightbulb flashed in her mind. *The fucking dolphins!*

"She bought you that Hermès tie," Sanya said as if the clouds had parted and the sky was blue and she could see everything clearly, especially that tie. "The blue one with the yellow dolphins. She got you that. I know she did. She told me how she's all about saving the fucking dolphins."

"You're crazy," Harry said. "I bought it in New York. Would you like to see a receipt?"

"Then she picked it out," Sanya said. "If you have a receipt, that is."

Harry shook his head. "Tara? I work with her. I'd never shit where I eat."

That actually could be true, Sanya thought cynically. But . . . They both lay there for a long while. Sanya was certain, *but* as Arthur had said, she *really* didn't have any proof. Otto had sort of confirmed it, but he hadn't said it directly, had he? And Harry wasn't owning up to it. Perhaps he didn't have an affair.

"I'm sorry," Old Sanya said. "Maybe I'm just jealous of her."

"Why?" Harry demanded, incredulous. "You're better looking than her. You're more successful than her, and you have a better husband than she does."

Sanya laughed then. "Only you would think that having a better husband is a badge of honor," she said. "Maybe it's because she has a job and I don't?"

"Sweetheart, once we go back, you'll get another job," Harry said. "You're just taking some time off. It's okay. Everyone needs to rest their brain once in a while."

"I am enjoying my time off," Sanya said. "Don't get me wrong; eventually I'll go back to work. But then again, who knows, and maybe not in finance. Maybe something else."

"And that's your choice, but you're really good at what you do," Harry said, obviously happy to be off the topic of adultery and Tara.

She let it go. She let him convince her that it was all in New Sanya's head.

❖ ❖ ❖

The next morning Sanya found Harry's blue Hermès tie with the yellow dolphins on it and took a pair of scissors and cut it up neatly into thin strips. Then she threw the pieces of the tie into the trash can.

Chapter 20

The Swedish Summer House

The summer house was gorgeous.

The lakefront house was surrounded by a garden and a wraparound patio with a view of the lake. The house's main attraction was the heated indoor pool. In the winter, Mandy explained, guests could get into the heated pool and look out of the glassed sunroom onto a snow-covered landscape. In the summer, they opened all the glass doors to let in the fresh air.

"I come here at least three times a year," Mandy said as she gave her guests the grand tour. "But then we also go to Norway, where the company has summer houses near Oslo and in Lillehammer. That one is busy in the winter because *everyone* wants to go skiing."

J Yu, Tara, and Otto were super impressed with the opulence and quiet sophistication *real* money could buy.

The massive chef's kitchen adjoined the patio. Sanya stood at the doorstep. She could see Mandy, Penny, and Katrine with their family friends, Leah and her journalist husband, Bjarke, pouring champagne and preparing snacks, blinis piled up with smoked salmon, sour cream with chives, or salmon roe.

Turning toward the lake, its waters quietly glistening in the sunlight, Sanya watched Harry and his colleagues. Then Penny appeared and handed her a glass of pink champagne with glistening raspberries floating inside. She took the glass and leaned against the doorway, looking away from the lake and facing Penny.

"Ravn, as always, is late," she said breezily. "I hear you went out for lunch with him."

Sanya couldn't imagine how Penny had found out, and it probably showed on her face, because Penny continued with smug satisfaction, "Ravn tells me everything."

"He was being nice," Sanya said. "He thought I must be bored and took me to lunch at the Glyp . . . something museum place."

"The Glyptotek," Penny said as if Ravn took all the women he had on the side to the museum. "Did you see the Monet? It's his favorite. And the Degas. Our Ravn does love those ballerinas. He has an original Degas in his office at home. He hides it, and if perchance someone sees it, he doesn't tell them it's an original. Did he tell you about it?"

Sanya could see how much Penny was enjoying telling her that she was nothing more than a piece of ass, that Ravn did this all the time.

"He did. The painting with a single ballerina leaning against a barre," Sanya said, even though she knew she was tipping her hand and letting this vindictive little bitch know her secret. *The hell with it,* she thought. Old Sanya had been a pushover, a naïve optimist and a pleaser. New Sanya was none of these things. She flexed her muscles and straightened her spine. *Chin up. Tits out. Go get her, Sanya.*

"And then you and Mandy were kind enough to take me to lunch as well," Sanya continued. "I'm sorry I had to leave in a hurry. I haven't been well."

"I'm so sorry. Are you okay?" Penny asked.

"I had a nervous breakdown a few months ago. I'm in recovery."

Her jaw dropped, and New Sanya started to enjoy herself.

"I hear that you took *my* husband out to lunch," she said before Penny could tell Sanya about all the people she knew with similar stories who were now doing fine.

Her jaw dropped again.

"Ah, well . . . we're friendly here in the IT Foundry family," Penny said.

"Ah, but you're not *really* part of the IT Foundry family, now, are you? I heard that Danes are not friendly to foreigners, but I have found all the Danes I've met to be very congenial," Sanya said. "And Harry has had the same experience."

"How nice for you," Penny said, looking for an excuse to walk away from Sanya.

"Penny, I'm going to say this once, and it's important that you listen carefully: *Harry is not available*," she said, as she sipped her champagne, looking at Harry laugh at some joke that Mark, who had just joined them on the patio, cracked. "Harry tells *me* everything."

Then Sanya watched Penny drain her glass of champagne, her high cheeks pink with embarrassment, her ears aflame like the red raspberries in Sanya's champagne glass. She made a hasty retreat into the house, and that was when Sanya heard a commotion in the kitchen. Ravn had arrived. He hugged and kissed his wife, who seemed so happy that her face burst open like a sunflower.

He saw Sanya at the doorway and leaned in to kiss her on just one cheek. "Hello," he said, then exited to the patio.

He stood right next to Harry, leaning against the balustrade with a beer in hand. They were so different, Sanya's blond man against Mandy's raven-haired husband, and yet they were so alike. They were equally tall, equally well-built, equally smart, equally deficient in moral character . . . and as they both looked at Sanya with focused intensity, she realized, they were equally available to her.

Sanya didn't swim in the heated indoor pool and lay on a lounge chair instead. She was wearing a pair of shorts (now that her legs were waxed) and a tank top; she had discarded a cardigan she had been wearing, because it was warm by the heated pool. Ravn, Lucky, and Harry didn't swim, either; they disappeared into a large meeting room upstairs.

Tara had abandoned her computer to put her lithe body in a bright-red bikini and swim the length of the pool gracefully. Mandy took a dip and then went into the sauna with Penny. Both of them wore black bikinis with gold embellishments, one of Penny's designs.

Katrine swam and then lounged on a chair with a book. It was the biography of Caesar her father had talked with Sanya about.

Mark, who had been swimming, hauled himself out of the water as soon as Bjarke and Leah dived in. They swam from the deep end to the shallow end of the pool, where Otto was leaning against the railing.

"Isn't Bjarke the editor-in-chief of *Børsen*?" Sanya asked Mark after he sat down next to her, and when he nodded, she mused, "Isn't it awkward to . . . ?"

"It's bloody painfully awkward," he said.

"But you're all still friends?"

"Penny is friends with this crowd. I don't really fit in, can't you see?" Mark said bitterly.

Sanya shook her head. "I don't know what you mean."

"This is *old* money," he said, waving his hand around. "I'm new money. Tolerated but never accepted."

"I'm sure that's not the case," Sanya said. "So, is the government investigation into your business over?"

Sanya had done research on Mark and used Google Translate to understand the articles in *Børsen* so she knew what was what. She still hadn't gone through Otto's files, and she knew it was because she was in denial. If something was wrong, would it tarnish her attraction for Ravn? Would it be best to not find out? But that was Old Sanya. New Sanya didn't think like that, though for this one time, she wished she did.

"So you've been reading the papers, too?"

"No *habla* Danish," Sanya said. "Just a little browsing and Google Translate. I was looking for your wife's online store to strengthen my paltry wardrobe. I didn't bring much from California." It was a plausible story.

"You'll look really good in her clothes," Mark said. "I have to say that you look really good in those shorts. You have nice wheels."

Sanya wasn't sure if he was being sleazy or complimentary, so she ignored the comment/compliment.

"Mandy said that Penny is very stressed about all of this," she said instead, to get him back on the topic she wanted him on.

"Penny has been losing her mind over it. She worries that we'll both go to jail," he said, and laughed as if that were an impossible scenario and it was bizarre to even think about it.

"Will you go to jail?" Sanya asked perversely.

"Absolutely not," he said. "These sodders are just making noise with this tax audit. In Denmark, they like to give it to white-collar crimes. You rape a minor and you get less than a year in jail, but you mess up your taxes and they'll put you away for years. My lawyers are sure it's going to be fine, as are Ravn's lawyers."

Sanya was careful to not seem too interested, in case she spooked him.

"How is Ravn's business connected to your business?" she asked.

Mark realized then that he had said too much. "Oh, he's just helping me out. Family, you know. Ravn's big on family."

"And here you thought you were just tolerated and not accepted," Sanya said.

How much trouble is Ravn in? Sanya wondered. He seemed so confident and self-contained that she couldn't imagine his business dealings were less than perfect. But then she was a woman with a crush; Ravn could do no wrong.

But Sanya knew she would have to look at those files Otto had sent sooner or later, just to be sure.

❖ ❖ ❖

That night Mandy served a dinner fit for kings, even though her Vietnamese cook couldn't make it because he was at a friend's wedding in Munich for the weekend.

"So don't mind the food; I just threw it together," she said like it was effortless.

It wasn't.

They had lobster bisque that she made fresh in the kitchen as an appetizer. For the main course they had beef tenderloin with a red wine reduction, roasted rosemary potatoes, an avocado salad, and a warm green bean salad. For dessert, she made a warm and bubbling berry cobbler with homemade vanilla ice cream she had brought from home, as she didn't have an ice cream maker or the time to make ice cream, she said, in the summer house.

They ate outside on the patio, and Sanya sat next to Bjarke. He was in his early fifties and had poise and dignity. His wife worked with handicapped adults and was down-to-earth and serious. They seemed relaxed as a couple. Comfortable in their own skins and the skin of their marriage. This was an isolated system, where the disorder had remained exactly as it had been the first day the system was created.

"How do you know Ravn and Mandy?" Sanya asked Bjarke.

"Oh, we've known each other for years," Bjarke said, and then shrugged. "I think his father and my father played golf . . . we're family friends, I think that's what they call it."

"Mark was saying that the Ravn family is *old* money, and that he's tolerated but not accepted," Sanya said to him. "I know the class system exists everywhere. What do you think?"

Bjarke snorted. "The reason that Mark is *barely* tolerated is because he's a sleazebag. It's all over the papers; everyone knows."

Sanya raised her eyebrows because that was quite direct. He certainly wasn't sugarcoating it.

"I read some of the news articles in your paper using Google Translate. You don't feel it's a conflict of interest knowing Ravn and Mandy?" Sanya asked.

Bjarke shook his head. "They have nothing to do with this. This is all Mark."

"What has he *really* done? There's plenty that's lost in Google translation," Sanya said.

"Ah, well, it's simple, and I'm shocked that Mark thought he could get away with it. He leased some properties out and then didn't pay taxes on that revenue," he said.

"Whom did he lease the property out to?" Sanya asked. She was starting to guess what could've happened. She knew that the ComIT people suspected a connection between IT Foundry and Mark, but they didn't know what it was.

"Some shell corporation," Bjarke said. "We tried to figure it out, but the trail ran cold. Doesn't matter. What he's done is illegal."

"Will he go to prison?"

Bjarke shrugged. "It's possible. We take white-collar crime very seriously in Denmark, unlike how you do it in the United States."

They discussed fiscal policy in the United States in comparison to the European Union, and Bjarke was impressed, he told Sanya, with her grasp of the financial business; and when he found out what she used to do for a living, he was further impressed and told her as much.

As they discussed numbers, Sanya started to see the Excel sheets in her head, and that part of her brain that had gone dormant since the implosion started to come back to life.

❖　❖　❖

"What is the holdup with this acquisition?" Sanya asked Harry when they went to bed that night.

There were fifteen bedrooms in total, and Mandy had given Sanya and Harry the one right by the swimming pool because it had the "best view" of the lake.

"You think they designed these small rooms with twin beds to prevent people from having sex?" Harry asked instead of answering his wife's question. He was lying in bed, his hands crossed over his chest, staring at the ceiling.

Mandy had explained to them that the summer house bedrooms were designed for corporate retreats like the old-fashioned Danish hotels, *Kro*, that came with two single beds so two colleagues could sleep in the same room more comfortably.

"Harry?" Sanya prodded, because it was obvious he was evading her question.

"We don't know," Harry said, frustrated. "We know something is not on the up and up; but we don't know how any of the dots are connected. If nothing else, Ravn is one slippery asshole."

"So you won't buy the company?" Sanya asked.

"Right now we're on track to acquire, and the delay, though not appreciated, is accepted," Harry said. "It's all hunches and gut feelings, Sanya. It looks like he padded last year's revenue, but it's within compliance—it just raised some questions for us that we have not been able to answer. We have to move on this soon, and if we don't, there's a good chance Ravn's going to sue us for breach of contract. And then the shit is really going to hit the fan."

"Otto didn't find anything?" Sanya asked.

Harry shook his head.

"I talked to Mark and Bjarke, and it looks like Mark is in some big trouble," Sanya said.

"Everyone knows that," Harry said.

"Mark said that I have very nice wheels," Sanya added.

Harry smiled. "Was he hitting on you?"

"I don't know," she said. "I don't think I'm the kind of woman that men hit on. Now, you are a whole other story." Old Sanya reared her head.

Harry got out of his bed and came to Sanya's. He got in and they managed to squeeze in together.

"I'll hit on you anytime," he said as he kissed her on her nose.

"And apparently half the women around will hit on you and save me the trouble to return the favor," Sanya said only half jokingly.

She expected him to respond with a joke, but he became serious suddenly. She put her head on his chest, and he stroked her arm.

"Remember that time when Sara had been just born and you were worried that you looked like crap?" he asked.

"Yes," she said.

"I'm sorry I didn't say or do anything to make you feel better," he said, and kissed her forehead. "I should've told you that you looked beautiful, that you always look beautiful. I'm sorry I forgot to tell you."

For nearly twenty years? Sanya wanted to kick him. It wasn't fair that he'd ignored her for two decades, and now, when she was ambivalent, he was making apologies.

They lay quietly for a while, during which time Harry fell asleep. Because the bed wasn't big enough for both of them, Sanya snuck out, planning to sleep in Harry's bed.

But as she stood up, she realized she wasn't at all sleepy. She could read, she thought. She could sit outside with a blanket and watch the sun and moon duel it out in the dark-blue sky. It was, after all, only one in the morning.

She was wearing a pair of short pajama bottoms and a top, so she just wrapped one of the blankets in the room around her and went outside, slowly closing the door behind her. She brought her Kindle along.

She could hear voices in the pool area, and when she peeked in she saw Otto and Lucky talking to Penny and Mark.

She made sure they didn't see her and went up to the kitchen. Light was spilling out of it. She stepped inside and saw Ravn sitting at the breakfast table with a cup of coffee, reading on his iPad. He wore a pair of jeans and a black T-shirt. His feet were bare. His hair was tousled. He didn't look like a corporate executive. He looked . . . ruffled and sexy.

Good god, Sanya, you have sex on the brain like a teenager.

When he saw her, he set his iPad aside and smiled this happy smile that said he was hoping she would join him, and now that she had, *everything* was wonderful.

"I was thirsty," Sanya said.

"What can I get for you?" he asked, standing up.

She told him a glass of water would be fine. She sat down at the breakfast table next to his empty chair and put her Kindle down so that it touched his iPad.

"You didn't reply," he said as he sat down.

Sanya smiled. "It takes time to respond appropriately to Shelley."

"Do you have a response now?" he asked.

She could see the scar on his face in the soft light of the kitchen.

"I do," she said. "I'll counter Shelley with Mirabai, an Indian poet from the sixteenth century."

> Only the wounded
> Understand the agonies of the wounded,
> When the fire rages in the heart.
> Only the jeweller knows the value of the jewel,
> Not the one who lets it go.

She had just finished reciting the lines when they heard a scream, a very loud one.

Chapter 21

Bad Penny

"She broke her nose," Mandy said, putting her iPhone on the kitchen counter next to the industrial coffeepot.

It had happened while Sanya had been reciting Mirabai to Ravn. Apparently Penny and Lucky had been alone by the swimming pool when Penny slipped on her Jimmy Choos and fell. The heel on the shoe broke and apparently so did her nose.

"Mark and Ravn are going to fly with her back to Denmark, where her plastic surgeon will work on her nose at Rigshospitalet," Mandy said.

They had congregated in the kitchen with cups of coffee. No one slept that night, except Harry, who showed up bright and early at six in the morning, as was his routine, ready for a run, surprised by all the commotion. He didn't miss his run.

Lucky looked miserable. All eyes were on him. He'd been the last person with Penny before she fell, and everyone wanted details.

"She just slipped," he kept saying, but he wasn't meeting anyone's eyes.

The weekend party as such was over. Mandy loaded up her Cayenne, Tara and Otto drove with Bjarke and Leah in their car, and Harry drove J Yu, Lucky, and Sanya in his Audi.

"She hit on me," Lucky said. He was sitting next to Sanya in the backseat.

"So she doesn't know you're gay?" Sanya asked. She knew she was being brazen. No one had ever said it out aloud.

Lucky stared at Sanya, then shook his head. "She pounced on me," he said. "And I'm not hiding the fact that I'm gay. I just don't mix business with pleasure."

Lucky told the story this way: Mark wanted Penny to come to bed with him. Lucky said he wanted to make some phone calls to the States, so he would stay by the pool.

But Penny had been adamant that she wasn't sleepy and told Mark to be on his way.

Once the others had gone, Penny had slipped off her robe and started pulling at the straps on her teeny-weeny black bikini.

"How about a late-night swim?" Penny suggested. "Let's go skinny."

"I couldn't believe it," Lucky told them. "She lay down on me."

"Okay, back up here," Harry said from the driver's seat. "Just so I have the right mental picture. You were lying on the lounge chair with your phone, and she came and lay on top of you?"

"Yes," Lucky said miserably.

"And she wasn't wearing her black teeny-weeny bikini, but she was wearing her high heels?" Sanya asked to complete the mental picture.

"And that gold chain around her waist," J Yu inserted.

"Yes," Lucky continued. "She lay on top of me, and my phone slid onto the ground. I tried to push her away, but then she mashed her lips against mine." Now he sounded disgusted.

"Oh . . . well," Harry said.

"This kind of thing *never* happens to me," J Yu said.

"I don't mind kissing a woman. I've done it, but it's not a first choice," Lucky added. "Then she has her hand on my crotch, and next thing she's lying half on me and half on the ground. I pushed really hard because she wouldn't give up the zipper of my pants, and she tried to stand up, lost her balance, and fell half into the pool and half on the tile . . . There was all this blood, ugh."

Sanya almost put her hand on Lucky's, but they didn't have that kind of a relationship so she refrained.

"That's how she broke her nose," Lucky finished his story. "You think she'll have me booked for assault?"

"That wasn't assault," Harry said. "That was a man pushing a rather persistent woman away."

J Yu sighed. "I don't understand why these things never happen to me. Women never throw themselves at me. Never, ever."

"I'm sorry. Next time a model type is all over me, I'll make sure to tell her to try her charms on you," Lucky said.

"Would you?" J Yu said. "That would be really great."

Sanya thought about it for a moment and then wondered aloud, "Why is Penny so adamant about getting into your pants right after she tried to get into Harry's?"

The car fell silent.

"She tried Harry also?" J Yu said.

"How do you know?" Lucky asked.

"I told her," Harry said.

"Maybe she's the slutty type," J Yu suggested.

Sanya wasn't sure.

"Next thing you know she's going to throw herself at Otto," Lucky remarked.

"Not until the nose heals," J Yu said.

That night after they'd arrived back at the apartment and Harry had gone to bed, Sanya opened her computer and the email Otto had sent her.

Chapter 22

Sanya Can't Handle the Truth

"What have you been doing all night?" Harry asked in the morning when he saw Sanya was awake and working on her computer.

Sanya thought about telling him the truth and then decided she wasn't going to, not yet. She needed time to digest this information.

"Just browsing useless shit," Sanya said. "I couldn't sleep."

"Are you okay?"

"Yes," Sanya said.

The lovely weeks of summer had made a sharp turn into gray skies and howling wind. The temperature had dropped to the sixties and it was pouring rain. Copenhagen was matching her mood, Sanya thought.

Once Harry left for work, Sanya called Bjarke. She asked him for details about the shell corporation that Mark had leased the properties in Sweden to, the rent money he was in tax trouble for.

"I'm just running a theory," Sanya told him, when he asked her why she wanted to know.

Bjarke was apparently no fool and didn't mind her help in cracking the story. "I'll connect you to the journalist who's working on this. Anette Sørsensen. She's a smart lady, just like you."

After she spoke with Anette at length, Sanya called Otto, her heart heavy.

"I went through your files," Sanya told him, but didn't add that she had also gotten access to documents that Anette Sørsensen had been collecting, which helped her complete the picture. And the picture wasn't pretty, not for Ravn.

"What do you think?" Otto asked.

"First, we keep this between you and me. Got it?" Sanya said.

"Okay . . . but why?"

"Otto, those are my terms," Sanya said, and waited until he acquiesced.

"Okay," he said.

"Have you heard of a shell corporation called Lala Associates?" Sanya asked.

She heard Otto typing away on his computer. "No, I don't think so."

"How about Cirque Fernando?" Sanya asked.

"That one I've heard of. It's an IT Foundry shell company," Otto said. "It's legal and on the up and up."

"Have you heard of a Degas painting called *Miss La La at the Cirque Fernando*?" Sanya asked.

She heard Otto sigh. "Are we talking about a painting? You're not making any sense. What the fuck has any of this got to do with IT Foundry?"

"Can you tell me what happened to the CFO of IT Foundry?" Sanya asked. "Lots of signatures by a Jens Jensen."

"That's the thing that has us worried. Jens Jensen left the company a month after we started to show interest in buying them. Ravn doesn't have a new CFO, and he's acting CFO. We have tried to contact Jensen, but he's off on holiday in Sardinia or something. IT Foundry paid for that trip outside of school vacation, and he has kids," Otto said. "We can't reach him and . . . we can't validate several financial documents and reports. But we haven't found anything illegal."

Sanya sighed. "You shouldn't buy IT Foundry," she said.

"Why? What did you find?" Otto asked.

Sanya hesitated. "Look, just find a way to stop it. I . . . I need some more time." *To do what, Sanya?* she asked herself.

"I can't just stop this without proof, and the courts are not going to buy it that a CFO out on vacation and a few noncritical books not being validated are enough to stop this acquisition," Otto said.

"Do you know who Ole Mejby is?" Sanya asked.

She could hear Otto's frustration. "What the fuck do you know, Sanya?"

"He's a director of the board at the Dansk Sjællands Bank," Sanya told him. "I looked him up. According to people who know the Ravn family, he's good friends with Ravn and actually even distant family. Ole Mejby's grandfather and Ravn's grandfather were cousins."

"How do you know this?" Otto asked.

"Because I do research," Sanya said. "Mister Mejby is in the IT Foundry documents. He signed off on some very interesting debts that IT Foundry took on last year."

"Those loans are legitimate," Otto said.

"Look at them again," Sanya said. "I think you'll find that they're not."

"But you won't tell me?" Otto asked.

"This is the best I can do right now," Sanya said.

I don't want to lead the man I suspect I have fallen in love with to the gallows, she thought, and sighed. She was starting to sound like a heroine from a doomed opera.

❖ ❖ ❖

By the time Harry came back that evening, Sanya was back in her bed and under the comforter.

"What's wrong?" Harry asked her. "You've been doing so well."

"I'm tired," Sanya said.

"Is it because you were up all night?" Harry asked, as if that was what he was hoping for. Sanya felt an overwhelming urge to cry, and her voice cracked. "I want to be left alone, Harry."

She felt Harry's hand stroke the top of the duvet. "Sweetheart, have you taken your pills?" he asked finally.

"Don't want to," Sanya said childishly.

"Did you see Arthur today?"

"No, I told him I had the flu."

"Come on, Sanya," Harry said. "Alec is coming soon."

"Alec is coming next weekend," she responded. "That means I can spend five days in bed. Now please leave me alone."

It took a while, but she finally heard Harry's footsteps leave their bedroom.

Sanya had a trigger point, and it was being made to feel small by others—but this time she had made herself feel small. She had trusted New Sanya, and she had led her astray. How could she trust herself again? Here she was falling in love with a thief. A part of her was excited that Ravn wasn't perfect at all like Harry, and yet another part was conflicted. Morality was a strange thing. Flexible at times but so rigid and unyielding at other times, and Sanya didn't know what to do with how she felt. She knew, she'd known for a while, that she was in love with Ravn—the wild and irresponsible, head-over-heels kind of love. Or was this something else? Lust? Attraction? What did it mean to be in love anyway?

Because she couldn't figure out how to sort through her feelings, she stayed in bed. This was known territory.

When Alec had asked her how she felt right after she'd come home from the hospital, she told him she was comfortable in the darkness of depression. "Once you stay in bed for a while, it becomes habit and the body starts to crave the rest. You doze off, you wake up, you use the bathroom, you go back to bed and you . . . repeat."

Nervous breakdowns can be so repetitive.

Chapter 23

Chaos Theory

Sanya ignored Ravn when he sent text messages and didn't pick up the phone when he called.

The turmoil inside her was becoming too much for her to deal with, and after her sojourn under her comforter, she started to come out of it when Alec came to visit. The rain that had come stayed as long as Sanya stayed in bed, and once she shrugged the cobwebs off, the skies let the clouds go, giving way to long July summer days.

When she told Alec everything she knew and how this knowledge was creating chaos, Alec told her that the chaos in chaos theory was not the chaos in the English language that means confusion. It actually meant a lack of order within a system that still somehow follows some of the rules.

"You can predict random events from simple equations using chaos theory," Alec said as they sat outside at the Cap Horn restaurant in Nyhavn, a glass of crisp Sauvignon Blanc in his hand, and a glass of champagne in Sanya's.

"So the chaos I'm feeling is actually a predictable random event?" Sanya asked.

Alec took a sip of his wine. "You haven't done anything yet. Nothing has really happened except that you've shared poetry. Stop behaving like you slept with the entire Danish soccer—excuse me, football, team."

"Isn't it bad enough just to think it? Isn't that cheating?" she asked. "And isn't it worse that now I know, now that I have proof that he's a *bad* guy?"

"You're so straitlaced sometimes. It's almost endearing. Why call it cheating? Are you cheating Harry of anything and giving it away? And what does *bad* mean anyway? Smile, Sanya, it's a beautiful day," Alec said, raising his glass.

In July in Copenhagen, Nyhavn was the place to be. Actually it was the place to be all summer. A string of restaurants and bars lined the cobblestone path—where people sat outside under colorful umbrellas. The most beautiful thing about Nyhavn was that the buildings were all different colors, from bright red and bright blue to yellow and orange. It gave the harbor a touch of whimsy, and this was the place that showed up in pictures when you Googled Copenhagen.

Nyhavn was, as the Danes would say—very *hyggelig*.

"There is no literal translation for that word," Sanya told Alec. "The closest is 'cozy,' but the meaning goes deeper than that."

"How Danish you've become," Alec said.

❖ ❖ ❖

Sanya had met Alec at a rooftop pool party not long before the Silicon Valley bubble burst. Their hosts, Shawn and Cindy, were one rung up the power couple ladder from Harry and Sanya. Shawn's company had just gone public, and Cindy was a partner in her law firm.

Sanya was getting a glass of Scotch, her drink at the time, and as the bartender poured her a finger of Lagavulin, a man standing behind her asked for the same.

"They're all money crazy here," he said to Sanya. He introduced himself as Alec, Cindy's cousin, new at Stanford via the University of Chicago.

"This is Silicon Valley," Sanya said in agreement.

"Did your company go public? Did Microsoft make a bid? How much are your stock options worth? Is that all people talk about around here?" Alec asked.

"More or less. They also talk about what car they drive," she said.

"What do you drive?"

"A Lexus," she said.

"So you're one of *them*," Alec said, with suspicion in his eyes.

"I'm not sure about me, but my husband is definitely one of them," she said. "He drives a Porsche."

"Right," Alec said. "You're one of those women who blames her husband for everything."

Sanya thought he was being a tad judgmental for someone she'd just met. "Yes, I believe so. Isn't that what husbands are for?" she asked.

"Why not take responsibility for where you are and what you are?" Alec suggested.

"What's the fun in that?"

And that was how they'd become friends. He was judgmental and Sanya was flippant.

They stayed friends after the Silicon Valley bubble burst—and became even closer through everything that had happened since.

❖   ❖   ❖

"Are you okay?" Alec asked as they watched a little boy standing with his mother, a chocolate ice cream in a waffle cone in one hand and his mother's hand in the other. The mother was fashionably dressed in a white summer dress and a brown hobo Prada bag that Sanya recognized from Birgitte Green's store. The mother wore big sunglasses and was chatting energetically with a man in a pair of jeans and a white polo shirt. They were all Danish. Blue eyes, blond hair, and light skin, still not kissed enough by the sun to be tanned.

"I'm just in an uneasy place," Sanya said to Alec, looking away from the boy when his precariously positioned ice cream scoop fell off the cone and he started to wail in earnest. The moment of harmony was lost. The man excused himself, and the woman with the Prada bag was left hopelessly consoling her child.

"Are you still upset about Harry and Tara?" Alec asked.

Sanya shook her head. "It's just sex. It's a bit of excitement—a respite from boredom, and god knows we all need respite from boredom. I understand marital jealousy—but it seems so useless. I mean, what do you do? You catch him with his pants around his ankles. You can leave him; that's a choice, or you can say that you want him to end his relationship. He ends the relationship and tries to save his marriage. He's miserable. Suddenly all the stuff he was getting from his affair—the excitement and the thrill—needs to come from his marriage. And if he was getting the excitement and the thrill from his marriage in the first place, he wouldn't have had an affair. Now suddenly your marriage is under pressure because he got caught cheating, and now you both need to make the marriage work. It was working fine before—except after *x* amount of years it got a bit boring—but now it needs to become this fabulous thing that it never was."

Alec nodded appreciatively. "So if Harry was to be a good boy, you'd have to provide him what he's getting from his affair, and that's too much pressure?"

"Exactly. And that either makes me the laziest wife in the world or the least loving one. But I can't suddenly make this marriage something it's not. I wouldn't know how," Sanya said.

"But you still cut up the Hermès tie," Alec pointed out.

"I have a mean streak," she said, and then sighed deeply. "I didn't want him to have the tie. I guess that means that I'm not *all* okay with it, but I don't know if I really care or if I even want to."

"When would you care?"

She shrugged. "If he came home and said he'd fallen in love with someone else, if he shoved it in my face and showed me no consideration. Or maybe I'd be just fine if he did all those things because I don't love him anymore and don't want to be married to him. Or maybe I'm in love with him, and I'm also in love with Ravn. I'm in that place in life where I doubt everything."

"But do you even know what love means?" Alec asked. "Love means different things to different people. Love means something to you, and it might not mean the same thing to Harry."

Sanya looked at Alec and mulled over the word *love*. Poor bandied word. Everyone used it all the time. So easy to say.

Over the phone: "I'll buy milk on my way home. Love you."

Or as a husband kisses his wife, who's in bed all the time, before leaving for work: "Have a nice day. Love you."

But what did that love mean? Did it mean I forsake all for you? Did it mean I can't live without you? Did it mean I'll die for you? What the hell did it mean . . . to Sanya?

"I don't know what love means to me," Sanya declared.

"Define that, and you define how you want to live with Harry . . . or without Harry," Alec said.

"For someone who's single, you're very smart about relationships," she said.

Alec grinned. "That's why I'm so smart about relationships—because I'm single. If I was in a relationship, I'd be mired in the intricacies of one."

"You like being single because you're selfish," Sanya said.

"All true," Alec agreed. "What if Harry tells you he knows how you feel about Ravn and he wants it to stop?"

"Stop feeling attraction? He can say don't sleep with him, but he can't say stop feeling attraction," Sanya said. "I can't stop feeling or start feeling anything by design. And if I have to sacrifice Ravn for my marriage with Harry . . ."

"Then that puts pressure on Harry to start quoting Shelley or Byron," Alec said, and smiled. "For someone as whacked out as you are, you sound pretty grounded."

She smiled back at him and downed the rest of her champagne. "Let's go to Christiania." She grabbed his hand and drew him to his feet. "I want to smoke some weed," she said brightly.

Alec pulled out some Danish kroner from his pocket and left it on the table and enfolded Sanya's small hand in his big one.

"Show me the way, fair maiden," he said. "Is this Christiania the hippie place?"

"Yes," she said. "I've never been, so this will be a first for both of us."

Chapter 24

Rainy Day Woman

The sign marking the entrance to Christiania said, YOU ARE NOW LEAVING THE EU.

The taxi driver dropped them off right at the entrance. The walls were covered with graffiti, a stark contrast from suave and über-clean Copenhagen. The taxi driver, a second-generation Dane as they were called in Denmark, and a Pakistani by ethnicity, was first disappointed that Sanya had not seen any Shah Rukh Khan movies (a Bollywood hero popular in all Hindi- and Urdu-speaking countries) and then appalled that their destination was Christiania.

"I'm visiting from San Francisco," Alec explained, "and I've heard so much about Christiania."

"Garbage place," said the Pakistani taxi driver, whose license said his name was Hamud Ansari. "They should shut the place down. Do you know the people who live there don't pay any taxes? Bastards."

"Danes pay an insane amount of money in taxes, like sixty-five percent top income tax," Sanya told Alec after they were out of the taxi. They waited at the entrance, slightly intimidated. Were they walking into a haven of drugs and debauchery?

"Brian, *pas på*," a man called out to a toddler running ahead of him into Christiania. Following him was a woman with a pram and a soundly sleeping baby inside.

"Apparently, this place is rated G," Sanya said.

"I don't know whether to be disappointed or scandalized," Alec wondered.

A small pathway wound through the eighty-four acres of the self-proclaimed autonomous neighborhood.

"How about coffee?" Sanya suggested, because the first stop close to the entrance was a café.

The barista smiled at them when they ordered their nonfat lattes and then smiled even more broadly when Sanya asked him if this was the place to buy weed in Copenhagen.

"Go down the pathway and past a square to Pusher Street," the barista, a twenty-something Danish kid told them. "Are you tourists?"

"I guess so," Sanya said, looking at Alec. "I mean, am I a resident?"

"Well," Alec said, "maybe a short-term resident."

The barista did warn them before they left with their to-go coffees. "The police raids are escalating, so if you see people running, just run along with them. No point getting arrested."

"Arrested?" Sanya's eyebrows shot up. "Why?"

"It's a crime to buy and sell weed," the barista explained. "But it's not a crime to smoke weed."

"Now that's truly diabolical," Alec said.

The barista shrugged. "It's to protect the pothead. Just like prostitution is legal in Denmark, but it's not legal to buy sex."

"The crime is legal and to commit it is legal, yet the instigator is the criminal," Alec said, his blue eyes glinting.

"Isn't the instigator always the criminal?" Sanya mused.

❖ ❖ ❖

As they walked down the wicked path they realized that the path wasn't that wicked. There was art all along the pathway—paintings on stones, sculptures made of discarded metal, and stray car headlights that might have been just stray car headlights or some sort of art installation, they couldn't tell. Musicians seemed to be scattered everywhere, and they hadn't smelled any weed yet or seen a junkie shoot up, but they had listened to parts of the Violetta aria from *La Traviata*, "Black Hole Sun" by Soundgarden, and even a strain of ". . . Baby One More Time" by Britney Spears—vintage stuff.

The first square was devoid of weed. There were several stalls surrounding the square, and all were selling nearly the same nonsense as the souvenir shops on the tourist-heavy streets of Copenhagen. They went to one of the stalls where both Indian and Native American handicrafts sat next to one another, not quite authentic to either region, and probably made in China.

"There's a kindergarten here," the woman at the stall told them and pointed to a yellow door that led into a shed that had a park next to it, populated with the colorful bits and bobs that children's parks usually contain—slides and swings and merry-go-rounds. "That's why we moved the weed guys."

The weed guys were less than a hundred meters away, and when Sanya pointed that out to the stall owner, she grinned and said, "Legally, they're far enough."

❖ ❖ ❖

At the weed square they walked up to the first stall, and a man in a Hawaiian shirt and a pair of worn jeans shorts smiled at them. "How can I help you?"

They peered at his wares. Glass bottles with some waxy stuff stood in front of rolled joints in capped plastic tubes.

The names were intriguing: Buddha's Breath, Monk's Deliverance, Blond Smoke, Crying Weed, Goblet of Jam, and Sanya's favorite, Rainy Day Woman.

"We want something strong but not too strong," Sanya said confidently.

The man nodded. "They're arranged in order of intensity."

"How about Rainy Day Woman?" Sanya asked.

"Medium to high strength," he said, like he was talking about something as banal as chilies. *This is the pimento, this is the jalapeno, and this is the Carolina Reaper. Eat at your own risk.*

"We'll take three of the Rainy Day Woman," Sanya said and then paused. "And one of the Monk's Deliverance."

"That is very strong, so be careful," the man warned as he put the four joints in plastic cases into a brown bag. "Hundred and fifty kroner."

"Where can we smoke this?" Alec asked.

The man shrugged, "Wherever you want, dude. Best thing, take it home and enjoy the toke. Here, there could be a police raid."

Alec grabbed Sanya's elbow and whispered, "Let's get out of here. I really don't want to get arrested in a foreign country."

❖   ❖   ❖

They pulled two chairs over to one of the big windows in the living room that Harry used as a study and opened the window wide. Sanya assured Alec that even though the window was big enough for jumping out of, she wouldn't attempt it.

Alec peered down and said, "We're only a floor up; you'll just end up with broken limbs, so go for it, if you like."

Alec washed down his toke, Rainy Day Woman, with a glass of whiskey, and soon they both were high and happy.

They heard the front door open, and Sanya turned to look at her husband.

"Do you know what love means, Harry?" Sanya asked him as he walked up to them. He sniffed the air and then noticed that his wife had transformed one of their expensive Royal Copenhagen saucers into an ashtray.

"She's high," Alec said in explanation.

"So are you," Sanya said, and giggled.

"I can smell that," Harry said, and pursed his lips.

"We went to Christiania," Sanya said proudly. "And between us we smoked almost . . . all of a joint of Rainy Day Woman."

"Right," Harry said, trying to conceal his bewilderment. He looked at Alec for an explanation.

"That's a type of marijuana," Alec offered helpfully.

"I figured that," Harry said, and put his computer bag on the floor against the wall next to where Sanya was sitting.

"You didn't answer my question, Harry," Sanya said.

"What was the question?" Harry asked.

"One for the ages," Sanya said, and a giggle escaped her again. "What does love mean to you? When you say, 'I love you, Sanya,' what do you *really* mean?"

Harry looked at Sanya cautiously and then at Alec. "This was irresponsible," he said to Alec.

"I'm not her father," Alec said. "And neither are you."

"You need to answer my question, Harry," Sanya said.

"Love is just love," Harry said. "It means I care for you, a lot. And you're my wife and my life. I think you're the most beautiful woman in the world. And I can't imagine my life without you. Happy?"

"But love doesn't mean fidelity to you, does it?" she asked. She didn't mean to bring up his dalliance with Tara again, but it slipped out. Oops.

Harry closed his eyes for a second, almost a blink but it was more than that; he was reining in the lies. "Are we back to the nonsense about me having an affair with Tara?"

She smiled. "Love means that you can't imagine life without me, but it doesn't mean that you will forsake all others for me. Right?"

"Sweetheart, I love you, but I have reasonable expectations of my marriage," Harry said, and she could see he was becoming angry. "You can't give me the professional satisfaction that I get from work. You can't be a male friend to me. You can't give me the pleasure I get when I watch a football game or go to the opera or see a piece of art. I can't forsake the world for you. I have to live in this world."

"Very articulate," Alec said, and held up his whiskey glass.

"Whose side are you on anyway?" Sanya asked peevishly. "But can you forsake the others?"

"Yes," Harry said.

"Have you?" she asked.

Pause. "Yes," Harry said quietly.

"Right now, right here?"

Harry's Adam's apple bobbed. "Yes."

"Forever?"

"Be careful what you wish for," Alec said in a singsong voice.

"Stay the hell out of this," Harry said to Alec, who smirked. "Yes, forever. From this moment on."

Harry and Sanya looked at each other, his eyes digging into hers, saying to her that he was open and being honest and demanding her to respond in kind. When she didn't, he said tightly, "I can't believe I'm trying to have a serious conversation with a woman who is high as a kite."

"This is turning into a bad theater play," Sanya said, and looked at the ashes on the saucer. "Can we go out for dinner? I feel like a *big* burger . . . with fries."

❖   ❖   ❖

That night as she lay in bed listening to the slow hum of Harry speaking on the phone with his office in California, she sent Ravn a text message. She'd not been in touch with him since she had gone through the IT Foundry financial documents and found out all the naughty things Ravn had done. But the temptation had been there all along, and now it overcame her.

What does love mean to you?

She wasn't sure if he'd respond. Rainy Day Woman wasn't playing havoc with her system anymore, especially after the burger, but she was still there, making Sanya reckless.

After five minutes of no response, she put the phone down on Harry's pillow and stared at it.

Ping.

Ravn's opening salvo was philosophy.

Love is the madness of the gods.

And who said that?

It's an ancient Greek saying.

Do you say "I love you" to your wife when you leave for work in the morning? she typed. He could respond and say none of your business, but he didn't.

Yes, he responded simply.

What does that love mean?

Nothing. Everything.

Can you imagine your life without her?

Yes. Easily. Can you imagine yours without him?

Sanya didn't know what to say to that, so she put the phone down as if it was too warm to hold. Then after a moment she replied, I don't know. What if she finds out about your affairs?

She won't.

What if she does? What will she do? What will you do? Sanya typed.

I don't know.

That's honest. Will you lie?

Did Harry lie?

Outright.

I would lie as well. Not out of malice. Out of respect.

She got annoyed at this point and picked up the phone and called him. "Why not stop screwing around on your marriage out of respect?" she demanded.

"Because one thing doesn't have anything to do with the other," he said.

"That's bullshit."

"Yes," he admitted.

Sanya hung up on him.

I'm sorry. Let's not fight.

Do you want me? Rainy Day Woman asked.

Yes.

I went to Christiana with Alec and got high.

Is Harry high, too?

Never.

Did you have sex with him after you got high?

None of your business, she wrote with a surprising thrill running through her.

This was what a new relationship felt like, an intoxicating mix of delirious emotions—love, jealousy, excitement—all blended together running through the bloodstream like pheromones.

I have no rights, I know. I'm jealous, he wrote.

How often do you have sex with your wife?

Once a week. Sundays. We're on a schedule.

Schedule? That's nuts.

She doesn't know that I know there's a schedule. It's how she feels connected to the marriage and me.

Is the sex good?

It's okay.

But you still have it.

For men sex is like pizza. Even when it's cold and a day old, it's still okay.

Harry and I have good sex, Sanya wrote on purpose, because she knew he wouldn't like it.

Don't say such things.

Do you think you and I will have good sex? She only asked because Rainy Day Woman was curious.

Yes.

How do you know for sure?

Because love is a madness, not just of the gods, but us humans as well.

Are you in love with me? How long had it been since she felt an honest-to-god butterfly fluttering in her stomach at the thought of a man?

Madly.

How madly?

Enough that I want to drive down to your street right now and take you away.

And make love to me? Her heart was beating so incredibly fast that she had to put a hand to her chest to slow it down.

And fuck you hard.

Heat pooled inside Sanya. Oh my, was this sexting? She didn't respond to his message. It was crude. It was not what she had expected. It was exciting and yet off-putting all at the same time.

The phone rang, and she picked it up.

"I'm sorry for my lack of finesse," Ravn said.

"Good night," Sanya responded.

"Sleep well," he said.

She did no such thing.

Chapter 25

Good Mandy

"I can't stand the humiliation," Penny told Mandy.

Mandy understood. It was bad enough that Lucky had rejected her; now she had to have her nose repaired again. The bandages on her face and her wrist, which was sprained from the fall, were a constant reminder of everything in her life that was not working.

Mandy looked at Penny in despair while Ravn was on the phone in the dining room of Penny's house. Penny had settled down in the sunroom, which faced the Charlottenlund forest. It was her favorite room, but in the past two weeks while she recuperated it had become a hated room, she told Mandy. The Queen Anne–style furniture seemed gaudy and unclean as the July sunlight streamed in from the glass doors and windows and danced on top of each dust bunny and flaw on the couch and the three chairs that surrounded the coffee table. Penny sat on a leather lounge chair, facing the forest. The coffee table had been moved close to her and was covered with a box of Kleenex, prescription painkillers, bottled water, and for now a teapot and a cup of green tea.

"Are you in a lot of pain?" Mandy asked.

"It's not too bad," Penny said as she flipped through the latest *Elle* magazine. "Princess Marie and Stine Lund both wore my designs to the opening of *Giselle*. God knows how long I'll be able to sell. I don't think they let you design in prison."

Princess Marie was married to the Crown Prince Frederik's younger brother, Prince Joachim, and Stine Lund was an up-and-coming musician who had last year won the Danish *X Factor* contest. How Penny could find this news an omen for disaster, Mandy couldn't understand.

"Come on, you're sulking," Mandy said.

"Look, Mandy, I know you care and, babe, I'm grateful you do. But I'm not a project of yours, okay?" Penny said.

Mandy was offended. "What do you mean *project*? I don't have any projects."

"Sure you do," Penny said. "You're always trying to save someone or the other. What was the name of that woman you picked up at Ruby's the other day?"

Mandy licked her lips. "You know, when Ravn and I first married and moved to Denmark, I didn't have a single friend. I was so alone. I just think it's hard for foreign women who come to Denmark. You Danes are not particularly friendly."

"But that doesn't mean you pick people up everywhere you go," Penny said, obviously happy to divert Mandy's attention from her nose.

"I don't do that," Mandy said, and pouted and turned to Ravn, who stepped into the room just then, his phone in his pocket. Mandy beamed at him. "Do I pick up people everywhere I go?"

Ravn smiled and kissed his wife lightly on the lips. It was something he did often, Mandy thought with delight. Something he just did offhandedly. They'd been married forever, and he still kissed her as if he liked it. She was the luckiest woman in the world.

"Yes, you do," Ravn said. "But only because you have a big heart, and we all love you for it."

"See," Mandy said triumphantly.

"See what? He agrees with me," Penny said. "And the latest one was a *weal* disaster."

Penny was referring to one of Mandy's new friends, Rosaline, a Frenchwoman who had recently moved to Denmark with her Danish husband from Lille. Mandy wanted to help Rosaline, but her family couldn't stand her because the woman was a complete snob and show off—and pronounced *really* "weally." It had taken just one dinner at Mandy's house for her to realize that she needed to get rid of her new friend even though she *weally* wanted to help poor Rosaline acclimate to cold, damp, and dark Denmark.

"She was an odd duck," Mandy admitted.

"And let's not forget that Russian woman," Penny said, and both Ravn and she in unison said, "Olga Ivanovich."

Mandy made a show of weariness, but she enjoyed the attention they gave her. They were saying that she was kind, bighearted, and welcoming. This was how she wanted people to see her. Not as the girl she had been in Oregon. No, not that gauche girl, but this wonderfully sophisticated philanthropist.

"She was a complete ho," Penny said.

"*Penny*," Mandy protested.

Olga Ivanovich had been married to a Russian diplomat. Mandy met her at some embassy to-do, and they had chitchatted politely over a glass of champagne for maybe five minutes tops. The second time they met had been at the Illum Bolighus department store in the city center, where Olga had dumped her three-year-old son with Mandy while she used the restroom. Mandy had played with little Andre and had bought him a Thomas the Tank Engine set, much to his delight. The third time they met had been at the local Irma grocery store, and Olga had brought her bag of groceries to Mandy's house, where she had insisted they have a cup of coffee.

Olga burst into tears even before the coffee was poured into cups. They never made it to the living room but sat in the kitchen, sipping coffee while Olga unloaded the whole story.

"My life is falling apart," Olga told Mandy, a veritable stranger. "My husband and I are having problems. He's sleeping on the couch and . . . I have Andre, and it's really difficult."

"I'm so sorry to hear that," Mandy said.

"My husband cheated on me," Olga explained.

"Oh dear," Mandy said.

"But that's okay. I forgave him. But . . . see, I'm . . . oh god," she said and burst into thick tears again.

It took a while for Mandy to coax the story out of Olga, but it went a bit this way: A year ago, Olga's husband had had a torrid three-month affair with a Russian opera singer who had been in Berlin while they had been living there. They had moved to Copenhagen with the hope of a fresh start to save their marriage, but Olga slipped when she met an older man. A much, much older man whom she was helping with his orgasms.

"Excuse me?" Mandy asked, as she gracefully managed to not choke out the coffee she had just sipped.

"Well, he's older and has trouble with reaching orgasm, so I help him," Olga said. "And I think I'm in love with him. But he's married and I'm married. I don't know what to do."

Mandy didn't think this was a difficult issue. "Do you want to stay in your marriage?"

"Yes," Olga said to her. "I love my husband."

"Well, then, you should stop *helping* this old man," Mandy suggested.

"But I think I'm in love with this old man," Olga said.

"He'll never leave his wife for you," Mandy said. "Danish men don't do that . . . actually, no man does that."

When Mandy had told Ravn and Penny about this strange woman with her strange story, they had both said that it underscored how Mandy needed to stop bringing home people she didn't know.

But Mandy loved to help—she loved being needed. She had purpose then. And now, as Penny lay injured while Mark was in Switzerland meeting with some investors, Mandy was more than happy to run Penny's house, keep an eye on the au pair, and take care of the girls.

"You're like a sister to me, and you're no project." She looked at Ravn and added, "And you need to put her mind at rest. She's very worried about her husband and the business."

"Of course," Ravn said. "Penny, there isn't really anything to worry about. I'll take care of you. You're family."

Chapter 26

Harry Wants to Be Married

Ravn sent Sanya several text messages. She resisted responding to any of them.

She had two tubes of Rainy Day Woman and Monk's Deliverance in her underwear drawer, and she was staying away from them. Post-implosion Sanya was difficult enough for her to put her arms around, but post-implosion Sanya on Rainy Day Woman was a bit too much.

The weather in Denmark was as moody as Sanya felt. July was always reliably warm, Sanya had thought, but not in Copenhagen. One day the sun was shining and the sky was blue, and the next day the clouds had gathered and the temperature had dropped to where Sanya was wrapping herself in a trench coat as she went out to meet Madeline, the University of Copenhagen professor she had met at Café Bopa a few weeks ago, for lunch at a French bistro, L'Education Nationale, in the city center. She'd advised Sanya to catch the 1A bus on Aarhusgade and get off at Nørreport Station, after which it was just a short walk.

This would be Sanya's first time catching a bus in Copenhagen, and she was a bit intimidated by the experience. She hadn't wanted to ask Madeline about bus tickets and how one bought them, so she asked Harry.

"Just take a taxi," Harry suggested, not looking up from his computer. He was sitting in his office, poring over what looked like a hefty Excel sheet that seemed familiar to Sanya.

She still hadn't told anyone what she knew. Otto had called her and told her that he had looked at the shell corporations, Lala and Cirque Fernando, and he had found no connection between them. If she knew anything, he told Sanya, now would be the time to tell him.

Otto was obviously not as good as he should be at uncovering information from financial data, Sanya concluded. But she didn't help him. Conflicted beyond belief, Sanya decided that denial would be better than dealing with her situation. Also, she didn't work for IT Foundry or ComIT. She was a jobless bum. This was not her responsibility.

"I don't want to take a taxi. I want to take a bus," Sanya said indignantly to Harry.

He looked up at her then, a bit confused, and seeming to say, *Then take the bus, do what you want, you're a grown woman.*

A foreign country was disorienting for her, but it was probably disorienting for him as well. It wasn't like he spoke Danish. Sanya had always been independent and able to run her own life, but here she was needy, lost, and . . . well, let's face it, Sanya thought, a little pathetic.

"It's okay; I'll ask . . ."

"No, I'll find out for you," Harry said and started to do a search on his computer.

After a few minutes, he said almost triumphantly, "Well, apparently, you can go to the 7-Eleven at the corner and buy a pass that gives you ten trips. You punch the card in the bus."

Sanya leaned over and kissed him on the mouth. "Thank you."

"Why don't we walk down together now and buy the bus ticket?" he suggested as he closed his computer.

Sanya's eyes narrowed. She didn't want to be *that* wife, the wife who was suspicious as soon as her husband suggested anything out of the ordinary, but she couldn't help herself.

"I can buy it tomorrow," she said, and then, when she saw his dejected face, said, "*Fine*. We can go now."

"We don't have to if you don't want to," Harry said as he pulled his computer toward him.

"I just said I wanted to," Sanya snapped.

"You should hear yourself. I should record it and play it back to you," Harry bit back. "I was trying to be nice."

"By buying me a bus ticket?" Sanya asked. Harry always had a bit of a short temper, but for the past several months he had reined it in for her sake. But now his impatience made Sanya revert to old habits, to give in to Harry, to please him.

"Let's go get my ticket," she said softly.

She slid her feet into her UGG boots because it was a tad nippy and wore a black dull-as-dishwater fleece jacket and waited for Harry to find his Armani or whatever leather jacket and Nike shoes. In other marriages men probably complained about their wives taking too long to get ready, but in theirs it was always Harry who needed more time, even though he looked so much better than Sanya did.

Harry put his arm around Sanya as they walked, and she almost jerked away.

What was up with him? Was he cheating on her . . . again?

This wasn't the usual Harry. She'd been with this man for two decades, and he wasn't the *let me put my arm around you while we stroll down to the nearest 7-Eleven* kind of guy. In their early days if Sanya tried to hold his hand when they walked, he always unclasped her hand from his, saying it was uncomfortable to walk like that.

"The weather certainly isn't summery. You still like it here?" he asked as they walked down Østerbrogade, the main street in Østerbro.

"I do," Sanya said. "How about you?"

"It's fine," Harry said. "It's just . . . Otto is all up in arms about us backing out of this deal, and he won't tell us why. This is business and we're professionals. I can't just go with Otto's gut. So Lucky and Otto are fighting all the time. Ravn is dropping hints about taking us to court if we don't move fast. But if Otto doesn't sign off, we can't finish fucking buying this company."

Sanya nodded but didn't say anything. Obviously Otto had kept his side of the bargain. He had told Harry nothing about her involvement with his business.

A young Danish man and woman passed by them. They were both holding hands. Young love and all that. The woman was talking enthusiastically about something while the man was walking with his iPhone in his hand, and he was paying more attention to it than her, even though he was holding her hand.

Harry suddenly pulled Sanya's hand and stopped. "Is something wrong?" she asked.

He kissed her on the mouth then. One of those quick, brush-his-lips-against-hers kisses. "I love you."

Say what?

"What's going on?" Sanya asked.

"Why can't a husband say . . ." He trailed off when he saw her raised eyebrows. "All right, I feel something, okay? I'm feeling . . . in love . . . I don't know, okay? I'm not the one in therapy, so I can't articulate how I feel."

"And that's what therapy is all about, articulating how you feel?" Sanya asked a little tightly, but her heart had turned just a little. She knew what he was trying to do. He was making an effort.

"Let's not fight," he said.

"Okay," Sanya said amenably. She didn't want to fight, either.

She leaned into Harry and pretended that they were good, a happily married couple with no problems at all, until they got to the 7-Eleven and Harry and she got into an argument over the fact that you could only buy a two-zone bus card and not a one-zone one, which Sanya thought was what she needed.

"This is the system; just follow the *fucking* system," Harry told her angrily as he thrust the two-zone ten-ride ticket into her hand while the pimple-faced teenager at the 7-Eleven stared at them in open fascination. "Sometimes, Sanya, stop questioning *everything*. You used to not be so . . . so . . ."

"So what?" Sanya demanded.

"So challenging," he said.

Chapter 27
Omelets at L'Education Nationale

"You have to have an omelet," Madeline told Sanya at their corner table at bistro L'Education Nationale. "With their baguette and a glass of the house white, it's *the* lunch."

A fixture of Copenhagen's Latin Quarter since the early nineties, L'Education Nationale was an authentic French bistro popular with locals as well as the French expat community. More lively than romantic, the tables were covered with red-and-white-checkered tablecloths, and the menu offered dishes like pissaladière, a Provençal pizza; a traditional French charcuterie with a variety of rillettes and French cheeses; and classics like coq au vin and boeuf bourguignon.

Madeline wore a pale-green summer dress with pink flowers that matched her hair, which was streaked with pink and blue, while Sanya wore skinny jeans, black leather ankle boots, a white sweater, a scarf, and a trench coat. She was even carrying her purse, an old Céline bag she had bought a long time ago on sale, in which she had put an umbrella in case the weather turned.

"You know it is July, right?" Madeline teased.

"It's not warm," Sanya protested as she took the trench coat off and hung it on the back of her chair. "The wind is biting."

"The sun is shining even if it is a little windy. You don't understand Danish weather," she said to Sanya. "We crave the sun, so the minute it's out we're all chasing it. Go to one of the big parks today, and you'll see many a topless lady, trying to get a tan even though the wind is a bit on the cool side."

"Is it a nude park?" Sanya asked.

"Not really. But no one cares. Parks are family places."

"I grew up in Boston, so I know what a cold winter feels like," Sanya said. "It's just that after twenty years in sunny California, this feels cold and . . . even in Boston in July it was never like this."

"Your blood has become too thin," Madeline said. "A few years in Copenhagen will fix it."

The waiter, a Frenchman from Marseille, suggested that Sanya choose the mushroom omelet, which she did. Madeline chose the ham-and-cheese omelet, and they ordered a bottle of the house white wine, a 2015 Château de Ricaud Bordeaux Blanc.

When Madeline asked what Sanya's plans were for her life, she said she didn't have any, because she hadn't been feeling well.

"There's only one way to get stronger," Madeline said. "You need to build a life that doesn't include your kid or your husband."

"I haven't had the time," Sanya said as smoothly as she could, but Sanya had realized, ever since she had opened up to Ravn, that she had missed living her life.

"It happens to a lot of women," Madeline said as she removed her napkin to make space on her paper table mat for their food, which arrived in record time.

Omelets, fluffy as dreams, were placed in front of them with slices of baguette and little cubes of foil-wrapped butter. Sanya hesitated to cut into the beautiful omelet, but Madeline immediately took up her knife and fork and dived in.

"Amazing," she said, and Sanya had to agree when she followed suit. It was the best omelet she'd ever eaten.

"What happens to a lot of women?" she prodded Madeline.

"This," she said angling her chin at Sanya. "This thing that has happened to you. You've spent your life taking care of others, and you've forgotten you exist and forgotten what it means to be just you. Babies do that. Husbands do that. Society does that. The expectations on a woman are ridiculous."

"I'm a recovering lunatic; it's going to take a while to be happy and fulfilled," Sanya said defensively, and shoved omelet into her mouth.

"Oh, please, don't pull the nervous breakdown card," Madeline said, but her voice was kind. "What are you doing tonight?"

Sanya raised her eyebrows.

"Come with me to Mojo," Madeline said. "Actually, after lunch let's go to the movies. They're playing film-school movies at the Nordisk Film Institute."

"I don't understand Danish," Sanya said, unsure if she wanted to spend a whole day with Gloria Steinem. *And what the hell was a Mojo?*

"That's okay; the student movies won't be good anyway. We'll find something else to do," Madeline said. "Come on, let your hair down."

"What's a Mojo?"

"The best blues bar in all of Copenhagen," Madeline said.

After they finished their omelets, they both ordered espressos, and as they sipped Sanya asked Madeline the question she had been pondering about her lunch companion.

"Have you always been a feminist . . . a free spirit?"

Madeline shook her head. "I met my husband when I was twenty-one. Very young. And I had a child and got my PhD and became a professor at the University of Copenhagen. I started to work and live that hideous bourgeois lifestyle so many of us claim as our own. We had people over for dinner. We went to Majorca for holidays. But then, when I was thirty-five and my son was eleven years old, something happened."

She paused to take a sip of her espresso.

"I had a breakthrough, though for a while it felt like a breakdown," Madeline said. "I was invited to a sociology conference in Paris to present a paper I had written about the social impact of the dole in Denmark or some such boring shit. My husband was busy with his book on the maritime history of Norway, so he was traveling to the ass-end of Norway quite a bit. I was alone. Not lonely, mind you. Why don't we walk and talk? We can go to the Round Tower. Have you been?"

Sanya nodded. "Recently, I did all the tourist stuff with a friend who was visiting."

They split their bill, fifty-fifty, and walked down Studiestræde toward the Skt. Petri Church. "So, what happened in Paris?" Sanya asked.

Madeline smiled impishly. "I had sex with a man who wasn't my husband for the first time in my life. And it was amazing."

"Who was he?" Sanya asked as they pushed past people thronging the pedestrian street by an Italian restaurant. It was getting warm, and Sanya had taken off her trench coat, and it trailed a little on the ground as she threw it over her purse.

"How does it matter? He could've been anyone," Madeline said. "And I have realized that. All my lovers could've been anyone, but Flemming, my husband, had to be Flemming."

"That's bullshit rationalization," Sanya said.

"Yes and no."

"Tell me about the Parisian," she said, thinking of Ravn and his scar.

"He wasn't a Parisian," Madeline said. "He was Scottish. One of those rugged and slightly unruffled types. He was nearly fifty years old then with graying hair, but I thought he was beautiful. He had a full head of hair, while Flemming had lost everything by the time he turned thirty."

Madeline insisted they buy ice cream on the way to Runde Taarn, the Round Tower. In the seventeenth century, Christian IV had built the structure wide enough to drive his horse carriage up to the top for a killer view of Copenhagen. He had proudly rebuilt the tower after the three-day fire of 1624.

So while they walked on Strøget, enjoying their ice cream, Madeline told Sanya about Wallace, her Scottish lover.

"He was married, of course, with two daughters. He was an editor at one of the big Dublin publishing houses."

Madeline stopped to throw the last bit of her ice cream cone into a trash can. They were next to the Hermès store, and from the corner of her eye Sanya caught sight of the orange purse that she had seen on Mandy's arm once. Was that a Birkin?

"I felt like a *woman*. A fertile, voluptuous, seductive piece of ass. He loved me, too. He couldn't keep his hands off of me. We were doing *it* everywhere. Back seats of cars. Restrooms of restaurants. You name it. It was the best and worst affair I ever had."

Floored by the depth of Madeline's emotion, Sanya forgot about the Birkin bag.

"What happened?" she asked.

Madeline sighed. "His wife found out, and he chose her. I didn't see him again, not for a long time, and when I did . . . let's say I wish I had not seen him again, because I couldn't recognize my Wallace in this man, because this man was old, bitter, and still unhappy in his marriage, which was devoid of love. I felt grateful for Flemming then. My life was full of love with him, and fun. But that affair was momentous because it opened my eyes to who I could be and how much I could feel."

Sanya bought tickets for the Round Tower, and they went up the winding path to the top of Copenhagen.

"Was the affair really that grand, or after all these years does it feel grander than it was?" Sanya asked Madeline.

"Oh, that sounds like a practical question," Madeline said. "Let's not bother to answer it and take the magic away from our memories of greatness."

Sanya sent a text message to Harry to tell him that not only was she out for dinner, but she wasn't sure when she'd be home.

He responded. Where are you? Do you need me to come and pick you up?

Why?

Just checking if you want a ride home.

I don't know when I'll be done at this blues bar.

Do you want me to come to this blues bar?

No. Why would I want you to?

If you can't find your way home or something.

For god's sake, Harry!

Chapter 28

A Lucky Break

Harry watched Lucky pace the meeting room.

"This thing is blowing up in our faces," Lucky said.

Otto had gone home and told everyone that IT Foundry was a bad bet but not why—the partners were freaking out, and all Lucky could tell them was that everything was on track.

"From what we know everything is on the up and up," Lucky said. "We should just buy this and get it settled."

Harry was distracted. He was standing at a window, looking out at the city. Even though it was a bit nippy (and it was July), the sky *was* blue and the sun *was* shining. It was the wind that made it cool. He liked this city, he realized, just like Sanya did. He liked how easy it was to walk around. How easy it was to find a cup of coffee. How he didn't have to pull out his car when he needed a carton of milk. It was *hyggelig*, as Danes would say.

"Harry? I'm stressed out of my wits, and you're all calm and cool," Lucky said.

"It's going to be fine," Harry said.

"Oh, and do you know anything about a Lala shell corporation? This is the shell corporation that Mark Barrett leased those nonexistent properties in Sweden to," Lucky said.

Harry looked at Lucky for a long moment and then said, "And what is the shell corporation that IT Foundry has, the legal one?"

Lucky browsed through his computer and said, "Cirque Fernando."

Harry thought about it for a moment and pulled out his cell phone. When he found what he was looking for, he smiled.

"Son of a bitch," he said. "Do you know about a Degas painting called *Miss La La at the Cirque Fernando*? It's now in the collection of the National Gallery in London. Degas painted the acrobat Miss La La hanging on a rope by her teeth at the Cirque Fernando in Montmartre."

"What on god's good earth are you talking about?" Lucky asked in exasperation.

Harry held up his hand to hold off Lucky and his inevitable outburst at what he thought was a non sequitur and called Otto. "Why did you start looking into Lala? It has nothing to do with IT Foundry business."

Otto sounded shifty and instead of answering asked Harry if he knew what time it was in California.

"You sent the files to her, didn't you?" Harry said exultantly. "And she connected Lala to Cirque Fernando."

"What?" Otto said.

"Go back to bed, Otto," Harry said. "We just figured this one out. And you're right; we won't be buying IT Foundry."

Lucky looked at Harry questioningly when Harry hung up on Otto.

"We need a lawyer," Harry said. "We need to find a way out of this deal."

"Ravn's not going to just lie down and let us walk away," Lucky said.

"He's not going to have a choice," Harry said.

"You know I'll do what you want," Lucky said. "But tell me this and give it to me straight. Are you backing out of this because you're worried about Sanya being attracted to Ravn?"

"Sanya is not the type," Harry said, but he knew that wasn't true. Old Sanya was not the type; but New Sanya was testing her boundaries and exploring the span of her wings.

"Man, look, she's a saint, okay? But we have a partners' meeting in a few hours," Lucky said. "We don't know yet what Ravn's been up to. And why should we doubt it? The biggest bank in Denmark signed off on those loans that Otto said were questionable."

"We need to look into that as well," Harry said. "Again. Because now I think I know what happened. I know how Mark Barrett and Ravn helped cook the books at IT Foundry to make them interesting for us to buy."

"You're making no sense," Lucky said impatiently. "And what really gets me is that you're not upset."

Harry looked at him in amazement. "What do you mean? I've never been more upset."

"Not about your wife," Lucky said, "but about this business deal going south. We came to buy a company and run it. Now we're going home empty-handed."

"As long as I can keep my wife with me, I'm not empty-handed," Harry said, and then breathed deeply. "Look, Lucky, there comes a time in a man's life when he needs to see himself as he really is. And I finally do see myself. I have for too long been the slick consultant who has been playing every which way possible to get ahead in his career, and as I stand as a partner in a really prestigious consultancy, I can't feel that it has been worth it. Do you think it has been worth it?"

"Of course it has been worth it," Lucky said. "You live a life most people envy."

"And Ravn lives a life I would and do envy," Harry said. "And maybe he's going to go to prison for it, or at least he'll be embarrassed in his own high-class society for being a fucking criminal. So tell me, what good did it do him? He got the fancy house, the big car, summer houses and holidays in wherever, and dinner with ambassadors and whatnot, but where has it gotten him?"

"Ravn's going to prison?" Lucky shook his head. "You are making less and less sense."

"I don't want to get divorced, Lucky," Harry said.

"Couples get divorced all the time," Lucky said.

Harry sat down on a chair and smiled sadly at Lucky. "People do. But not people like me. I can't be Harry Kessler without Sanya. She makes me who I am. She's my family. The only person in the world who gives a shit if I live or die. I wake up at six in the morning every morning and smile because she's in bed next to me. Even this past year, when a strangely erratic woman has replaced my happy, positive wife, I smile because she's *still* there. And this woman, this confusing woman, is full of fire and passion, and I love her even more than I did before. Sanya feels that she's lucky to have me—but the fact is, I'm fucking fortunate to have her. The irony is that I didn't find that out until now when she could walk away and I would have no defense, no way to stop her."

Chapter 29

A Mannish Boy at Mojo

The name for Mojo Blues Bar, Madeline told Sanya, came from the lyrics of old blues songs like "Got My Mojo Working" and "Went to Louisiana to Get My Mojo in Hand."

"Mojo is also a talisman that is worn to attract a true soul mate or lover," the man at the ticket counter, who overheard their conversation, told them as Sanya paid for her entrance. Madeline, who knew everyone at Mojo, got in for free.

The bar was smoky, and with muted light it impressively hosted people from eighteen to sixty—different skin colors, different ethnicities—it was the most diverse gathering of people Sanya had seen in Copenhagen, which tended to be white.

"Madeline, *hvordan har du det?*" a young man about twenty-five rattled off in Danish and lifted Madeline off her feet with a big hug.

"So nice to see you," Madeline said, and kissed the boy on both cheeks when he set her down. "Sanya, this is Asgar, my son's best friend."

In greeting, Asgar tipped his black porkpie hat trimmed with a small black feather and replaced it on his head at a rakish angle. He wore a hippie jazz chic ensemble of distressed gray jeans, a Dolce & Gabbana T-shirt, and a thick gold chain with a cross pendant.

Amulya Malladi

"Nice to meet you," Asgar said, and shook Sanya's hand. The kid was cute; Sanya had to give him that. He even had a dimple on his right cheek covered by carefully cultivated stubble.

"Asgar is on the bass. And he's fabulous," Madeline told Sanya. "We came just for you," she told Asgar.

"And you brought a beautiful friend along," Asgar said to Madeline as he looked at Sanya, who blinked.

Is this kid hitting on me?

Madeline smiled a knowing smile. "We're going to find a place to sit."

"Can I get you a drink?" he asked, still looking at Sanya.

Thick cigarette smoke wafted between them, and Sanya inhaled without thinking. It wasn't Rainy Day Woman, but it could be.

"At Mojo we only serve music and drinks, so you can smoke inside," Asgar said.

Sanya still had some of Chloe's cigarettes in her handbag, which she hadn't touched since the dinner at Kiin Kiin. Once Asgar took them to their seats, Sanya pulled out the pack and held a cigarette near her mouth. Asgar lit the cigarette, and she smoked, channeling Lauren Bacall in one of her many black-and-white movies with Bogart. Sanya smiled like she was a sophisticated cougar who had young men fall all over her all the time. This was New Sanya, with a slight sprinkle of Rainy Day Woman.

"You should go, Asgar," Madeline said. "They're waving to you. We'll find our own drinks."

Asgar grinned and winked at Sanya. "Showtime," he said, and then was gone.

"You want a drink?" Madeline asked.

Sanya licked her lips and nodded, "Yes, please. What would you like? I'll get them."

218

Sanya hadn't been drinking hard liquor, not since her Scotch days during the nineties tech boom. But it just felt right to have bourbon on the rocks at Mojo, especially since Madeline was having one, too.

As musicians were tuning their instruments, Sanya took her first sip of the bourbon and let it burn her inside.

"The best thing about live blues is how they improvise as they go, and Asgar improvises like a bad motherfucker. That kid is something else. He dropped out of university, which isn't a big surprise. He has an IQ of 150 or something outrageous like that, and university is just not challenging enough," Madeline said. "Sit back and be impressed."

There was a man playing the harmonica who looked like something out of a thirties movie; there was Asgar on bass, standing by a blond woman in fatigues at the drums; and a man who looked like a Harry Potter–style wizard with frizzed hair was the guitarist. A black man, the lead vocalist, introduced himself as Small Creek Slim and promised to entertain them with a variety of famous blues songs, including those by Nina Simone, B.B. King, Muddy Waters, and more.

As they tuned their instruments, Sanya watched Asgar, and slowly the cacophonous sounds of the instruments being tuned turned into "The Thrill is Gone" by B.B. King, and Sanya leaned back into her chair and started to enjoy herself, and not only because Asgar watched her as he played.

They moved from B.B. King to Albert King's "Born Under a Bad Sign," and then they moved to Muddy Water's famous "Mannish Boy"—and that was when Asgar popped a cigarette in his mouth.

"'Mannish Boy' was first recorded in Chicago in May of 1955, and accompanying Muddy Waters was the amazing Jimmy Rogers on guitar, Junior Wells on harmonica, and Fred Below on drums. The song has made it in Hollywood and can be found on the soundtracks of *Risky Business*, yep, the famous movie where Tom Cruise made his debut as a singer in his underpants," Small Creek Slim said, and the audience dutifully laughed at the joke.

Sanya smiled at the lyrics as Small Creek Slim sang them—"because it was apt for Asgar, he was a boy who thought he was a man."

As the song progressed the bass started to become more and more dominant.

"Watch this," Madeline said with a big smile.

Asgar winked at Sanya and then closed his eyes. His fingers started to play the bass as if . . . yes, as if it were a woman. He caressed the instrument, ran his fingers alongside her, and as he did, the cigarette hung in his mouth, the ash starting to take over what had been paper and nicotine.

The others stopped playing, the singer had stopped singing, and it was just the bass now, just Asgar, and there was pin-drop silence in the bar. The man next to Sanya had his cigarette in his hand, and he watched openmouthed as Asgar played, his eyes closed and the cigarette ash becoming more tenuous and longer by the second.

Would the ash fall? Would it not? How would he save it?

And then just as everyone gasped, the song came to a smooth end, and Asgar elegantly tipped his cigarette in the ashtray next to him.

The crowd went up in flames. People stood up and clapped. Sanya joined them, feeling the pump of the music, the crowd, and Rainy Day Woman within her, who she was starting to accept was here to stay.

When the next song, "Got My Mojo Working," also by Muddy Waters, started to play, Sanya asked the previously openmouthed man sitting next to them if she could borrow his lighter. He graciously lit her cigarette.

They played more songs by Muddy Waters and then announced a break.

"Give it up for Asgar on the bass, no treble, people," said Small Creek Slim while the crowd clapped. "We have Janus on harmonica, take a bow; Celine on the drums; and Mister Dumbledore, a.k.a. Buddy, on guitar. Time for a break, we'll be right back after we have soaked our parched throats. Don't go too far."

Asgar came up to them instead of grabbing a drink.

"You were amazing," Madeline said.

Sanya sat there, a sophisticated woman with her cigarette in one hand and a glass of bourbon in the other. If this was a black-and-white film, she'd say something along the lines of, "You know how to whistle, don't you?"

"What's next?" Madeline asked.

"'Catfish Blues,' 'The Sky is Crying' by Stevie Ray Vaughan, and I think some Aretha, because you've got to have Aretha," Asgar said to her, and then looked at Sanya. "Where are you from?"

She felt a little off balance at the question. "From Østerbro," she said, mangling the pronunciation of the place.

He smiled. "Is that where you live? Østerbro?" he asked.

"Yes," she said.

"But where are you *from*?" he asked again.

"California," she said.

"You're just what I always thought a beautiful American woman would look like," he said with a twinkle in his eye.

This boy was young enough to be her son, and Sanya wasn't sure if it was the bourbon or the smoke or the fact that a man like Ravn had shown interest in her, and now that he had, all the men in the world were also taking note of her; regardless, the attention was exhilarating.

"Really," she said.

"Madeline, will you stay until the end? We're going to go find a bar and get some drinks after," Asgar said.

Madeline shook her head. "Take Sanya. I turn into a pumpkin come midnight."

"Will you come?" the mannish boy asked.

"Absolutely, I'd love to," Sanya said, and then choked a little on the cigarette because she wasn't used to smoking and ruined the whole Lauren Bacall whistle thing from *To Have and Have Not*.

Chapter 30

Sinner Woman

"You didn't do the ash thing after the break," Sanya said to Asgar as they got comfortable on a sofa next to each other in a luscious swanky bar called 1105.

Named for the postal code where the bar was, 1105, which made many of the world's best bars lists, had a subtle décor with sophisticated soft lights, and the music they played was a mix of Motown and easy jazz.

Before they got their drinks, Asgar introduced Sanya to Mandeep Hardal, the bartender who was apparently *the* couture cocktail mixer in all of Copenhagen. Mandeep spoke with a British accent and clapped Asgar on his back several times and asked about a music tour and about someone called Helena. And then Mandeep got Asgar a Jack Daniels on the rocks and made Sanya his signature drink, a Cucumber Yum-Yum, a frothy pink concoction in which cucumber was the sole identifiable ingredient.

"You do the ash thing just once; otherwise it loses effect," Asgar said, and then laughed. "Actually, I didn't plan the ash thing; it just happened. It hasn't happened before. Might never happen again."

"Oh, please," Sanya said sipping her Yum-Yum, which was very yum. "This whole distressed jeans, D&G shirt, and manicured stubble; you're dressing to produce an effect."

He looked at his clothes and then at Sanya. "My mother is a designer. She dumps clothes on me and I wear them. The stubble is not manicured but a product of sheer laziness."

"Your mother is a designer?"

He nodded. "Straight down the pedestrian street from here and right after the Hugo Boss store is Big Legs, Tight Skirts, and that's my mother's designer brand."

"Is she famous?"

"Yes, in the fashion circle in Scandinavia at least," he said. "My father used to be a blues musician; he played the guitar and he sang, that's why she called her brand Big Legs, Tight Skirts. It's a famous song by John Lee Hooker. The story goes that she had come to a blues bar where he was singing this song and that's when she fell in love with him."

"Your father also plays at Mojo?"

"He's dead," Asgar said. "He died of a drug overdose. He died young."

"Oh, I'm sorry," Sanya said, immediately contrite. Lauren Bacall needed to reel it in and behave like a considerate forty-plus woman instead of some incarnation of Demi Moore trying to seduce young Ashton.

He shrugged. "It happened many years ago. I didn't even know him. It's not a tragedy. I was raised by my stepdad; he's a corporate type, but the coolest cat. I didn't have a scary childhood or anything. Well balanced, super good, and all that."

"So you're not the neglected child of famous parents?" Sanya asked.

"On the contrary, probably even a little spoiled," he said. "But enough about me. You have the most intriguing eyes."

Sanya had to laugh.

"I'm too old for this," she said. "I have a daughter who's eighteen."

"Does she have your eyes, too?" he asked.

"I'm married," Sanya said.

"All the good ones are taken," he said. "You have incredible eyes and incredible legs."

"I'm forty-two," Sanya added quickly.

"I'm twenty-three," he said. "And I've been playing in a band since I was sixteen."

"What's wrong with you? You seem a bit too mature for your age."

"Because I'm an artist," he said. "Have you gone dancing in Copenhagen?"

Sanya considered his question for a moment. "I haven't gone dancing since I was in university, I think. And that was a really long time ago."

"A tragedy, because those legs are meant for dancing," he said.

"Madeline said you have an IQ of 150 plus," she said.

"Yes," he said, and grabbed Sanya's hand to stand her up. "And because I'm such a smarty, I sound more mature than I am. But I'm a great dancer, and you're going to have the time of your life."

"Sold," Sanya said and downed the cocktail and felt light in the head but in a *really* nice way.

❖ ❖ ❖

Sanya thought they'd take a taxi, but Asgar borrowed the bartender Mandeep's bicycle. It was no ordinary bicycle but a Christiania bicycle, which came with a carriage in the front where Sanya sat, a lot like a rickshaw.

It was a joyride. Asgar rode across the cobblestones and Sanya waved at the tipsy pedestrians on the walking street, feeling energized as the cool night air splashed through her.

She deliberately didn't look at her phone, which was in her handbag.

"What time is it?" she asked, holding on for dear life to the sides of the carriage, commonly used by commuting parents to transport their children to school.

"*No es importante*," he said, not even huffing at carrying her weight. "Come on, Sanya, let's have some fun."

He parked the bicycle on the walking street alongside hundreds of other bicycles, some with carriages and some without. He locked it and slipped the key in his jeans. "I'll pick it up later," he said.

They entered the Jane, another cocktail bar in the heart of Copenhagen on Gråbrødre Square, where mannish boy seemed to know everybody. The bar had a *Mad Men* feel, with some of the rooms featuring bookshelves and where many hidden doors revealed themselves, and behind each door were more bars.

Asgar introduced Sanya to many people whose names she immediately forgot. The entire time, Asgar didn't let go of Sanya's hand. It wasn't sexual or even possessive; it was almost friendly, as if he was saying, *Just hold on to me and enjoy the ride.* Sanya had *never* been to a place like this. She didn't even know places like this existed.

Where was the dancing? she wondered, sipping on yet another mystery cocktail that Asgar had shoved into her hand.

"The DJ is a friend of mine," Asgar said to Sanya. He opened a door into a room where the dance music played on high volume and the warm air carried a hint of sweat.

She didn't recognize any of the music, except one Beyoncé number that wasn't quite the same one as on her Amazon Music but some mixed version.

And for the first time in her life, Sanya *really* danced.

Asgar, as he had promised, was a great dancer and an excellent partner. He swept Sanya off her feet, threw her around the floor, and she felt her heart bang against her chest as her blood alcohol level rose and everything turned into a misty dream.

She danced to the fast songs. She danced to the slow ones in Asgar's arms. She twisted. She shimmied. She didn't know how long they danced, but when her throat was parched she whispered to Asgar that she needed water or she'd die.

So Asgar took her to yet another room in the Jane that Sanya hadn't seen before. Doors opened and closed in the Jane, new rooms, new ambience; the change was constant.

In this room the music was quieter and people were having conversations. They couldn't hear the sound from the dance floor.

He brought Sanya a tall glass of water with bubbles and ice. She drank it all before speaking. "We can't hear the music," Sanya said.

"Soundproof walls," he said.

He leaned closer to her then, and for a moment she wondered if she should not turn away. Was her nearness a signal for him to kiss her? Did she want him to kiss her?

"Are you hungry?" he asked instead.

Sanya thought about it for a moment and said, "Starving, actually."

From the suave rooms of the Jane, they went back out into the streets and got in line in front of a hot dog stand in Kongens Nytorv where many of the city's revelers seemed to be getting their post-party fix.

"These hot dog stands are becoming rarer and rarer; that's why the line is so long. Today there are more sushi restaurants than hot dog places. This one on Kongens Nytorv is my favorite. The best," he said, and then proceeded to speak in Danish with the man at the hot dog stand.

Sanya had eaten hot dogs before. She had even eaten proper ones in Chicago and New York, but she had never eaten a hot dog this good. The sausage was crisp and covered in mustard, ketchup, deep-fried crispy onions, fresh onions, and pickled cucumbers wrapped in bread that held its ground.

One bite and she moaned. "Wow," she said with her mouth full.

"Fabulous, isn't it?" Asgar said. "Finish your hot dog, and then we wash it down with something that's going to blow your brains out."

They took the chocolate drink, Cocio, to go.

Hand in hand, they strolled down the street, sipping their chocolate milk. It was an unusually warm evening, or maybe she was flushed from the activity, or maybe she was hitting early menopause and having a hot flash.

He took Sanya to the lakes, Søerne. There were three rectangular lakes curving around the western margin of the city center, and they were one of the oldest and most distinctive features of the city. The paths around the lake were popular with strollers, bikers, and runners. Stairs from the street went down to the lake, and on a sunny day Copenhagen dwellers used the stairs for picnics or to just hang out.

They sat on the stairs that led from the street, Øster Søgade, to the middle lake, Fiskesøen, and drank their Cocio.

"When you asked me if I was hungry, I thought you were going to kiss me," Sanya told him.

"I was," he admitted, "but I got scared."

"Why?"

He shrugged. "I don't know. You're incredibly beautiful."

Sanya's eyes narrowed.

"Come on, you have to know this," he said in disbelief.

"I'm not being coy," she said. "I'm not beautiful. You should see my husband; now, he's Adonis. I was never a match. We weren't Brad Pitt and Angelina Jolie; more like if Brad Pitt married . . . I don't know . . . some plain Jane no one ever heard of."

"And in any case they're not together anymore," Asgar said. "Who told you that you're a plain Jane?"

"Are you sexually interested in me?" Sanya asked instead of answering his question.

Asgar laughed. "No. I just wanted to take you dancing and to a cocktail bar and am walking in the middle of the night with you to discuss world politics. Of course I'm sexually interested in you. I'm twenty-three. I like to . . . you know . . ."

"I've only slept with one man my entire life," Sanya said.

Asgar gaped at her.

"I know it seems antiquated, but I'm a bit antiquated, I'm afraid," she said. "And you really find me attractive?"

"Someone's done a number on you," Asgar said. "You're a good-looking woman with great legs, and I'd love to . . ." He paused and then smiled, "It's not going to happen, is it?"

Sanya sighed. She was cheating on Harry with Ravn and on both of them with Asgar, or was she just having a good time? Wasn't a little bit of flirtation necessary to keep the blood pumping? Wasn't it good once in a while to feel something that wasn't linked to reality?

"I'm afraid that you might become a midlife crisis," she said.

"I don't mind," Asgar said.

"I mind," Sanya said. "No one should be someone else's midlife crisis release valve. Not someone as talented as you. You should have good sex based on mutual attraction."

"You're not attracted to me?"

It sucked to be older and wiser, Sanya thought. "I'm attracted to the idea that a twenty-three-year-old Mensa-smart blues prodigy is attracted to me."

"But you're not attracted to *me*?"

"I'm too old for you."

"I once had an affair with a woman who was thirty-five," he said. "It was brief. It was in the Alps during a ski holiday. She was British. The cutest thing ever. Curly hair, freckles, tiny, and full of energy. We had a week, and we went skiing and made love in every possible way and place we could. It wasn't more than that."

"Of course," Sanya said. "Of course. No, don't get me wrong; I wasn't thinking that you were suggesting anything but an affair. I'm just too old for an affair. Or maybe I'm just too messed up for an affair. I recently had a nervous breakdown."

"Really?"

"Yes," Sanya said, "I'm a nut case. It happened several months ago in California."

"What happened?"

"I used to be a consultant with expertise in financial process optimization, and I worked in a consultancy firm, a prestigious one. I worked there for a decade and a half, and I was happy to be a director of strategy even though my husband was a partner at his firm and my parents were sure that I was a complete loser for not making partner," Sanya said.

"Your family is the corporate type?"

"No. My father is a surgeon and my mother is a surgeon; and my sister is a pediatrician married to a surgeon," Sanya said. "Overachievers. I was supposed to be a doctor, and barring that I had to have Condoleezza Rice's job."

"So you have shitty parents; lots of people do," he said. "Tell me about your breakdown."

Two swans floated close to the stairs in the lake, their white wings and bodies in stark contrast to the dark waters.

"I call it an implosion," she said, watching the swans. "One fine day the partners called me into a meeting and offered me a partnership. They said that I had done a bang-up job, and they wanted me to be a partner after fifteen years of grinding my soul to produce for them."

Sanya paused and Asgar waited, as if he understood that she needed time to say this because she hadn't told this to anyone.

"I got angry. That was my first reaction. I was angry. How could they? I mean, it took them fifteen years? Brian made partner six years ago, and he started three years after me. And Santosh became partner last year, and I had four years' seniority over him. So I was angry. *Really* angry," Sanya said. "I stood up."

She stood up then and dropped her empty bottle of Cocio on the concrete stairs, and the bottle crashed into pieces. The swans scattered. Asgar didn't move. He just watched her.

"I wanted to say *fuck your partnership*," she said. "I pointed my finger at the senior partner, a really nice guy called Miguel Herrera, and I wanted to say that even though he had hired me and I was grateful, he could shove the partnership up his ass. But I didn't say anything. Something broke inside me, and I sat back down on the chair"—Sanya sat back down on the stairs—"and I started to cry and I couldn't stop for hours. They had to knock me out in the hospital. I didn't speak for a week after. They put me on suicide watch. Gave me a psychiatrist and some drugs and told me that I had just had a nervous breakdown."

"That's a pretty disproportionate reaction to being offered a partnership," Asgar said. To his credit, he didn't seem shocked, or at least he didn't show it.

"I know," Sanya said, and blinked back tears. "You should have seen their faces. God . . ." And suddenly, just like that, she started to laugh. "I remember one of the partners saying they should call security. What did they think I'd do?"

"Maybe they thought you had a gun on you somewhere?" Asgar said, joking with her.

"In a Hugo Boss skirt suit that was a little tight on my waist?"

"Maybe James Bond style? Strapped to your thigh," Asgar said, and Sanya laughed some more.

"But you know what was even funnier? Harry. That's my husband. I called him, and he didn't pick up the phone, which was normal. I sent him a text message while I cried nonstop. It took him an hour to come to the office. He looks at me crying and then he starts to ask people if I'm hurt," Sanya told him. "Instead of asking me, he's asking Miguel what happened, and Miguel was just shaking his head and saying Harry needed to take me to the doctor because I wasn't feeling well. Harry then suddenly goes cockeyed and asks Miguel if I was raped."

"What?" Asgar asked.

"I know. I don't know where he got that idea. Miguel almost died, and even while I'm unable to stop crying I'm thinking this is ridiculous, but I can't stop crying and tell Harry anything, so I keep crying. Miguel says he's offended, blah, blah, and that I had lost it at a partners' meeting and he wasn't going to say anything until he spoke to the firm's lawyers," Sanya said. "Christ, it was a mess. After I felt better I called Miguel and apologized; he said it was okay and then said that he hoped I understood that I was officially on medical leave without pay."

"So they wouldn't make you partner anymore?"

Sanya started to laugh again. He joined her.

When they stopped laughing, Asgar asked, "Why did you call it an implosion?"

"Do you know what entropy is?" she asked, and he nodded. Of course high-IQ boy knew. "Well, when a closed system is in such complete disorder that it can't sustain itself, it implodes and a new closed system comes in its place."

"I'm not sure that's exactly what happens," Asgar said.

"Just go with me on this. It's my theory of entropy," Sanya said. "So I had an implosion, and now there's a new closed system, which is my marriage. And in this new closed system, I'm not the same Sanya I used to be. I'm the Sanya who goes off to a bar with a strange man and dances until . . . my god, what's the time? The skies are lighting up."

"Aren't summers grand in Denmark? The sun is up until nearly midnight and then rises again early," Asgar said. "It's four in the morning, Sanya. Do you need to get home?"

"Probably," Sanya said, looking at her bag and knowing that her mute phone was probably bleeding voice mails and text messages and missed calls.

"Do you think your husband called the police?"

"What would the police say?"

"That they can't do anything until forty-eight hours have passed; and you're a grown woman, not a child," Asgar said. "Where do you live? I'll get you a taxi."

Sanya told him her address and he punched it into his phone.

"Let's get up; taxi is here in five minutes," he said, holding his hand out to Sanya, and she put her hand in his. They walked up the stairs to the street, hand in hand.

The taxi was there before she was ready to leave. But she knew she had to, so she let go of Asgar's hand.

"I had a lovely time," he said as Sanya put a foot into the taxi. She suddenly stopped and turned, leaving the taxi, and stepped closer to Asgar. She put both her hands around his face and lifted hers up to him.

The kiss blew Sanya's mind. She had never tasted another man like this, leisurely, luxuriously, in the morning with a taxi waiting. It was lazy, this slow exploration of a tongue in the mouth—the taste, alien— a mystery that she would not explore, just dip her toe into and resist.

She got into the taxi afterward and said, "I had a blast."

"My pleasure," he said, and closed the taxi door.

The hell with a midlife crisis, Sanya thought. She had kissed a twenty-three-year-old hottie, and she felt great.

Chapter 31

The Lightness of Being

"Maybe you should've checked your phone," Sara suggested.

"But I was having such a good time," Sanya said. She touched the screen of her MacBook and sighed. "I miss you."

"You know what, so do I," Sara said. "When are you coming stateside?"

"I thought you'd come visit us here," Sanya said. "They have a great jazz festival in July, starting in two weeks."

"So now you're an expert on all things jazz because you went to a jazz club and hung out with a bass player?" Sara asked, but she was smiling.

"It was a blues bar, very different from jazz. Harry didn't enjoy it when I explained the difference to him," Sanya said.

"He *even* called me," Sara said.

"How did he think you could help?"

"I don't know—something about if you were dying then you would've at least tried to reach me," Sara said. "He went apeshit, Mama. I mean, I've never seen him this worried. You know, most of the time he never knows where you are and doesn't seem to care one way or the other. But this was different. He was afraid that something had happened to you."

"What would happen to me?"

"That's what I said," Sara said. "You know what, there's something different about you. Are you coming out of it then? Are you both coming out of it?"

"Harry didn't have a mental meltdown, my love," Sanya said.

Sara shook her head. "I think whatever journey you're on, he's on it, too. Maybe you're not on the same boat or train together, but something's going on with him as well. Look, I know Daddy isn't one of those attentive husbands or fathers. But he's attentive enough. I have no complaints, mostly because you were *always* there. I think we all got used to you always being there. And I suspect that he's starting to worry that now you're not *always* there."

"And how do you feel about that?" Sanya asked.

"About time," Sara said. "Sometimes I wanted to shake you. Even in the most difficult situations, you'd hold on to that never-failing optimism of yours. You'd let Mira Auntie and your mom walk all over you because you wanted to be nice to everyone. It didn't seem . . . don't take this the wrong way, but it didn't seem genuine, like you were a plastic doll playing a role. The only time I saw you being different was with Alec."

Sanya smiled. "I left the doll behind."

"Good," Sara said. "Really good. You're a fantastic person, Mama. You're smart, good, and lovely, and I love you."

Something had happened to her, Sanya thought. She felt lightness around her, as if a heavy fog had lifted.

❖ ❖ ❖

Sanya talked to Arthur about her evening with the blues, and he thought she had made a breakthrough by finally talking to someone about what had happened that day in the meeting room. She had purged it from inside her—finally she was on the right track, and the lightness she felt came from having freed herself of that day.

Of course, she had to figure out why being asked to become partner made her respond like this—but she thought that maybe she already knew.

Finally, when everything she had worked for was within reach, Sanya realized that she didn't want it. Her rejecting the partnership and her anger at not being appreciated for so long was really her rejecting her marriage and being angry at Harry for not appreciating her for the entirety of their marriage to chase down his corporate dream.

"Thank you, my love," Sanya said to Sara. "So, you're coming to visit, yes?"

"Mama, don't get angry, but my friends and I are thinking of going to Peru and doing the Mayan trail this summer," she said. "There won't be any time for Europe, and I already did Europe last year."

Disappointment stabbed through Sanya but so did excitement. The Mayan trail? She had wanted that. She had wanted that and other things that she had not pursued. But Sara had the freedom, the time, the energy, and her daddy's money, so why the hell not?

"I'd never be angry about something like this. It sounds like fun. Tell me about it," Sanya said.

She watched and listened to Sara as she excitedly told Sanya about the five-day hike to Machu Picchu and the other places in Peru she intended to visit.

This was victory, Sanya thought.

Unlike Sanya, who had been burdened by her parents and her husband's success, Sara was unfettered, happy to explore her life and universe the way she wanted. *I'm not a complete failure,* Sanya thought. She had raised a self-confident, self-assured woman, one who would never have her mother's emotional issues because she carried no baggage that made her feel small, ungainly, and irrelevant.

After she talked to Sara, her phone beeped with a message. She picked it up and smiled. Straight from daughter to illicit lover. Sanya was definitely not a plastic doll anymore.

I want to see you.

Why? Sanya typed.

For all the wrong reasons.

I kissed a boy.

Was it a good kiss?

Unbearably good.

I can do better.

She laughed and typed, **Prove it.** And then deleted it.

He didn't wait for her answer and wrote: I'll show you. **Come to Café Victor. Tomorrow. 4 p.m.**

Sanya didn't respond and turned her phone off to avoid further temptation.

Chapter 32

Harry Goes Right

Chief Inspector Hans Møller nodded from time to time as Harry explained the fraud that IT Foundry and Mark Barrett had perpetrated.

The meeting was taking place in the offices of HS, the law firm hired by Harry's company for the merger, close to Amalienborg, the royal palace.

Harry hadn't wanted to have this meeting, but their lawyer, Alice Risbjørn, insisted that they had to do this to protect themselves from a lawsuit that IT Foundry could bring against them for breach of contract. ComIT had officially decided to back away from acquiring IT Foundry based on revenue figures in the past year that didn't match up with revenues from selling consultancy services.

The chief inspector was just as Harry had thought a Danish cop would look. He was about six feet five inches tall, had a shaved head and blue eyes, and wore a pair of Levi's with a white dress shirt. Unlike an American television cop, he did not carry a gun. He didn't even have a fancy holster. He didn't wear a badge on his Marlboro-branded leather belt. He was fit, like he worked out every day and enjoyed it.

"You say that someone at the Dansk Sjællands Bank is involved?" the chief inspector asked when Harry came to that part.

"Yes," Alice said, looking at her papers. "Ole Mejby. He is listed as an executive vice president and is on the board of directors."

The chief inspector made a sound, which was mostly a snort, meant to indicate disbelief. "Big accusations, you understand, and you're all Americans."

He said *Americans* like they were immoral thieves.

"I'm not American," Alice said with a smile. She didn't sound defensive, just stating a fact.

The chief inspector raised both his hands. "You do understand that this is going to raise all kinds of hell. The National Bank. IT Foundry. These are reputable Danish organizations."

"Well, it's all here," Alice said, handing over an IT Foundry–branded black USB drive to the chief inspector. "You're welcome to have one of your financial people go over it."

"I will, but those nerds get too technical on me," the chief inspector said. "Can you explain this to me in English?"

Harry explained what they had found out. They had proof for certain aspects of the fraud, and they were speculating about others.

Mark Barrett had done some creative accounting to put together leases for properties in Sweden that didn't exist. He leased these properties to a shell corporation called Lala, and that corporation then rented the nonexistent properties to another shell corporation, this one owned by IT Foundry, called Cirque Fernando. Mark then paid no taxes on the income he received from these leases, which triggered his tax audit.

IT Foundry went to the Dansk Sjællands Bank and got loans based on these nonexistent leased properties. This wasn't common practice, but someone in the board of directors at the bank signed off on the loans, which added up to nearly five hundred million Danish kroner. This money was funneled back into IT Foundry as revenue to inflate the numbers and keep the share price high in the stock market.

"But why would he do this?" the chief inspector asked, shaking his head.

"Because he wanted to sell his crappy company to us," Harry said. "He hid it all very well, and if our experts weren't as good as they are, we would've been saddled with this mess."

"But eventually it would have come out," the chief inspector said.

"We think Ravn was planning to use the money from the sale to pay off the loan," Alice said. "That way he could clear the books and no one would be the wiser."

"What proof do you have?" the chief inspector asked.

"Only the loan papers from the Dansk Sjællands Bank," Harry said. "And they don't specify the Swedish properties clearly, so it's all a bit vague. It is poor banking practice, and maybe Ole Mejby will get into trouble but not Ravn. He can say he knew nothing."

"So you have no actual proof," the chief inspector said.

"The shell corporations are connected because . . . do you know a Degas painting . . . ," Harry began, but Alice interrupted him. She had warned him that his Degas connection would make him look like a fruitcake.

"We do have proof that earnings from last year do not match the sales, as the loan has been put into the revenue column. Again, this is noncompliant, and IT Foundry will be expected to pay a fine and fix processes. *But* we're coming here in good faith and telling you that we have found discrepancies and that you should investigate," Alice said.

"And you have proof that these properties in Sweden do not exist?" the chief inspector asked.

"That needs to be investigated by you; we have done our investigation and have not found these properties," Alice said.

"So we have at least that against Barrett," the chief inspector said, and then, as if coming to a decision, he stood up and put the USB drive Alice had given him in his front jeans pocket. "I'm going to take this, and we're going to investigate and fast. No one talks about this to anyone. You continue as if it's business as usual. We don't want Ravn, Barrett, or anyone else to find out that we're investigating. Got it?"

They all nodded.

"Looks like you walked into a solid cluster fuck," the chief inspector added, looking at Harry.

"Like you wouldn't believe," Harry said, and stood up. He shook hands with the chief inspector, and Alice's assistant, who was in the meeting with them taking notes, walked him out.

Once the inspector left, Lucky, Harry, and Alice collapsed into their chairs in the HS main conference room, which overlooked the impressive Amalienborg.

Lucky, who hadn't said a word the whole time during the meeting, asked the inevitable question, "What happens next?"

"I am meeting Penny Barrett at Café Victor at one, in about fifteen minutes," Harry said.

"What?" Lucky asked shocked.

"I'm going to give her a heads-up," Harry said, and before any-one could speak, he held his right hand up to silence them. "She isn't involved, and we all know this."

"But she might tell Ravn," Lucky protested, and looked at the law-yer in the room.

"Legally, as long as you don't talk details, you're okay. You can tell her that she should maybe get divorced or that she needs to distance herself from her husband but nothing about Ravn. Don't go there," Alice said.

"That woman shouldn't get caught up in the mess her cousin and husband have made," Harry said.

Alice shook her head. "In any case, we don't have much on Ravn. He could easily skate and let Barrett and Mejby take the hit. It's impor-tant he doesn't know. We'll let the police figure it all out."

"Penny doesn't seem the type who would try to save her cousin's neck over hers," Harry said.

❖   ❖   ❖

Lucky followed Harry as he left the room and pulled him into an empty office.

"You don't owe Penny anything," Lucky said.

"It's the right thing to do, Lucky," Harry said. "And you know it."

"What's up with you?" Lucky asked, frustrated.

"What do you mean?"

"When did you start giving a shit about what the right thing to do is?" he demanded.

Harry's eyebrows furrowed. Was this the kind of man he was, the kind that wasn't supposed to give a shit about the right thing? Where had he veered so off track that he had become such a man, that his closest friend thought him to be such a man?

Lucky breathed deeply. "I'm booking our tickets for California for the end of next week," he said.

Harry shook his head. "You go ahead and book your ticket; I'm not sure about Sanya and me," he said, and knew this would surprise Lucky.

"What do you mean?"

"Sanya likes it here. I like it here," Harry said. "Maybe we'll stay. Go on vacation. Will you give J Yu and Tara a report about this meeting?"

"Vacation? You?"

"Yeah, Lucky, I'm thinking that I need to start living my life," Harry said.

Lucky looked even more perplexed, but Harry didn't know how to explain what was happening to him. Harry was starting to see things clearly. For the first time the fog had lifted, and all it had taken was losing Sanya. Oh, she hadn't left him or anything as dramatic, but emotionally she had checked out of their marriage, and he couldn't blame her. He hadn't checked into their marriage, and they'd been married for over two decades, so he didn't have any moral ground to stand on and question her burgeoning attraction to Ravn.

Of course he knew.

She was changing right in front of his eyes. She was altering her personality. She was always the tough one. The strong one. The one who smiled through adversity. She could juggle Sara and work and him. Sanya was a superwoman.

She had raised a kickass daughter, and he was man enough to admit that Sanya had done the raising; he had written the checks. Sanya always said that her child's accomplishments were not hers, but her child's failures would be Sanya's. He didn't believe in that bullshit, because his successes were his and his failures were his and had nothing to do with his parents. Sanya had been the model wife. He had never had any complaints. No nagging. No "where are you?" No "you work all the time." None of the bullshit that his friends faced with their wives. He hadn't had to change his lifestyle at all after he got married or after they had Sara. And what had Sanya gotten in return?

Now, after years of ignoring his wife, his wife didn't give a shit if he ignored her or not. Harry hoped it wasn't too late to save his marriage and maybe in the process even save himself.

Chapter 33

And Then She Falls Off the Mountain

Sanya had never before lain down on the couch when she met with Arthur. She always sat on the couch. She sat cross-legged, Indian style, and put a cushion on her lap when she spoke with him. But this time she felt she needed to lie down, change her perspective.

"I had a dream. It was cold, winter, and snowy," she said to Arthur, looking at the ceiling, which was typical of old Copenhagen apartments, decorated with intricate molding. "I was on top of a mountain and I slipped. I struggled, grasping to hold on to something, and then suddenly I decided to not. I let myself fall. I closed my eyes and thought of Sara and whispered, 'I love you,' and then I opened my eyes, in the dream I mean. If I was going to fall, then I was going to be relaxed about it and enjoy it, I told myself. The snow that was falling changed into little white flowers, and then as I reached the ground . . . the dream shifted and I can't remember anything after that."

She turned to look at Arthur, who smiled his little smile. "And why is this dream more important than any other you've had?"

"It just is," she said. "I let go. I never let go. But I did and I decided to fall. Do we die in real life if we die in our dreams?"

"No," Arthur said.

"But they say that if you dream you've died, like this, like you fell down and died, then your brain thinks you died and you're dead, *finito*," Sanya said.

"No, that doesn't happen," Arthur said. "You're dodging the real issue. So let's get back to the importance of the dream."

"Do dreams say what's happening in our heads even though we don't know clearly what's happening?" she asked.

"Yes and no," Arthur said. "Dreams don't have significance as popular myth says they do. So if you have a snake dream, it doesn't mean you have a nasty aunt or whatever it's supposed to indicate. But this dream that you had, it seems symbolic to you."

She sat up. This lying-on-the-couch business wasn't working.

"You've definitely had an eventful few days. First, you meet this boy, Asgar, and tell him about your nervous breakdown. Second, you unravel the mystery your husband's company has not been able to solve, and you confirm that Ravn is a crook, and third, you had this dream that you feel is a sign," Arthur said.

Sanya nodded.

"You appear to be very restless," Arthur said.

"I'm meeting *him* today," she said. "I'm going to meet him at a café. And I think my falling off the mountain means that I want to have sex with Ravn."

Arthur nodded. "But you're evading the bigger moral question. What will you do with the information you have about Ravn's illegal dealings?"

"I know what I have to do, but that doesn't mean I *want* to do it," Sanya said. "What do you think I should do?"

"I can't tell you what to do," Arthur said. "That's not what we're here for."

"So you don't recommend that I jump off the mountain?" she asked.

"I want you to make an educated and intelligent decision. After that, if you want to jump off the mountain or hump it, that's up to you," Arthur said.

She knew what she had to do. She was *maybe* in love with Ravn, but it didn't change what needed to be done. Old Sanya would have smoothed it over with rationalizations. New Sanya left Arthur's office and called Anette Sørensen, the journalist with *Børsen* who was investigating Mark Barrett, and asked to meet her for coffee at Café Victor, an hour before she was to meet Ravn there.

She had decided to jump off the mountain.

Chapter 34

A Penny for Your Thoughts

Harry had to give Penny credit. She didn't miss a beat. She just sipped her champagne and popped a plump tomato from the chef's salad she had ordered into her mouth.

She should've looked ridiculous with that bandage on her nose, her sprained wrist in a cast, but she still managed to carry herself with grace. You could take the model off the catwalk, but you couldn't take the walk away.

They were sitting outside at Café Victor because it was nearly eighty degrees, a veritable summer day in Denmark.

"You need to talk to the police before Mark is arrested," Harry said. "Make a deal. Protect yourself."

Penny took a deep breath and then looked at Harry speculatively. "Why are you telling me this?"

"You mean why am I helping you?" Harry asked, and when Penny nodded, he smiled. "Because I want to do the right thing. You knew nothing about any of this."

"How do you know?"

"Because you were ready to sleep with me to get information. Ravn's wife and you have been interrogating my wife to get information. Obviously you know nothing," Harry said.

Penny nodded again. "I expect this kind of shit from Mark, because he's a goddamn weasel. But Ravn, now that I didn't expect. He was always the righteous one. The good one. When we went to the south of France on holiday as a family and the parents would stay in the house and drink themselves silly and the cousins would head to Cannes to party, Ravn would be the designated driver. He'd drink sparkling water all night so that he could drive us all safely home. It was always my brother and me, two brothers who were family friends, and another cousin of ours who now lives in San Francisco. We all looked up to Ravn. He wasn't the oldest, just the wisest. We all leaned on him. When Ellie, our cousin in San Francisco, was going through her divorce and needed money, she didn't call her parents, she called Ravn. We all have always relied on Ravn. He's the rock."

"Maybe that pressure of being everyone's rock forced him into this," Harry suggested.

Harry understood Ravn's dilemma. Everyone was always counting on him. He had to make it work. He had to succeed because failure wasn't an option.

"But Ravn has family money, Harry," Penny said, and then shrugged. "Maybe it's all gone. Maybe there really wasn't much, and Ravn made the money. We should've known. I should've known. Last year, Ravn asked my brother, Peter, to get his money out of IT Foundry, right around the time that Mark leased those Swedish properties out. I didn't know he leased them to Ravn. I didn't know they didn't exist. Peter was pissed. He felt that Ravn was screwing him."

"Maybe Ravn knew that Peter needed to be protected, and Mark, well, maybe Mark was a casualty he could afford," Harry said.

"You and he are very alike," Penny said. "Down to how attracted you both are to your wife."

Harry didn't let her bait him. "My wife wouldn't be interested in a man like Ravn. She has high integrity."

Penny smiled. "It's the scar that gets the girls. He used to tell tall tales about it. Sharks, fights, whatnot. What did he tell your wife?"

"I don't know," Harry said. "Maybe it never came up."

"Oh, it always comes up," Penny said. "He got it when he was a kid. He fell into a well at our family farm. But it's so boring that I think he tells the big stories to get attention. After all, even big bad successful Ravn is insecure."

Aren't we all, sweetheart, Harry wanted to say. *All us big bad successful men are driven because we're insecure fools. We're always waiting to be found out. We're waiting for the world to see that we're frauds, and Ravn's time is up.* Even though he hated the man's guts, Harry felt Ravn's colossal embarrassment, the burn inside when the real Ravn was revealed.

"I'm nothing like your cousin," Harry said.

Penny dropped her fork on her salad plate. She gave up the pretense of eating. "Whatever helps you sleep at night is fine by me. I do appreciate your telling me, though. I didn't expect you to be this nice."

Harry opened his wallet and dropped a few hundred kroner on the table and pulled out a business card.

"You should have your lawyer contact Chief Inspector Hans Møller immediately," Harry said.

"And I shouldn't tell him you talked to me?" Penny asked.

Harry shrugged. "Say what you like. Hans Møller can't charge me with a crime. I met with a friend and advised her that she should extricate herself from a situation that she had discussed with me in the past, the situation being her marriage. I haven't told you anything else."

"Doing the right thing but carefully?"

"I'm a good man—rather, I want to be a good man, Penny, but that doesn't mean I should take leave of my senses," Harry said. "If you don't mind, I have a conference call."

"Of course," Penny said and watched Harry leave.

Chapter 35

Penny Deals In

Penny sat still for a moment, not sure what to do.

She called her lawyer first and asked him to contact this chief inspector. She needed to make a deal. Both Mark and she couldn't end up in prison. Who'd take care of the girls? Mandy? She was going to be a basket case once Ravn was arrested. Even though Harry hadn't said the words, Penny knew. She hadn't taken leave of her senses, either.

She felt sorry for Mandy. What would poor Mandy do? And Katrine? And Jonas? She felt a pang of fear for her niece and nephew. They were good kids. Jonas was a lot like Mandy, a little calculating but in general not so bright. Katrine was all Ravn. She talked like him and she thought like him. Katrine would be devastated. Her father was her hero. Her superman and now the hero would fall.

Penny played with her iPhone and looked up her favorites in the contact list. Before she could put her finger on Anders Ravn's name, she put the phone down. Should she? Shouldn't she? Ravn had always been there for her. He had held her hand through every shitty situation that had come her way. And there had been a few. The time she was arrested in Bulgaria with cocaine, he and Mandy had come running and had not lifted an accusatory finger, but managed with money and a local lawyer to get her out and get her record cleaned up.

She couldn't call him. No. That could get her into trouble with the police, who could and would check phone records. So what could she do?

She looked at the napkin on her lap and pulled out a pen from her white Valentino bag. She wrote carefully on the napkin: *They know about Mark and you. Take care of yourself.*

She didn't ask for the check, knowing that the money Harry had left would cover their meal and tip with some to spare. She walked down the street, past the Louis Vuitton store and then the Burberry store, past Magasin and came to Kongens Nytorv.

And then, just to be sure, because she worried someone might be following her, she went back and entered Magasin and became part of the crowd. She sprayed some perfume on her wrist as if trying it out and then walked through the lingerie department to the exit. She was being silly, she realized. No one was following her. She wasn't relevant enough.

Penny came out of the department store and then walked down Gammel Mønt, the street with the posh shops and the IT Foundry offices. She would have to be careful so no one saw her.

She went into the underground car park, balancing carefully in her Stuart Weitzman sandals. The parking garage was packed with cars but no people.

She spotted Ravn's Audi A8 by the elevators. She folded the napkin and put it in his windshield. And then she all but ran out of the parking garage as gracefully as her sandals with five-inch heels would let her. Once out on the street, she cut to Pistolstræde and started to breathe again.

❖ ❖ ❖

Penny had never paid much attention to Politigården, the police headquarters, which was also known as the Yard. It was close to Hovedbanegården, the main train station. It was an impressive building.

"Neoclassical style, I think," she said to Leo Vestergård, her lawyer, trying to keep an air of indifference when she came to the building with him the day after she had met with Harry.

"Excuse me?" Leo said. He was one of those pretty-boy lawyers from one of the top law firms in Copenhagen, Lexsos. Penny had been assured by her divorce lawyer, whose services she had acquired after speaking with Harry and who was from the same firm, that Leo Vestergård was a badass lawyer with a reputation of managing "situations such as these" with ease.

"I was talking about the architecture of the building," Penny said.

Leo stopped walking through the main corridor they had entered before getting to the reception desk, where they would have to leave everything electronic and go through a security gate.

"Mrs. Barrett, I know you're nervous. But there isn't any need. We're not the criminal parties. You're here of your own volition," he said.

Penny eyed the blond, blue-eyed man carefully. Ah, that chiseled mouth. He was probably a tiger in bed, or maybe he was the selfish type; the pretty ones usually were. It was the ugly ones who tried hard because they knew they had to.

"I'm not nervous," Penny said. "I'm anxious. There is a difference."

She spoke authentically and with strength, and she could see that she had changed Leo Vestergård's opinion of her, from a fashion floozy to a woman of substance.

Chief Inspector Hans Møller asked them if they wanted coffee or anything else to drink, and even before they could decline, he said, "Okay then, let's get started and get this show on the road."

Penny's hands were trembling, and she was afraid, not just for herself but for her kids, for Mandy and Ravn and their children. Her family was unraveling. Everything was falling apart. This beautiful life they had built, this high-society living was all coming to an end. Would people still buy her clothes after all this?

The chief inspector appreciated that Penny wanted to get in front of this and assured her that she was not under investigation.

Leo whispered to Penny then, "Are you ready?"

Penny nodded. During their prep meeting at Leo's office, Penny had given Leo everything she had found when she went snooping after her conversation with Harry and found that Mark's underwear drawer had a false bottom. She discovered everything she needed there: the real estate deeds to the Swedish properties that didn't exist; the papers about the shell corporation Lala; and the papers that Lala had rented the nonexistent properties to another corporation, Cirque Fernando.

She had checked and Ravn was in the clear, but not Mark. It was obvious he had made up the real estate deeds and whitewashed them through Lala. She hoped that Ravn was smart enough to not be connected to Lala, the shell corporation Mark had set up, because that would be proof he knew the real estate properties didn't exist.

"My client is showing her goodwill, and we're prepared to hand over everything, but we need to ensure that she has immunity," Leo said.

"What does she have?" the chief inspector asked.

"We would like to speak with a state's prosecutor," Leo said.

The chief inspector seemed to know this was where the conversation would go and stepped out of his office and had a muffled conversation with a secretary and came back in.

It took all of three hours. Just three hours, Penny thought, to sell out her husband. Three hours to save her and her children's lives.

Penny got her deal. Immunity.

She signed papers and nodded like a robot throughout the process. She held her face strong as she had during a modeling shoot a million years ago in Provence. It was dusk, and the photo shoot was at some uppity villa by a pool. She was being bitten by mosquitoes while she maintained her pose of pouting sexiness in a bikini. After the shoot she needed to put calamine lotion all over her body, which was puffy and red with mosquito bites. They had bitten her everywhere, even her face. But the pictures for H&M, which were in all the major magazines, had been flawless.

"Good job," Leo said when they both were seated in his Audi TT, driving away from Polititorvet, where they had parked, and past the Tivoli Gardens on H. C. Andersens Boulevard.

Penny put her face in her hands and burst into tears.

Chapter 36

Kidnapped

Her meeting with Anette Sørensen didn't take very long, even though it was fruitful for Anette, who gave Sanya a hug and told her how grateful she was before she left.

Sanya waited for Ravn with a glass of champagne under the green awning on the patio of Café Victor with other patrons who were enjoying the summer. She paid for the champagne right after she ordered it, as instructed by Ravn in one of the many text messages he had been sending her for the past hour.

Tell no one. You have to promise to tell no one.

And when she promised, he responded, like a schoolboy who was wet behind his ears and in love, in that incandescent way that only a schoolboy can have.

I can't wait. I just can't.

And then there was the message that brought tears to her eyes. Not out of pain or fear or even excitement but in response to his passion, like she was some ingénue who was going to be deflowered by her very first lover. It didn't help that she had already betrayed him.

Sometimes I think about you in the middle of the day, and that is the hardest because I have to get through the rest of the day without you. Because at night, I can close my eyes and pretend that you're mine.

We'll run like the wind. It'll take us far. Will you come?

She typed as her breath caught in her throat, **Yes.**

Yes, damn it. This was it. This was the passion that she'd been missing her entire life. This was what she didn't have with Harry. It was all so sensible. So damned proper, and she didn't want proper. She wanted sex against the wall. She wanted passion, the kind you see in the movies, like Dennis Quaid and Ellen Barkin have in *The Big Easy*, which she bumped into the other night while cable trawling.

She wanted fire. She wanted the opposite of security. She wanted spontaneity. She wanted adventure. She wanted to have a story to tell her grandchildren.

When Grandma was old, like in her forties, she left Granddad and ran away with a pirate, she would say.

And little whoever would ask, *Did the pirate have a false eye?*

No, but he had the deadliest and meanest scar on his cheek.

Her wholesome grandchild would grin with glee and say, *Wicked.*

❖ ❖ ❖

In between text messages from Ravn there was one from Harry. Sanya didn't even look at it. She didn't have the courage.

She was betraying Harry, and she had already betrayed Ravn. There was a good chance, Sanya thought, that by the end of this she'd have no man in her life. And . . . that would be okay as well, she thought.

Alec said that loyalty was all about opportunity, and the only reason people were loyal to their spouses was that they hadn't had the opportunity to cheat on them. Because if, say, Scarlett Johansson took her clothes off and said, *Take me*, there weren't a lot of red-blooded men who would say, *No, please put your clothes on. I'm married and I don't care how great your pussy looks. I won't eat it.*

Had she simply not had the opportunity? Arthur didn't think so. He thought that she never paid attention. That she never looked at the men who looked at her. That had changed, because New Sanya was paying attention.

Ravn didn't pick her up in his Audi but in a black Ford S-Max. She almost didn't notice it. But then he honked, and she looked up at him.

"Get in," he said, and he had the most unholy look in his eyes, and if he had a diamond on a tooth, it would've glinted.

Sanya got into the car.

"Hi," she said, and gave him a brilliant smile. "Where are we going?"

"Is that your cell phone?" Ravn asked, and when she nodded he asked her to give it to him. And when she did, he threw the phone out of the window.

"What was that about?" she asked, shocked as he revved the engine.

"I'm kidnapping you," he said.

Sanya then looked out of the windshield and saw J Yu on his bicycle; he saw Ravn and her in the car and had a bewildered look on his face. He screamed something to Sanya, but she couldn't hear him over the din of traffic. The next thing she knew, Ravn was driving fast, making another bicyclist veer off and bang into J Yu, who was focused on them and not the road. As they sped away, violating several traffic laws, Sanya turned to see J Yu on the road next to Café Victor. She couldn't make out if J Yu was hurt, and just as she was about ask Ravn to stop, she saw J Yu stand up and pull out his cell phone.

"Are you *really* kidnapping me?" she asked, because things like this didn't happen in *real* life.

"Yes."

"What's the ransom?"

"Your husband destroys all the proof he has against me," Ravn said.

She looked at Ravn and then out the window, wondering how Ravn would feel when she told him what she had done. They were hitting the motorway now, and he was starting to do 150 kilometers an hour in a 130 zone. But what was a speeding ticket under the circumstances?

"What if he doesn't pay up?" she asked.

Ravn smiled. "Then I'll have you all to myself. But don't worry; he'll pay up. A man like Harry needs his wife."

"And you know this because you need yours?" she demanded, irritated that Ravn thought of her as Harry's wife and not just her.

"Harry and I are not alike, Sanya," Ravn said. "I'm not him."

"What does that mean?"

"I want to be here with you; I don't need to be here with you," he said.

"Am I free to leave right now?" she asked. She wasn't taking this kidnapping seriously, and she wondered why he had set this up the way he had.

"No, I'm afraid not," he said.

"Where are we going?"

"Somewhere incredibly beautiful," Ravn said.

And then she started to suspect what he was up to and smiled at him. She was hardly kidnapped, and she was already a victim of Stockholm syndrome. Pathetic!

"Maybe we'll have some time together until he comes and gets you," Ravn said softly.

"Ah . . . did you take me by force, so to speak, so that I could be relieved of the blame of running away with you?" Sanya asked. It was almost sweet. He wanted her to have an excuse for being with him. He made her. She didn't have a choice. It was gallant.

Ravn grinned but didn't respond.

"He won't come; the police might," Sanya said. Harry was no knight in shining armor. He wasn't going to *save* her. He was going to call the cops and be sensible about the whole thing.

"We'll deal with that when it happens. Why don't you take a nap, and in a few hours I'll bring you to paradise," he said.

"I'm too excited to sleep," Sanya said, and curled her legs under her on the seat. "So, you're a criminal?"

"Yes," Ravn said without hesitation. "I've always been. This time it got a bit out of hand, but if your husband would just keep his mouth shut . . ."

"Maybe he already called the police," Sanya suggested.

"He did," Ravn said, and his eyes lightened with mischief, like this was a game. "Penny warned me."

Sanya laid her head on the leather headrest and closed her eyes. "Here we are. The kidnapper and the kidnapped. Two barren humans in the middle of a desert, looking at a chimera." She opened her eyes and asked, "How's your wife going to feel about this?"

"One thing has nothing to do with another," Ravn said aggressively. "My wife has nothing to do with how I feel about you. I'm madly in love with you. I think about you and I feel drunk, like I've been sipping Scotch all day, fine, fine Scotch so that the drunk is elegant and refined, and it doesn't give you a hangover but this delicious feeling of freedom."

She closed her eyes again. She was in a movie. A romance film by Nicholas Sparks with a sappy title. Or maybe she was in a tragedy. No, she knew where she was; she was in a dark comedy. She stood at the precipice, and there was a crowd around her, egging her on.

JUMP. JUMP. JUMP. They all screamed. *Do it now. Do it already.*

And she had definitely taken the leap—all the way from a very tall mountain.

"I don't want to be kidnapped," Sanya said. "I would've come with you if you'd asked."

He shifted his right hand from the gearshift and put it on Sanya's left. "I'm not Harry. I'd never let you implode if you were mine."

"This is important to you, isn't it, this ownership business, this mine and yours and Mandy's and Harry's?" Sanya said, holding his hand in hers, letting her fingers run through bumps and creases. "This makes a difference to you. This is what stimulates your hair follicles and gets you up in the morning, this sense of ownership."

Ravn didn't reply. As he drove, they stayed quiet, holding hands. After an hour or so Ravn took an exit and drove into a gas station. He parked under a tree, a little away from the gas station building. Sanya could see people milling around, walking to the kiosk in the gas station, buying gas, getting coffee, getting on with life.

"Do you need the bathroom?" Ravn asked.

Sanya shook her head. She could escape, she thought. If this was a real kidnapping, she could escape, run away, but run away from what, and run away from whom? She could run away from Ravn, but she'd have to deal with her inner psyche sooner or later.

"I want a Mars bar," she said suddenly, because she saw a child at a distance bite into one, and the memory of the taste of the gooey caramel exploded inside her mouth.

"And . . . ?"

"Coffee, a latte," she said.

"I'll be right back," Ravn said.

He didn't say, *Don't go anywhere* or *Don't leave*. He just left, as if confident that she wouldn't leave. He hadn't even locked the car doors. She could walk away. No harm, no foul.

But she couldn't go, not until she saw this through. Also, she had to tell him what she had done. And now there was another enchanting morsel of life to investigate: Would Harry actually come and rescue her? Not that she needed rescuing.

Ravn came back with a Mars bar, a latte, and a bottle of Dansk Kildevand *uden brus*, Danish springwater without bubbles.

"We have to change cars," he said, and put his arm on her elbow and led her to the gas station parking lot.

"Are we getting a better car?" Sanya asked.

"Of course," he said.

It was an old black beautifully maintained Mercedes convertible parked at the far end of the parking lot. The tan leather seats inside were immaculate and looked delightfully comfortable.

"Yours?"

Ravn shook his head. "I'm borrowing from a friend."

"Does he know?"

"Know what?"

"Your friend, does he know that you're borrowing his car?" she asked.

Ravn handed her the Mars bar and latte and ushered her into the car.

As they drove with the top down, the wind in her hair, Sanya ate the Mars bar greedily, washing it down with the gas station latte.

"This is the best kidnapping ever," she said to Ravn.

Chapter 37

Off the Mark

"You've lost your mind," Mandy said to Penny. "You're in shock because of Mark."

The day after Penny had that horrible meeting with Chief Inspector Hans Møller, both Mark and Ravn went missing. Mark never returned from Switzerland, and now Penny knew he never would. Ravn didn't come home the previous night, and his cell phone was going directly to voice mail.

"Sometimes he just takes off; you know how moody he is," Mandy said as she poured tea in her white-and-blue Royal Copenhagen cup with shaking hands. The teapot was also Royal Copenhagen. Everything in her house was Royal Copenhagen, Mandy thought bitterly, Royal Copenhagen and Georg Jensen and Erik Bagger and . . . all Danish design. She had done this. She had made this Danish home. And now her house of Danish cards was falling apart.

She sipped the soothing green tea, which unfortunately couldn't soothe her nerves.

"I got a call from Harry Kessler, Mandy. Ravn has apparently *kidnapped* that Indian wife of his," Penny said.

"That's absurd," Mandy said. "Your husband is a crook who has taken off with your nanny; that doesn't mean my husband ran away with that drab fashion victim."

Penny looked at her empty teacup, which stood on the large granite kitchen counter next to the teapot with green tea, as if wondering what to do with it.

"Screw it," she said. She marched to the liquor cabinet, pulled out a bottle of Lagavulin, and poured a good measure of it into her cup.

She took a sip and sighed.

Mandy looked at her Chopard wristwatch pointedly. It was nine in the morning. But it was not a usual morning. Whiskey was made for mornings like this. She emptied her cup of its contents into the sink and poured whiskey into it instead.

"Skål," she said to Penny. They raised their cups. "To husbands," they said, and downed the whiskey.

"So Mark was having an affair with the nanny?" Mandy asked, as she, with a more steady hand than before, poured more whiskey into their teacups.

Penny raised her shoulders and let them drop. "His note said that he was in *love* with Jinny and that he would be somewhere in the Philippines. He loves the girls, but he wasn't going to go to prison. And he added that Ravn is a corrupt asshole who should burn in hell."

"I'm sorry," Mandy said.

"The son of a bitch cleaned out some of our accounts. The joint ones," Penny said. "Months ago. This was not a dash for freedom. He was planning this for months. And here I was feeling guilty about divorcing him and handing him over to the police."

"Are you short of money?" Mandy asked, and then bit her lower lip. "Am I going to soon be short of money?"

"I don't know. Ravn told Harry that if he wants his wife back, he needs to destroy all the evidence he has against him, which means the only evidence the police will have is what I gave them, and that's against

262

Mark. I have no idea what Harry has," Penny said. "And if Harry agrees, Ravn might go free."

"Will he?"

"I don't know," Penny said.

"And what will Ravn do if Harry doesn't agree? Kill his wife?" Mandy demanded. "What the . . . ?"

Mandy's words were already slurred. She wasn't used to drinking hard liquor in the morning.

"He's not going to kill Harry's wife, Mandy," Penny said, as simply as she could.

"Then what's he going to do to her that's going to make Harry listen to him?" Mandy demanded and then blinked. "No. No. No. She's so plain. She's so . . . weird."

Penny drank more whiskey from her teacup.

"Oh my god . . . it's been there all along, hasn't it," Mandy said. "I knew something was going on, but I didn't think it was *her*. She dresses like a bag lady. And she told us she doesn't even get waxed down there."

"I don't think Ravn gives a shit about that," Penny said.

"Oh, he certainly cares about waxing. I can attest to that. So, he's in love with her what . . . her mind?" Mandy demanded aggressively. She was now on her third teacup of whiskey.

"You should stop drinking," Penny suggested, and then sighed. "Fuck it! You know what, if anyone deserves to get drunk this morning, it's you and me. Two women on the brink of a nervous breakdown thanks to our thieving, cheating husbands. It's pitiful."

"Do the police know about the kidnapping?" Mandy asked. She slurred on the word *kidnapping*.

Penny, who knew how to drink and would not be slurring anytime soon, shook her head. "Harry said that Ravn had specifically told him not to tell anyone. He called me . . . because . . . well, he did me a favor and he hoped I'd do him one."

Mandy sat down on one of the barstools by the kitchen counter. "I feel like saying, *What will I tell the children?* It's such a goddamned cliché, you know? They say it in the movies all the time. But, Penny, *what will I tell the children?*"

"I don't have to tell mine anything. Apparently Jinny and Mark talked to the girls before they ran away—the girls told me. They're going to some beach in the Philippines for Christmas next year. But I don't think that will be possible; the statute of limitations for his kind of white-collar crime is five years—I checked," Penny said. "I told you, I saw some expensive lingerie in Jinny's room and . . . I should've put two and two together."

"You never suspected?" Mandy asked, even though she remembered having done exactly that. She wished she had said something to Penny.

Penny shook her head. "Mark has an okay dick. And now he's even lost his looks. He's got the potbelly, the balding head . . ."

"Ravn has a *big* dick," Mandy said, and held her hands an arm's length apart. "*Huge.* When I first gave him a blow job, my jaws hurt the next day."

Penny stared at Mandy in disbelief. "Did you just say that?"

"Why? Am I not allowed to say things like this?" Mandy asked belligerently.

"Hey, feel free. I'm not one to take offense," Penny said.

"Lately, we've still been having sex once a week as we always have, but it's lost that . . . loving feeling," Mandy said.

"You have sex once a week?" Penny asked.

"He's busy . . . swindling money apparently, so we have to schedule," Mandy said. "Plenty of people schedule. You can't judge. Your husband was sleeping with your nanny. Talk about a cliché."

"And he ran away and took all our money," Penny said. "Well, as much as he could, so I can still keep the house, but the cars might have to go. I actually have no idea what my finances look like. My accountant has been calling, but I told him I was busy having a nervous breakdown and we would have to talk some other time."

They decided then that the barstools at the kitchen counter were not comfortable and went into the sunroom, where Mandy plopped onto an extra-soft beige sofa with her teacup and bottle of Lagavulin.

Penny sank into a couch across from her.

"I never gave Mark a blow job," Penny said.

"Never, ever?" Mandy asked.

Penny shook her head. "I can't have a man cum in my mouth."

"It's Ravn's favorite thing," Mandy said. "But now I have practice. My jaw doesn't hurt so much." And then she giggled. "All my life I've told myself that sex between Ravn and me was sensational, but you know what—it's really not. Can I tell you a *secret*, Penny?"

"Sure," Penny said.

"The best sex I ever had was with . . . remember Vladimir Markencho?" Mandy asked.

Penny shook her head.

"He was a violinist. The Russian ambassador then . . . forget his name . . . Ivan something or the other, he introduced us to him. One look, *just* one look, and I felt things that I'd never felt before," Mandy said.

Penny gaped at her. "Not even in my wildest imagination where I'm married to George Clooney and winning an Oscar at the same time could I have thought that you would've cheated on Ravn. *Bravo!*"

"Do you remember him?"

"The violinist?" Penny shrugged. "I think so. Big guy with big hands. There was this quietness about him, or was that someone else? This was almost . . . what five, six years ago?" When Mandy nodded, she said, "Wow! That long ago, and yet so very recent."

"I had sex with him in the Russian ambassador's coat closet—the first time," Mandy said. "He made me come with his mouth. I didn't even know that was possible. Ravn just sort of does things down there, but he never makes me come. Vlad played my pussy like a violin. Why are you looking at me like that? Shocked, are you?"

"I don't know, I use words like *pussy*, but coming from you it sounds dirtier, like Miss Manners is sitting with her legs uncrossed," Penny said.

"Oh, my legs were uncrossed for sure. He leaned me over someone's fur—beautiful, beautiful fox—anyway, he leaned me over and took me from behind," Mandy said, the fingers of her right hand sliding down between her breasts.

"I came back to the party with his semen between my legs," Mandy said. "It was intoxicating. Drinking champagne and eating caviar and all the while being wet from Vlad. He watched me when he played the violin. I saw him a couple more times at Hotel d'Angleterre where he was staying. The sex was still good, but it wasn't the same. It wasn't the same as holding his semen in between my legs while I held Ravn's hand and had Vlad watch me as he played the violin. I orgasmed with Vlad that day on top of that fox fur like I never had before. It was explosive. Ravn has a big dick, but you know what? He's never fucked me over fox fur."

"Maybe when he comes back home, it could be one of the things you ask of him," Penny suggested.

"If he comes back and he wants back into the marriage, he's got to stop sleeping with other women," Mandy said. "He's had oh so many affairs."

"You knew?" Penny asked.

Mandy made a face. "Please. I know the blond hair makes it hard to believe, but I do have a ticking brain underneath the golden tresses."

"Ravn thought he was being careful," Penny said.

"So you knew?"

Penny shrugged. "He's blood."

"And I'm not a real blonde, anyway," Mandy said wearily. "He *was* careful. He did it all rather professionally, I must say. Not a word out of place. Not a . . . nothing. But I knew."

"Well, they do say the wife always knows. I didn't," Penny said. "I can't believe Mark ran away. I told that odious chief inspector, and he said that there wasn't much they could do and it would have to be handled diplomatically. So Mark is going to live it up with Jinny somewhere in Southeast Asia . . . *with my money.*"

Katrine came into the sunroom when the bottle was empty and Penny and Mandy lay on the couch, talking about love lost.

"Oh, darling," Mandy said. "How lovely to see you. Is your brother with you? We have important . . . fam . . . family stuff to discuss."

Mandy stood up, her body swaying, the world swimming around her.

"Have you both been drinking?" Katrine asked as she steadied her mother with hands on her shoulders.

"Yes," Penny said. "I'm afraid that between our husbands we had no choice but to finish that lovely bottle of Lagavulin."

"It *was* lovely. Aged how many years? Sixteen?" Mandy wondered, shrugging away Katrine to pick up the bottle and look keenly at it to spot the number of years it had been aged. She set the bottle down with a thud on the coffee table. "Doesn't matter how aged the whiskey was. It's all gone now. So, go get Jonas and we can have a family meeting."

"Jonas is not in Denmark, Mom. You know that, right?" Katrine asked.

"Where is he?"

"Traveling. Last I heard, the Philippines," Katrine said.

"The Philippines?" Mandy repeated and then squealed. "Maybe he can say hello to Mark and Minnie."

"Jinny," Penny said right before they both started to laugh uncontrollably. They laughed until Mandy had to rush to the guest toilet and throw up. It was a nice distraction, Mandy would think later on, a way to hold off from telling her daughter about her husband.

Chapter 38

Harry Meets an Angel

It was Penny who suggested that Harry meet Michael "Tandhjul" Øvesen. Tandhjul was Danish for "gear," and Tandhjul was the leader of the biker gang Iron Angels, a supporter of Hells Angels.

"And you think this biker can help you find Sanya?" Lucky asked while they drove to the biker bar that Tandhjul used as his office.

"Penny said that Tandhjul is his best friend and that Ravn listens to him," Harry said.

"Why am I not surprised that Ravn's best friend is a biker?" Lucky said. "How does a guy like Ravn even know a biker?"

The ambience at the biker bar was the antithesis of what Harry had expected and not hostile at all. The music was Iron Maiden, and several bikers were scattered around the bar. Some were playing pool, while others were drinking beer at the bar. There were a few bikers playing a board game. It seemed very congenial.

They went to the bar, where Harry ordered beer for both of them. "To blend in," he said to Lucky, who stared at him in bewilderment. Harry then told the bartender that he was there to meet Tandhjul.

"Also, you know that he didn't *kidnap* Sanya; she probably went with him willingly," Lucky said while they waited for Tandhjul. "This Copenhagen trip has fucked with your head. You're going cuckoo."

"I'm not losing my mind," Harry told him.

"Then maybe I'm losing mine, because if I was in full control of my faculties, would I be standing in this biker bar in my Missoni suit, holding a cheap bottle of Tuborg beer in my hand as a way to blend in?" he said. "And here you are wearing a pair of jeans and a T-shirt, which you never do, and we're here to meet a *biker*. Are you aware of how incongruous this is with the way we live our lives?"

Harry ignored him when a man came up and introduced himself as Tandhjul. Harry shook his hand, as did Lucky.

Tandhjul was a large man, not overweight, just big. This is what Thor would look like, Harry thought. He was bald but had a nice thick blond beard. He was dressed in a traditional biker outfit: jeans, boots, T-shirt, and leather vest, and looked just as badass as Harry had thought someone called Tandhjul would look.

"Ravn and I go back a long way," Tandhjul said.

His English was accented, and he had already apologized for not being articulate in the language. He had suggested German, which neither Harry nor Lucky spoke. Romanian was also not an option for them, so they settled into English.

"You say he's kidnapped your wife?" Tandhjul asked. He didn't seem surprised at all. "And what did he say he'll do with her if you don't destroy this evidence you have against him? Will he kill her?"

"Of course not," Harry said.

"Rape her?"

Harry looked aghast and then shook his head.

"Then what?"

Harry cleared his throat. "He'll . . . well, he'll take her."

"Take her where, dude?"

Harry sighed. "Look, my wife may be in love with Ravn."

Tandhjul looked at Harry in surprise. "Dude, are you here because your wife ran away with Ravn? I don't do that kind of couples counseling. Okay?"

Harry showed Tandhjul the message he had received from Ravn.

She's with me. If you want her, you need to make sure I can go back, unharmed.

Tandhjul read the message and gave Harry's phone back to him.

"This has to do with that asshole Mark Barrett, doesn't it?" Tandhjul said, and when he saw Harry's surprised expression, he sighed. "I told Ravn that Barrett was a loose cannon. But he didn't listen."

"Do you know where he would take her?" Harry asked.

Tandhjul nodded. "I have a good idea."

"I don't have any evidence to destroy; the police already have it, and in all honesty with a good lawyer he'll probably get away with it," Harry said. "I need to get my wife back."

"Why?"

"What?"

"Why do you want your wife back, dude?" Tandhjul asked.

"Because I love her," Harry said.

Tandhjul looked at Lucky. "Does he?"

Lucky sighed. "Sure."

"Are you a faggot?" Tandhjul asked him.

"I'm a homosexual," Lucky said. "And *faggot* is not a nice word to use."

"You must excuse the language. We Danes learn English from Hollywood movies, so we don't know it's not okay," Tandhjul said. "Are you seeing anyone?"

Lucky didn't respond for a long moment and then said slowly, "No."

"Hey, Raphael," Tandhjul called out to someone in the bar, "This guy is a fa . . . a homosexual and he's single."

Lucky visibly gaped at Tandhjul, and then another large man called Raphael, with a thick dark beard and a full head of long black hair, came close to him, gave him a once-over, and shook his head. "Not my type. Sorry, man. No offense."

"None taken," Lucky said wearily to Raphael's back as he walked away from him. He looked at Harry and sighed. "How has my life come to this, where a biker is rejecting me? Damn you, Harry, and damn your wife and damn that son of a bitch Anders Ravn. I'm out of here. I'll Uber."

"Uber is illegal in Denmark," Tandhjul said. "Relax, dude. Someone will drop you off wherever you need to go. And it's not personal. Raphael likes them more . . . less corporate. But he broke up with someone last month and he's still a little unhappy so . . . I thought maybe he'd take a chance."

Lucky held his hand up. "I'm not taking it personally."

"Will you help me?" Harry asked.

Tandhjul looked at him for what seemed like an eternity and then nodded.

"Can you ride a bike?" he asked.

Harry nodded.

Tandhjul threw him a keychain and then put on his leather jacket. "Pick up a helmet on your way out."

"I'll see you later," Harry said to Lucky, and handed him his car keys.

Lucky stared at the car keys and then his best friend. He looked at the beer bottle in his hand and toasted Harry with it. "Good luck."

Chapter 39
Mythical Indian Villains and Heroes

He took her to a summer house on an island off the West Coast of Denmark. It was the only summer house on the island, which wasn't very big.

They left the Mercedes in an empty parking lot. It was early, just seven o'clock, and the sun was still high and bright.

"There is a bridge on the other side, but it can't handle a car," Ravn said. "Motorbikes and bicycles only. It's too narrow."

Ravn rowed them across the water in a small rowboat. She watched him as he rowed, one oar down, another oar down, while she sat across from him, their knees touching.

"Do you know there is a Ravn in Indian mythology and he's a villain?" she told him.

"The family name refers to the bird."

"In Hindu mythology Ravn is Ravan, an extra *a*, and a bad guy, what they call an *asura*, a demon," she said.

"He sounds promising," he said, rowing steadily.

Sanya dipped a hand in the water, which was cool but not unpleasantly so.

"Once upon a time, a prince named Ram married a princess named Sita. Ram's brother Lakshman was always by his side, devoted to Ram. When they were exiled . . . there is a melodrama here with a stepmother and dying father, blah, blah, blah . . . so where was I?"

"They were exiled," Ravn offered.

"Right," she said. "They were living in a hut in a forest where a demoness called Shurpanakha saw Ram and immediately fell in lust with him. She hit on him, and he turned her down and asked her to try Lakshman, who also turned her down. And somehow one thing led to another and Lakshman cut the lady demon's ear and nose off."

Ravn paused in his rowing. They were midway between the mainland and the island. "That's a bit harsh."

"What can I say? Temper, temper," Sanya said. "So lady demon gets justifiably angry and goes to her brother."

"Ravan?"

Sanya grinned. "Yes, and he comes to take revenge. But then he sees Sita and *he* falls in lust with her. He kidnaps her and takes her to his island, Lanka."

"And does she fall in love with him?" Ravn asked.

"No, she is pious and makes a circle of honor around her so Ravan can't touch her," Sanya said. "Ram and Lakshman make some new friends, monkeys, and then come and save Sita. Of course Ravan is killed."

"Of course."

"But then comes the strange part," she said. They were getting closer to the island with the sole idyllic wooden summer house. "Ram says to Sita that he knows she's pure, but he worries people will doubt her because she's been living with Ravan for so many days. So he asks her to take a fire test. She has to walk into fire, and if she doesn't burn, she's all good, but if she does, then, well, it's all for the better."

"That's a tough crowd. I'm assuming she passes the fire test," Ravn said as they came close to the sandy beach of the island. Once they were out of the boat, he added, "If you're worried that Harry will ask you to take the fire test, let me assure you that you won't pass; you know that, right?"

"The problem is not the fire test but . . . Ravn, that evidence you're hoping Harry will destroy to get me back? He doesn't have it. *I* found out what happened. *I* connected Lala and Cirque Fernando," Sanya said.

She could see his surprise. He had not expected this. They stood on the sandy beach, and Ravn shook his head as realization struck him. "Damn Degas."

"Before you came to Café Victor today, I met with Anette Sørensen; she is . . ."

"I know who she is," Ravn said. He closed his eyes as if coming to terms with what Sanya had done, who she was.

"I gave her everything I had, and I had everything," Sanya said.

Chapter 40
Helen of Troy Maybe Had a Similar Problem

Unlike the summer house in Sweden, this one was basic. The house was just a small wooden structure with a living room, a bedroom, a kitchen, and a toilet. There was a shower outside. Next to the summer house was a small well-maintained greenhouse where chilies, tomatoes, green beans, and spinach were growing. Ravn told her that there was a gardener who took care of the greenhouse and kept the house stocked as needed.

The bedroom had a wall of glass, opening onto a wooden deck toward the waters. The porch had an old coal grill that Ravn used to cook the fish he caught in the fjord for dinner.

He hadn't railed at Sanya after she told him what she'd done; he simply said, "We'll see what happens. For now, I'm hungry and we need to eat; and so I need to fish."

They had dinner on the wooden deck, where there was a small worn wooden table and two weathered wooden chairs. There was a bench on one side, and Sanya sat there and watched Ravn cook. He told her how his grandfather had taught him to fish and that it was one of his favorite things to do alone. He made her laugh with fishing stories, and she forgot for a while that this wasn't her *real* life; this was a place away from time.

For dinner, they ate grilled sea trout with a spinach and tomato salad. They shared a bottle of Muscadet from the Loire Valley in France that Ravn said was very good with trout, and it was. And when they finished the meal and the bottle, they started on another bottle of the same wine.

The domesticity of it was not uncomfortable but surprisingly familiar. Maybe because both of them had done something of this nature with their spouses and their roles hadn't changed. Sanya didn't grill or open wine bottles, but she was excellent at setting the table and drinking the wine.

It was a romantic getaway. The conversation flowed easily between them like they were familiar lovers; the magic between them stayed alive despite her betrayal of him.

"Is there anything for dessert?" she asked as they sat and watched the sun flirt with the edge of the water. It was late now, around one in the morning, and the sun was just below the horizon, getting ready to bounce right back.

"Of course there is," Ravn said with a smile.

"And a blanket?" she asked.

"And that, too," he said.

He brought back a box of Summerbird chocolates, a chocolatier that Sanya had seen all around Copenhagen. The box was pink and wrapped with a silk ribbon. The blanket was beige and woolen. He wrapped the blanket around Sanya and set the box of chocolates on the table next to the wine.

He opened the box, and Sanya chose a chocolate that promised to be filled with Armagnac, and he chose a chocolate filled with Grand Marnier.

"You're not angry with me," she said.

"No," Ravn said. "I'm hurt that you didn't love me enough to protect me. But I'm not angry. I brought this upon myself. However, I'm still hoping to get lucky tonight."

Sanya had known, deep down, as she had played this conversation out in her head, that he would not be angry, even though a part of her refused to believe that could be possible.

"So you think we're going to have sex tonight?"

"I'm hoping," Ravn said, smiling.

"I knew you wouldn't be angry with me," Sanya said.

"Love is recognizing yourself in another," Ravn said.

Sanya smiled. How easily he had unraveled the question that had been plaguing her. *What is love to me?* Sanya had wondered. And how simple it was to recognize oneself in another. To be seen. Arthur had said that Sanya wanted Harry to see her. This is why Ravn had been so attractive, because he saw her when no one else had, because his propensity for depression was also Sanya's.

They sat in silence for a small while, drinking their wine, choosing their chocolates.

The implosion seemed like a million years ago. The old isolated system had disappeared, and the chaos was clearing now, Sanya thought. Whether she slept with Ravn or not, a new isolated system was forming, and the waves were quieting.

He stretched out his hand and Sanya put hers in his. He squeezed gently.

"I never believed in soul mates," he said.

He rose and came to kneel in front of her, not letting go of her hand. He put his head on her lap. She touched his hair, letting her fingers explore his scar.

The sun was slowly rising, painting the sky in shades of gold and orange.

"I'm scared," he said.

He didn't have to tell her what he was afraid of; she knew, because she feared the dark abyss of depression just as much as he did. And as they stood at a crossroads not sure what the future held for either of them, the risk of slipping, of falling through, was greater than ever before.

"Yes. I know. Me, too," Sanya said as she held him close.

❖   ❖   ❖

Sanya woke to the sound of motorcycle engines.

He didn't ride in on a white horse but a red-and-black Harley Davidson. Sanya didn't even know Harry knew how to ride a motorcycle.

He and Ravn's friend had come to the summer house as the sky started to turn a warm blue, bathed in the light of the risen sun. They had not taken a boat, as Sanya and Ravn had, but had taken the narrow wooden bridge to the island that was designed for pedestrians, bicycles, and motorcycles.

Sanya and Ravn had fallen asleep on the bench, wrapped in each other and the woolen blanket.

Harry's eyes flickered.

"Good morning," she said, and rose, disentangling herself from Ravn, waking him in the process.

"Good morning," Harry said, and walked toward her.

Sanya eyed the man with him.

"Tandhjul," Ravn said, getting up slowly, the blanket falling to the ground. "Sanya, this is my friend Tandhjul."

She nodded at the man, who looked like a biker, just like the ones from the movies. This was the friend who had been there for Ravn when he had attempted suicide.

"Good morning," she said to the man.

They all stood and looked at each other. They had many things to say . . . well, maybe all of them except Tandhjul.

"Let's go inside," Ravn said, making a peace offering. "I'll make us some coffee."

Tandhjul pulled out a paper bag from the saddlebag of his motorcycle. "I brought breakfast," he said. "We had to take a leak, and there was a bakery at the gas station."

Sanya looked at Tandhjul in disbelief and then at Harry, who shook his head, as if saying, *Don't ask.*

They went inside the summer house. Sanya brought the blanket along, for security. She sat on a barstool, still wrapped in the blanket, and watched Tandhjul put Danish pastries and croissants on a plate.

Harry stood next to her, saying nothing, as if preparing himself to say something but afraid of what he would say, afraid that one word out of place might make her take off.

They drank coffee. No one but Tandhjul had the stomach to eat. The morning sunlight sliced through the room.

"This man loves his wife," Tandhjul said to Ravn when he finished his *wienerbrød*, a popular Danish multilayered pastry.

"I love his wife, too," Ravn said, not insolently but matter-of-factly. "And she loves me."

Harry drew in a deep breath and looked at Sanya, who said nothing and showed no emotion.

Maybe the implosion wasn't a hundred years ago. Maybe she was going to have one again . . . now, Sanya thought. Maybe the new isolated system that had just formed was erratic, unstable, and it was going to fall apart and yet another new one had to be created.

Sanya didn't think she could handle yet another breakdown, and she willed herself to walk away from the abyss, the dark hole she knew she would have to live with for the rest of her life. So she calmly drank her coffee and waited for the storm inside to pass, for the sun to shine through and warm her insides. For the first time since that day in the meeting room when she started to cry, she felt—no, she *knew* she would be okay. She could handle this.

"I'm sorry," Harry said to her, as if Tandhjul and Ravn had not spoken.

"What are you sorry about?" Sanya asked.

"I'm sorry I slept with Tara. There were two other affairs. They lasted about three months each or so. Tara . . . that's been on and off for two years," he continued. "I'm so sorry that I wasn't there for the most part, and I get it; I get it that somewhere down the line you stopped wanting to be with me. I get that. I don't want to harp on here about history and say we've had twenty years and don't throw that away. They were not all shitty, but they weren't all great, either. So, here's what I will say to you. I love you. I know the man with the scar feels like the right thing, and who knows, if you had a chance he *might* be the right thing. But I'm a sure thing. I know I'm the right man for you."

Everyone remained silent for a long moment.

Tandhjul nodded appreciatively and clapped. "That was good, dude. That was real good. Honest and no bullshit."

Ravn looked at Sanya and smiled. She smiled back.

"I did fall in love, I think, with Ravn," she said to Harry. "But it isn't *that* kind of love. It's about recognizing yourself in another."

"Before you go into marriage counseling," Tandhjul said, "dude, the police are looking for you. I checked my Twitter feed when we bought breakfast, and *Børsen* has released a story about your connection with that asshole Mark. Didn't I tell you not to go into business with him?"

Well, Sanya thought, that solved the question about Bjarke's loyalty, as she had wondered if he'd somehow block publication of the story.

"What?" Harry asked. "How did the newspaper get the story? We went to the police but . . ." He saw Ravn look at his wife, and he turned to her. "You went to the newspaper."

Sanya nodded and then asked, "What did you go to the police with?"

"Some fact and some innuendo," Harry said. "I figured out the connection between Lala and . . . you told me he was a Degas fan.

What I don't understand is, if you say you love him, then why did you turn him in?"

"Because I have integrity," Sanya said, and then added angrily, "which is more than I can say for you." Harry was taken aback by her sudden change in mood.

"What?" Sanya demanded. "You think you can just show up and talk about how you cheated on me, and what am I going to do, forgive you?"

Harry sighed. "No. That's . . . no . . . Hey, just a minute, you spent the night here with Ravn."

"And?"

"And I'm not asking any questions," Harry said quietly, and raised his hands in defense.

"Fire test," Ravn said, and Harry glared at him.

"Like hell," Sanya said, and let go of the blanket and straightened her spine. "Harry, I kissed someone recently . . ."

Harry's eyes moved to Ravn, and his look said, *Sweetheart, I think you did a lot more than kiss.* But he didn't say it out loud.

"No, not him, another man in the city," Sanya said, shaking her head.

"Jesus, Sanya, we came to Copenhagen ten weeks ago; how many men could you have met?" Harry said.

"This was a young musician, a bass player," Sanya said. "I did it because it was fun. I'm not being provocative; I'm trying to tell you that I'm not the *old* Sanya anymore."

"I think that's pretty clear," Harry said.

"Can we go now?" Tandhjul interjected. "I think we should leave them alone to solve their problems and try to keep you out of jail."

"I'm not going to jail," Ravn said. "I'm probably going to get into some trouble."

"You're already in trouble," Tandhjul said. "I think you need to ask your lawyer to meet you at the police station."

"Or I could run away," Ravn said, his eyes gleaming with mischief. "Take Sanya with me."

Harry seemed to want to say something, a hundred things, but he watched Sanya instead.

"I'm not running away," Sanya said, and let out a laugh. "And neither are you."

"Then what are you doing?" Harry asked.

"I'm contemplating," Sanya said.

Ravn poured fresh coffee into their cups, and they all sipped silently. Tandhjul ate another Danish pastry.

"Where's Lucky?" Sanya asked.

"On his way to California," Harry said.

"And you?"

"I'm waiting for you," Harry said.

To be honest, Sanya never thought he'd come. She really had been expecting police sirens, not Harry on a hog.

"It's not good enough, Harry," Sanya said.

"I quit my job," Harry said. "I called the partners and asked them to buy me out."

That silenced Sanya. She couldn't believe it.

"Wow," Ravn said. "Even I wouldn't do that for my wife."

"Shut the fuck up, will you, Ravn?" Harry said.

"What's your plan now?" Sanya asked Harry.

"I have *no* plan."

"You've got to be kidding me," Sanya said. "Are you doing this to manipulate me?"

"Yes, absolutely," Harry said honestly. "But I'm also doing this for me, for us. You keep talking about Old Sanya and New Sanya. Well, when you changed, I changed as well. I had an implosion as well. And this is the new Harry. He wears jeans and he doesn't have a job. He may not wake up every morning at six and go for a run, and who knows, you might even catch him eating a burger and drinking a milkshake at a fast-food joint."

Sanya looked at Ravn, and he raised his hands as if in defeat.

"Sometimes soul mates don't meet at the right time," Ravn said.

"Oh, I don't believe in soul mates," Sanya said.

"Is it fair to say that you've been using me to crawl out of your depression?" Ravn asked.

"She's a nice-looking lady," Tandhjul said. "I wouldn't mind being used by her."

"I don't," Ravn said with a smile. "Tandhjul, I think you're right; it's time for us to leave. I'll call my lawyer. The Mercedes I borrowed from you is parked on the other side of the island. Maybe you can give me a ride on your motorcycle; we'll get the boat back later."

"Hey, Ravn," Sanya said as he walked to the door, picking up the car keys that he'd left on the fireplace mantel when they had come in. "Try to stay out of prison."

"Oh, don't worry, I've been doing this for years," he said, and walked out of the little cottage with a swagger that made Sanya laugh.

"This has been the weirdest morning," Tandhjul said, following him.

"Hey, Tandhjul, how much for the hog?" Harry called out.

"You want to keep it?" Tandhjul asked, surprised, and when Harry nodded, he said, "Take it. Ravn will pay for it. He owes me."

They heard the motorcycle engine start, and once the sound disappeared Harry sat down on the barstool next to Sanya's.

"I don't want to go back to California," Sanya said. "So if you want to go, you'll have to go alone."

"If you don't, then I don't," Harry said.

Sanya looked at him. "I know you don't have a plan, but I have a plan."

"Tell me," Harry said.

"I just came up with the plan . . . like now, so I don't know if it's a good plan, a solid plan," Sanya said.

"We'll figure it out," Harry said.

"Why don't you and I manage the ComIT Europe branch together, here? Instead of buying a company, why don't we build a company? ComIT can invest, and we can then slowly acquire new consultancies as needed," Sanya suggested.

Harry nodded slowly. "And you want to do this from Copenhagen?"

"Yes," Sanya said. "I love Copenhagen, even with the weird weather. People here have work-life balance. They have free health care. They pay their students to go to university. Don't get me wrong, there's also stuff that's really unpleasant here, just like anywhere else . . . but I feel at home in Copenhagen."

"I can't promise I can pull it off. But I can run it by the partners and—"

Sanya shook her head and interrupted him. "No, we'll strategize, you and I, and then we will run it by the partners together. Equal partners from now on, Harry. And we will live in separate apartments, to start out at least."

"What? Why?" Harry asked.

"Because I want space," Sanya said. "I want to be independent again, find out who Sanya is, outside of being your wife and Sara's mother. And I need time to forgive you, Harry, for cheating on me; and I need to forgive myself as well for allowing it to happen, for not paying attention. We both need to heal and grow."

"But what does it mean, Sanya, to live apart?" Harry asked. "Does it mean we'll date other people? Are we getting divorced? What does it mean?"

"Fuck if I know," Sanya said.

"Maybe we need to think this through and plan this out and . . ."

"Oh no," Sanya said, shaking her head. "No, no. No more of Harry Kessler's incessant planning and maneuvering. I don't know what this new relationship, this new system of ours will look like. But I do know that if we want to save this marriage and me, I need to figure out who I am and *you* need to figure out who this new Harry is."

Harry poured himself a cup of coffee and nodded as he drank it, as if he understood, but Sanya wasn't sure. His whole body was tense. He didn't like the idea of staying apart. He didn't understand it. Maybe she was wasting her time, Sanya thought. Maybe he'd never get it, get her, this *new* her. It wouldn't be easy to let him go, but she'd rather be alone than be lonely in a relationship like she had been before.

"You and I, we need to *date*. We need to learn to have fun together outside of raising our child or working. We need to go on vacation. I don't know, spend a weekend in Paris. *Something*. I don't want to plan our life in its entirety before living it. I want spontaneity. I want . . . no, I *need* adventure," Sanya explained.

Harry continued to nod and then slowly, as if letting what she had said sink in, he let his shoulders drop and relax.

"I'm game." And then he added, almost gleefully, "You know what? I have a hog, a spare helmet, and a fully loaded credit card. If we leave now, we could have dinner in St. Germain with a view of the Eiffel Tower. Is that spontaneous enough for you?"

Maybe, just maybe, Sanya thought as hope sparked within her, *Harry does get it.*

After all, she had never ridden on a motorcycle or gone to Paris.

AUTHOR'S NOTE & ACKNOWLEDGMENTS

I lived in Denmark for fourteen years, and in and around Copenhagen for nearly eleven of those before moving back to the United States in 2016, where I now live in Orange County. I love Copenhagen and I miss the city. I miss the food, the ambience, the outdoor café culture, my friends—I miss my life there.

This book is my love letter to Copenhagen. I have described various restaurants, cafés, museums, and bars that Copenhagen offers—but some of these may have closed or changed in the time it has taken for this book to be released from when it was written. For example, you used to be able to buy cannabis in Christiania, but that changed after a shooting incident in August 2016, and Pusher Street is now closed. In addition, I have embellished here and there for effect but without, I feel, taking away anything from the *real* location.

I have many people to thank for helping me bring this book to my readers—both in Denmark and in the United States.

Thanks to Alice Verghese for reading this book in its initial terrible draft and still encouraging me to finish it, and to Fatima Aller, because of whom I will always have a home in Copenhagen.

To my friends in Copenhagen who used to be colleagues: Annette Lindorf Thurø, Oliver Brunchmann, and Soumitra Burman—thank you for your continued friendship, which I'm convinced will last despite us living in different continents. (You should all come and visit. I have better weather.)

Thanks to Julie Timmer, Loretta Nyhan, Amy Perschini, and Jeanne Frederiksen for being early readers, and to Denise Roy and Tiffany Yates Martin for editing this book—your critique means that this book is now actually readable.

Thanks to Rayhané Sanders, who is the best agent any writer would want. I'm lucky to have her even though I feel undeserving. I have great respect and affection for Lake Union's editorial director, Danielle Marshall, who doesn't mind that I go into "neurotic writer" mode—without her support, there would be no new published Amulya Malladi books.

Love and gratitude to my husband, Søren Rasmussen, who patiently read every draft and put up with me when I didn't bathe or eat, and when I generally snarled at everyone around me during the periods of time when I wrote and edited this book (which were holidays and weekends—yes, he's a saint).

Enormous thanks to Isaiah and Tobias, my sons, for their patience and support. When they get older, they'll probably talk to their therapist about how often they heard their mother say, "I'm in the middle of a sentence" very loudly when they disturbed her while she wrote. Since art needs pathos, I feel I'm helping them to become artists. You're welcome, kids.

And last but not the least, my gratitude to Valerie Soulier, who I sometimes failed to appreciate when I had her and whom I now miss immensely.

AUTHOR Q&A

Amulya and her husband Søren have been together for twenty-two years and married for nineteen years. Amulya started to write this book when she was depressed and wanted to laugh. And as she reads everything she writes out loud to her husband, she thought it would make him laugh as well, which it did. Since this book is about depression and marriage, this Q&A is more of a conversation between Amulya and her husband.

SØREN: We've been married a long time. What do you think about our marriage?

AMULYA: It's been good. It's been bad. And it's been everything in between. It's my only marriage. I have nothing else to compare it to, either, so I can't benchmark. Overall, it's been like life—some ups and some downs and still alive.

SØREN: You wrote this book when you were depressed. What does depression mean to you?

AMULYA: I am what they call a high-functioning depressive. Unlike Sanya, who stayed under the covers, I didn't. I went out and worked and was a mother, a wife, a friend . . . and I was also terribly sad, miserable, and the whole world was covered in gray. I couldn't write. I had no creative outlet. It wasn't much fun.

SØREN: You are high functioning. Even I didn't know until much later how bad things were. I learned a lot about depression from your experience. Now I think I can detect if something is wrong before it goes wrong. Going through depression, what was the most important lesson you learned?

AMULYA: I learned two things. First, the opposite of depression is not happiness but vitality. It's being able to see all the colors of the rainbow, feel everything (good and bad), and live life to the fullest. The second thing I learned is that you can't make me happy. That no one can make me happy. I have to make me happy. I have to make a choice every morning if on that day I will be happy or indulge myself to go into this gray state of feeling nothing. It sounds really simple, but that's the truth. I control my destiny.

SØREN: Speaking of controlling destinies, how come Sanya doesn't end up with Ravn? I always thought that she would.

AMULYA: I had no idea how it would end. I actually talked to Tobias (our son) about it. I explained Sanya to him and Ravn and Harry. Tobias said that Sanya should dump both men and go on a long vacation. I think that Sanya knew all along that Ravn was a distraction she was using to get better. Sometimes distractions divert you from fixing your life, and sometimes they help you get out of your situation. In Sanya's case, Ravn helped her clear the gray and find herself.

SØREN: Sanya and Ravn never consummate their relationship. Why not?

AMULYA: We actually don't know if they do or don't. We don't know how they spent that night in the summer house. And neither does Harry.

SØREN: I loved Sanya's voice. She's quirky and sarcastic, batshit crazy and fun. How did you put her together?

AMULYA: Of all the characters I have written, Sanya is the one who's closest to me. Not Old Sanya but New Sanya. I'm slightly irreverent, and I look at life with cynical glasses at times; and I never have a problem with being blunt and up-front. I'm sometimes a bit of a drama queen. I also am afraid of the darkness of depression.

SØREN: I thought Mandy and Penny were fun. Do we know these people?

AMULYA: Well, parts of them are similar to some people we know, but the rest is conjured up. These are *my* characters, and they are created by me and don't exist in reality.

SØREN: What actually inspired this story?

AMULYA: One day I was at work and walking past an office and I saw a sign with the name Anders Ravn. The Danish *Ravn* is from the bird raven. In Hindu mythology, we had a Ravan who is a bad guy. This was also the time that there was the whole IT Factory scandal in Denmark, where a leasing carousel scheme meant that the CEO of that company did prison time. So I started to think about a modern version of *The Ramayana*—where Sita, my Sanya, has had a nervous breakdown and . . . bit by bit the story emerged.

SØREN: The Copenhagen you describe in this book is *your* Copenhagen. How do you feel about the city?

AMULYA: You know that Copenhagen is my favorite city in the world. And I love it very much, even more than Paris, which is a city that I adore. The Copenhagen in the book is definitely *my* Copenhagen. The places I went to and the experiences I had. Some of these experiences I had with you, some with friends, and some alone. I get so nostalgic when I think about Copenhagen that I even forget how terrible the weather used to be. I miss it very much, and when I sometimes go there because of work, I'm once again enamored and feel all the feelings. I also have friends in the city—friends who are nearly family. So Copenhagen is very special and will always be this special city—like a long-lost lover, the one who got away.

READER'S GUIDE

1. Sanya and Harry have been married for a long time, and maybe not so well the entire time. What did you think of Sanya and Harry's marriage?

2. Sanya is clinically depressed and doesn't want to get out from under her duvet. We have all felt the blues at some time or another. Could you relate to Sanya and how she felt?

3. Why do you think Sanya is attracted to Ravn? And why do you think Ravn is attracted to Sanya?

4. Sanya is at the center of this story, but *The Copenhagen Affair* is full of colorful secondary characters like Penny, Mandy, and even Lucky. Who were your favorites?

5. We find out that Ravn is not who he seems to be—and is in fact a white-collar criminal. How did you feel about the fact that even after knowing this, Sanya continued to be attracted to him?

6. *The Copenhagen Affair* discusses marriage as a closed system. How true is this in marriages you know?

7. What were some of the big differences between Old Sanya and New Sanya?

8. As Sanya changed and evolved, so did Harry. What were the most significant changes that Harry made, and do you think they were enough to save his marriage and himself?

9. Did you think, in the end, Sanya made the right decision?
10. At the end of the book, Harry and Sanya decide to try again to be a couple. Do you think they'll make it?
11. The book takes the reader on a tour of Copenhagen. What places from the book would you like to visit if you went to Copenhagen?

ABOUT THE AUTHOR

Photo © 2017 Justin Odom

Amulya Malladi is the author of seven novels, including *A House for Happy Mothers*, *The Sound of Language*, and *The Mango Season*. Her books have been translated into several languages, including Dutch, French, German, Spanish, Danish, Romanian, Serbian, and Tamil. She has a bachelor's degree in engineering and a master's degree in journalism. When she's not writing, she works as a marketing executive. After several years in Copenhagen, she now lives outside Los Angeles with her husband and two children. Connect with Amulya at www.amulyamalladi.com or on Facebook at www.facebook.com/authoramulya.